D1060576

FISHMONGER'S FIDDLE

FISHMONGER'S FIDDLE

TALES BY

ALFRED EDGAR COPPARD

Short Story Index Reprint Series

BOOKS FOR LIBRARIES PRESS
FREEPORT, NEW YORK

First Published 1925
Reprinted 1970

STANDARD BOOK NUMBER:
8369-3313-3

LIBRARY OF CONGRESS CATALOG CARD NUMBER:
78-106276

PRINTED IN THE UNITED STATES OF AMERICA

to
GAY

Contents

OLD MARTIN   9

THE LITTLE MISTRESS   32

WILLIE WAUGH   64

THE HIGGLER   73

ITALIAN WHIRLIGIG   114

THE JEWEL OF JEOPARDY   121

ALICE BRADY   145

THE WATERCRESS GIRL   155

AT LABAN'S WELL   175

A WILDGOOSE CHASE   181

DUMBLEDON DONKEY   217

A THREE-HANDED REEL   225

THE SNARE   252

FISHMONGER'S FIDDLE   260

A LITTLE BOY LOST   284

A DIVERSION WITH THOMAS   295

MR. LIGHTFOOT IN THE GREEN ISLE   303

OLD MARTIN

THREE BARNOVER MEN DIED, AND DIED BADLY TOO, within a month of each other; a succession of mortality so swift as to be almost terrifying. Barnover was proud of its folks' longevity; it was four or five years since anyone had died there; but the alarm had its mitigations, for the three dead men were drunken, lecherous, swearing fellows.

Barnover was hidden in an oval pan-like hollow surrounded by turfy hills, a very quiet stolid place. The railway was four miles distant and the main road as far off in another direction. A kennel of hounds was kept there, and a mill for the weaving of thick cloth. There was also a brown dumpy church, the tiniest of graveyards chock-full of headstones, and a large portly vicarage with suitable vicar. Of the two inns, the *Fox* was favoured by the Oddfellows, while none but Foresters foregathered at the *Angel*. In summer there was cricket on the green, in winter there was nothing; but the people were prosperous enough to be contented; their natures were simple to the point of superstition; they were happy even though not very wise. If Barnover men had a vice at all it was toping; the Oddfellows and Foresters were strong, thirsty men — something in the air, perhaps — but things were easier now the three drunken rips were dead and buried. Ephraim Stinch, the last of them, had been the worst of all.

'Those three scandalous drunkards are at rest now, and the place is all the better for it,' people said, and

George Bartlett, the huntsman, said it when he came to supper with Old Martin and Monica about that time.

But *were* they at rest? Old Martin had his doubts. He was a retired seafaring man living with his orphan niece, the schoolmistress of Barnover.

'Your grandmother in Galway,' he began to his niece, Monica Doyle, 'your grandmother, Eva Martin — she was second-sighted — often told me the dead have no rest; they do not rest, they do not rest at all. And what's more, Bartlett, the last-comer to the cemetery, the last one to be buried, that one, she said, has to slave and to serve all the other lost souls that lie in the same consecrated patch waiting for their judgment; the last one,' he repeated, 'always.'

The tall girl stared at her Uncle Martin. The huntsman, a plump, twinkling person with crooked legs, said:

'So I have heard, too; ah, and Ephraim Stinch will have his hands full of it rushing to Limbo or Tophet or wherever he is ordered to go.'

'Go he must,' Old Martin asserted. 'Until the next poor soul dies and gets buried there, he'll fetch and carry, carry and fetch. But at last his own turn is bound to come.'

'Yes, I can believe that; ha, ha!' cried old George. 'Ho, ho, yes, that I can.'

But Monica shuddered; she did not like to hear of this. She had feared the living Ephraim Stinch, a powerful, ruddy, unruly farmer, of forty or thereabouts, with a large horn-like nose and an ox-like moustache – he resembled a Swiss; now he was dead she wanted to think of him as done with. His house had been dim and dirty, his farm harsh and hungry, with stealthy cats, lean dogs, and famished hens. He had ogled Monica, very often he had ogled and affronted her when he was drunk, sometimes even when he was sober. Oh, he had been fond of her according to his lights, and indeed in spite of the drink he had money in the bank, but Monica could not think of him or look at him without repulsion. He had drunkenly sworn to get even with her.

'In fact,' continued the huntsman, ' I *know* such things be true, for I'd the proof of it, the very warrant of it; three nights ago – or four if this be Thursday.'

A rotund little squirrel of a man, still dapper in mind and body, was this huntsman, whose healthy shaven face looked as if he washed in tomato soup. Without a vein of contrariety in his frame, or a useful conception in his mind about anything but the hunting of a fox, he was just a genial person who delighted to agree with everybody. A teller of tales and a retailer of news that he trilled off his jolly mind and forgot. All information was grist to him, he affected to believe everything he was told, and he hoped for similar faith in his own hearers. His mishandling of the truth amounted to genius, but there was no harm in him at all.

'I tell you I know,' he asseverated to Martin, 'because I have seen that man since he died.'

Old Martin glanced at Monica and at George in turn. Certainly the principal emotion expressed in his glances was scepticism, but he only said: 'God bless us!'

'I have seen the man,' repeated the huntsman.

'I knew it!' declared Old Martin. Monica begged to be told about it.

'He walks,' the huntsman said, his gaze dropping to the table. 'As I'm a living man I saw his ghost four nights ago if this be Thursday.' He was groping thoughtfully with his left hand for a morsel of bread. ''Twas past eleven o'clock, and I'd just popped out in my shirt-sleeves for a smoke, not thinking it would be so dark. Dark! I could scarcely find my way out of my own garden gate. I be got into the road when I see something.' George here swallowed the last pickled walnut and took a deliberate swig at his glass of beer. 'For all the darkness I *saw* something and I said to myself, "That's a good visible man, for this dark night seems to choke my very eyesight. I wonder who he may be." And before I knew it the words popped into my head and out of my mouth: "Is that you, Ephraim Stinch?" It didn't make no reply, no reply at all, but 'twas Ephraim Stinch as large as life. "God help me," I said, and I wanted to run, but I couldn't, so I gave a few damns to myself and stood till the thing was by me, and I knew that but for the dark I could ha' seen right through him to his spinal column. He did not look like e'er a ghost I ever heard tell of; no skeleton, nor no white sheet, nor no brimstone fire; was just the man himself, same's we all knew him, though if it hadn't been dark I'd a seen right through him, like that glass.'

12

Monica silently filled it.

'It took no notice of me, but — this is the awful story — that ghost was roaring drunk (thank you, Miss Monica), as I'm a living man, full to the gob, but no sound coming from it. Cussing and damning, ramping and roaring — you could see — staggering from here to yon, you could see but you could hear nothing, not a word, not a footfall, and that's how it passed behind me, close as the back of my chair. A very strong murderous man, sir. When it was gone by I pulled myself together. A man has got to be a man, whether or no, but believe you me, my flesh wherever I touched myself felt like that blancmange. I didn't know rightly whether I burned or froze. My hair was just grass and my elbows were stiff and chill as the handle of a jug. What I want to know is where he got it.'

'Got what?' they both interrogated him.

'The strong drink — and how could he carry it. Whatever it was it should by rights have dropped clean through him — begging your pardon, Miss Monica.'

'It was devil's drink,' murmured Old Martin.

'Yes, I suppose,' agreed the huntsman, 'the devil's own drink. But where he got it! eh! Ah, well, some will perish their mortal souls for anything — for anything. But not me, would you?'

'He is working out his fate, Bartlett, you may depend.'

'Sir,' said the other solemnly, laying his right palm confidently upon the tablecloth and inclining his head towards the Captain, but at the same time slewing a glance towards Monica, 'I don't envy the poor lost souls he's among, the devil himself would be a greater comfort to 'em in their strange situation. Young lady, ghosts are terrible things, terrible!'

Old Martin was much impressed by this sound confirmation of his ghostly theme. A good man's simple credulity was his: 'You are sure it was Ephraim?'

'Why, bless you,' protested the huntsman, 'I knew him as a boy. A hard man, sir, his own mother died in bearing him, and he was a sickly child until his father, who was a butcher, fed him on spoonfuls of raw ox-blood. Then he thrived, I do assure you; ha, ha!'

'O, but that is horrible!' Monica put her fingers into her ears. George was dismayed and hastened to change the subject.

'Talking of tipple, d'ye know, James, it is not a great many years ago when our parson himself was fond of a cup of strong drink. Ah, many a firkin of good stingo have gone down his gullet and laid to rest. Mind you,' — he lowered his voice — 'that is between ourselves; but truth's true, and let it be known.'

Old James Martin had followed the sea for nigh upon forty years; then had he suddenly cried, 'Done!' and severed himself from it, retaining not a single maritime reminder, not a flag, telescope, barometer, whistle, uniform, or cutlass. Clad in a grey tweed suit and a white panama hat he came to live with his widowed sister in Barnover, carrying only a mirror given him by a strange woman in Java. It was a foot square, bound in copper, and he hung it up on the wall of his bedroom.

When Monica was fourteen, eight years ago, Mrs. Doyle died. Martin had installed a maidservant in the little house, enabling his bonny niece to qualify as a teacher by the time she had grown into a handsome woman. Then indeed the pleasures of life and home were deepened and enlarged. What a pleasant little house it was, thatched with bright straw and coloured with saffron wash; the fruit trees, much cherished by the old sailor, almost hid it. But most of the homes in Barnover were like that, and a fantastic stranger once looking down from the encircling hills when fruit bloom was flaunting in every garden had declared that Barnover village resembled an omelette lying in a green dish.

Old Martin lived on there, loving his niece and his garden, but nothing else, maintaining a simple but not uncharitable reserve to all but George Bartlett, the huntsman, and disliking nobody, except, perhaps, the Reverend Coberly Nashe. The parson had a fat, expensive-looking stomach, lean legs, and as far as could be discovered, a lean mind that did not cost him a penny. But Martin was a regular attendant at his church and a subscriber to his funds.

The sturdy old mariner, with his clipped grey beard, suit of tweed, hat of straw, always carried a malacca cane trimmed with a silver knob when he walked in Barnover. If occasionally he spoke to casual acquaintances such as the policeman and the postman, he would genially address them as: 'Well, my son, how is it with you to-day?' If it were a child he recognized he would always stop and, fumbling in his pockets, inquire, 'Well, old man!' or 'Well, old lady!'

When Monica died Old Martin began to hate the parson and ceased to attend his church. Monica died soon, and suddenly, almost mysteriously. The tragedy crushed the old man's mind, and it physically weakened him. She was buried in the church-yard, a new white stone was set at the head of the mound; a new mistress taught in the school, and no one seemed a penny the worse or a penny the wiser. But Old Martin was in anguish, not so much for his personal loss as for Monica's own fearful fate. For it was in vain he tried to repudiate that wild notion of her grandmother: *The dead do not rest. The last-comer serves the lost souls.* Deep down it was an instinctive belief; grafted upon his childhood it clung to him. Dreams of the dead girl flocked into his sleep, terrible dreams that drove sleep from him and brought agony and madness. These were dreams not alone of Monica, for he saw, or his distracted mind thought it saw, the dreadful sodden form of Stinch dogging, enslaving and destroying his beautiful girl. He visibly aged, he recognized no one in the streets and was greeted by none — even the children stood unnoted at his side. All refrained from touching the deep wound of his sorrow; they could do no other, he was so changed. He walked in loneliness on the hills above the village, and the countrymen, seeing his ambling figure there, would mutter: 'Old Martin again. He takes it badly; the poor man.' Daylight gave him no relief, for he sought no relief for himself; all his malady was a vast anxiety for Monica whose doom floated ever about him, touching and maddening him until his wits went wandering. Casting his thoughts around upon his neighbours, he wondered: 'Who then will die soon? On what poor unfortunate will it fall to take this load of evil from Monica, and she be free and sleeping?' He ran over in his mind all the old people of the place, but none was sick or sorry, all were hearty, the least of them might last another ten years. Then, all at once, a great light broke upon him. Why, he could kill himself! Of course he could! That would trim Ephraim Stinch's ghost, leave *him* alone for that! But he would have to disguise his intention, for they would not bury a suicide in that same consecrated ground. Not all the dead bodies in the world could help Monica unless they were buried there. They must not bury him at a cross road.

That night the old man lay sleepless in his bed, but with a mind more tranquil now he had seen a way of hope, when his gaze was caught by the faint gleam on the wall of the square mirror from Java. Suddenly from the floor beneath it something puffed like a spirt of thick white smoke. It rolled and lolled right up to the ceiling, and then resolved slowly into a round mass like a balloon. At last that began to droop and flag and fold itself into the shape of Monica, tall and frail, wearing a blue robe with gold beads and bands, the blue of succory. She had a face of marble whiteness and pale gold hair.

He knew it was she though the darkness was complete. Had it not been so dark he would have seen right through her body, he felt sure. It was she, though he had never seen her in a robe of that kind. In the morning he felt that he had had a beautiful dream, but he could not remember it.

His friend George came to see him, but could make nothing of him. The old man was gone wavering in his mind, he was dull, until George said, 'Come, my old friend, you must get yourself out of this humour. Sorrow don't last for ever.'

'Does it not?'

'It will bring nothing back to ye. Sorrow don't give, it only takes away. You must come out of your shell and ockipy your mind with things.'

'I see too many things, Bartlett.'

'What things?'

'Not of this world. Stinch and my Monica!' The old man broke into tears.

'Au but . . . but . . .' spluttered the huntsman, 'that can't be true, my old friend, they're . . . they've passed away!'

'I know, I know, but I see her. And you have seen him.'

'Me!' cried the dapper one. 'Never in this world, never in this life! Mind you, I don't say as spirits are not to be seen, but they never come my way, never on your life, James.'

The old man gazed at him in dismay. 'But you

yourself saw Ephraim Stinch, you told us, you told
us, you told Monica.'

'Pshaw!' the huntsman stood up, fiddling with his
hat. 'You been adreaming, James. I ain't seen
Ephraim Stinch, I ain't seen him' — he reflectively
cocked his eye — 'no, not since a week afore he died.
Come you along now. This kind of thought is no
good to you, it's too depressing. You want a cheer-
fuller outlook, all the gossip of the town that goes on
round about ye. Did ye hear now of old Harry
Chalgrove? Died last night — in a fit!'

'Dead! O heavens,' quavered the old man, 'is that
true? Good news, George, it is good news indeed!
What a load that takes from my mind; it's gladness.
When will he be buried, George?'

The huntsman was so amazed at this outburst that
he could not speak. Noting the concern in his friend's
eyes, Old Martin continued: 'Don't you see? My
girl's spirit has been roaming and restless — Monica
— fetching and carrying — in mortal danger from that
Stinch. Horrible! You remember, don't you — the
last soul buried slaves for all?'

'Well, to be sure, I can't tell whether or no. But
Harry Chalgrove will not be buried in the churchyard. 'Tis full up! They will put him aground in
the new lot!'

It was true. Barnover churchyard was now as full as
it could be; it was recently completely and finally
filled. Monica's corpse was the last; not another
body would it hold. The Council had already procured another half-acre in a different part of the

parish. It had been trimmed and consecrated, and now awaited the inevitable procession of luckless mortality. Harry Chalgrove was to head it.

This was a circumstance of dreadful, shocking import to Old Martin, to whose diseased comprehension it was plain that nothing now could ever release the soul of Monica from its horrible task. That stricken soul was doomed to drift in ceaseless agony till the Day of Judgment.

The huntsman comforted his friend. 'Go see Parson Nashe about it. Something may be done yet.'

Martin went to bed determining to ask Nashe's assistance in the morning. In the middle of the night the ghost came in a cloud again, and this time it appeared to fade away into the Javanese mirror as if that were a portal to the Unknown. Old Martin did not sleep, and at an early hour, trembling, he sought the help of the parson.

The Rev. Coberly Nashe received him in his study, a comfortless, heartless, linoleumed room with a great looking-glass and a carafe of water on the black mantelpiece. Columns of dusty books were piled in the corners or against the knee-hole desk of pale wood lined with dark green leather. The window was closed, though the morning was warm, and the room smelled of upholstery that seemed to be decomposing. There was little else in the room but some chairs and the Rev. Coberly Nashe, who had a stomach that could be delicately described as buxom and a countenance that might have seemed all mouth and teeth but for the spectacled eyes that glistened and gloomed at the visitor.

Old Martin's request to him was that Chalgrove's body might be buried in the old churchyard instead of the new cemetery lot; the dead man had no relatives or friends; he was old, he had been forgotten.

'I fear it is an impossibility, Mr. Martin. I fear so. But why do you ask for this? It is kind and considerate, but it is . . . singular.'

The visitor sat silent. Nashe got up and filled a glass with water from the carafe. Sipping it occasionally, he straddled before Old Martin.

'Extraordinary difficulty, you know,' he went on, between his sips. 'Act of Parliament — that sort of thing — absurd, of course — but there you are.'

Nashe very carefully replaced the glass and leaned with an elbow upon the mantelpiece, twirling his watchguard with the disengaged hand. It was of black cord hung with a medallion of copper, a cross of gold, and a seal of silver.

'I would do anything to oblige you, Mr. Martin, anything, but this is not a case for obligation; it is a thing beyond my power to do. Anything, I assure you, to oblige . . .'

'Do you believe in ghosts, Mr. Nashe?'

The vicar was silent. Old Martin raised his musing head:

'From the day of death the soul may be in grief or pain to the Day of Judgment, and if we neglect it, it haunts its friends and its home, seeking relief. Such things are seen and known, for sure, sir!'

'Oh, come, Mr. Martin, different men, different vision. I like to keep an open mind. These things are hidden from our mortal eyes, we can but conjecture. But the human eye, the human eye, mind, can only see human objects . . .'

'Then maybe you'd not see what I do see and have seen. In three latitudes of the world's waters, very far apart, I assure you, I saw the Flying Dutchman! And that's a fabulous ship, the ghost of a strong vessel, full of the moving souls of dead men.'

'That is very wonderful, my dear sir,' said the vicar.

'And I saw,' quavered the old man, 'the ghost of a person lately dead in this parish. For the peace of that soul I want to see Chalgrove buried in the old yard.'

'But why? But why?'

Old Martin did not care to give his fantastic reason to this sceptic. He only said:

'He should be buried with the friends of his bygone days.'

The vicar was all at sixes and sevens. Queer man, Old Martin! He observed the alteration in him (poor old chap!), and he was very sympathetic, but there was nothing he could do; there was not a foot of space left. What could he do? Nothing!

The old man went away despondently, but in half an hour he was back again in the vicar's room. He felt he had not been frank enough with the parson. Now he told Nashe how the spirit of his niece visited him in a ball of smoke, how she was being ceaselessly harried by the dire menace of Stinch. And so he wanted the body of Monica, already three months in its grave, transferred from the churchyard to the new cemetery lot. Let Chalgrove have her place.

Of course it was an impossible request. Sacrilegious! Preposterous! Nashe bluntly told him that his mind was perhaps a little unhinged by grief. He was unwell, ill, must look after himself carefully, consult a doctor, and so on. Mr. Nashe was intensely sympathetic, but just then he was also very busy.

'My dear sir, it cannot be done without a faculty, and a faculty could not be procured for love or money in such a case. Only by an order of the higher authorities for an extraordinary occasion. My dear sir, my sympathy is with you, needless to say, entirely with you. But it would be impossible, ludicrous even, for me to approach them on such an errand. You see it's impossible, don't you? Why, my good man Martin, you know in your heart of hearts it is absurd. That you should see the spirit of your niece is, I am of firm belief, due to hallucination, pure hallucination; and to see the soul of Stinch in a state of insobriety is undoubtedly an hallucination of the Evil One himself. Fix your thoughts upon the Almighty and this madness will leave you. Oh, and see a doctor.' Alternately looking at his watch and burbling in this fashion, the vicar burbled Old Martin out of the vicarage door and through the vicarage garden into the road, where, patting him on the shoulder and howling 'Hallucination!' at him twice, as if it were the name of a sovran remedy, he left him.

The ghost of Monica allowed her uncle no peace.

Her own restlessness, her trouble, was to be shared
with him. In the middle of the night she came again.
The cloud of smoke puffed from the floor below the
mirror from Java. It spun into a lolling globe that
sank and declined like drapery round a whirling
dancer, and there was she. The man felt no terror,
only an anguish of human helplessness. The girl did
not look at him; no sound, no sign, pale and unbe-
seeching, a figure whose pitiful appearance clawed
at his heart, she stood peering into the mirror.

'Monica!' he gasped. At the word she faded and
died; it seemed that she passed, a little whorl of
smoke, into the mirror itself. After a few moments
he rose from his bed and looked squarely into the
strange glass from Java that hung upon a wall. At
that momentary glimpse a shriek of horror burst
from him; he sank trembling upon his bed. Credence no longer wavered; all his mind's foreboding
flamed into terrible confirmation. He lay almost
senseless until the cocks began to crow and day
came once more, but not to lull his fears.

George Bartlett called again the next evening and
they sat in the garden under a walnut tree. He was
startled at Old Martin's terrible appearance.

'There, there,' he soothed the trembling man when
he heard of his experience. 'By God, what is it,
James? I tell you what, my old friend; say but the
word and we'll dig her up together and plant her
elsewheres, some dark night, but not to-night, for
I've an early job to-morrow. But when you like,
James, whenever you choose, I'll stand to you.'

"'Tis no good, Bartlett, no good. You can't play tricks with an evil that comes from hell itself. There is nothing mortal can deceive it. Its course must run for ever and ever and ever.'

In the dim air of that thick and moveless evening the bell in the church tower deeply hummed its nine o'clock. A distant flock of sheep baaed in a preposterous bass. A young owl kept up a shrill snarl, a mixture of bird whistle and the bark of a puppy. Martin looked up into the tree:

'O trees, trees, you should have some springy elastic growth so that if you pulled down a branch, Monica, you could shoot yourself into the skies, like a catapult!' He recovered himself and looked at his friend. 'Except, of course, for gravity, Bartlett. She couldn't conquer gravity, nobody ever has. Gravity, graveyard, graves – oh, when shall I go – what shall I do – where shall I be buried!'

The old man's tears were shocking to the jolly huntsman. He tried to rally his friend, and to persuade him to that body-snatching effort.

'James, it can be done, it has been done. I know the man as done it, too, and all. He worked for a gentleman in Scotland, in some castle it was, where the king of Scotland used to live when the wars were on. The queen's chair is in it now. Bless you, yes.'

But Martin declined the impious offer. The huntsman went home and declared to his wife: 'Old Martin is mad. There is not a doubt upon it. I do believe he is mad.'

Then, although it was so late, Old Martin took his

stick and called upon the vicar. He was in his study, sitting between two candles with a book in his hands. He listened to the man's fresh evidence, and then said with a snort of irritation: 'There is nothing in the whole world I can do for you. I have told you how impossible it all is, but you have given your mind to it, I suppose. Now you see the result. You can believe anything if you let your mind dwell upon it, anything, James Martin,' he said sternly. 'The mind is an obstinate thing, it goes its own way. I am reading this book now, you see, a book of divinity, to help me in my sermons. But I cannot attend to it well, for I keep thinking of a piece of business I have in hand and intend to do. I go on reading my book, but I cannot understand it, not one single word, for all that business I intend to do keeps pressing itself forward like a child that is bothering me and will have my attention. At last I put down my book, lean back in my chair, and let my mind dwell upon that piece of business I have to do. And then, what do you think? my mind dismisses that business, it refuses to contemplate anything but the book I have been reading, although I have not absorbed its contents. How is this now, tell me?'

But Old Martin could not tell him, he could not understand him, he could only realize that the soul of Monica was harshly suffering. Nashe reclined in his chair, linked his fingers across his stomach, and gazed at his visitor with a smile that endeavoured to be benignant, but uncommonly resembled a grimace. He sat up and said: 'So you see! you see! Concentration! You must concentrate your mind.' He accompanied the old man to the vicarage gate, loudly exhorting him not to let his mind dwell upon goblins and cantrips, they were a kind of intemperance, an intoxication, they would pass. And when the vicar saw the old man disappear in the darkness, he too murmured: 'Poor old chap, all the tiles loose, quite gone. It's excess of grief, he is mad. I must speak to the doctor about him; it makes me uneasy.' He walked up to a glow-worm in his garden path, and taking it to be a spent match carefully put his foot upon it. And when he got back into his study his mind leaped to his own absorbing busness. For he was a widower, contemplating a new marriage to a spinster who had five thousand pounds and a moustache.

Martin carried his grief locked in his own breast for days; he scarcely stirred from his home; if he did, the people eyed him furtively, children avoided him. Once more the huntsman called:

'Do you know what I've done, James?' he began impressively. 'I killed our best hound, Glossary, prince of the pack – and last night, listen James, Mr. Martin, I buried him myself in the churchyard. He's in the corner there behind the monkey tree. That's cooked the business. Don't tell me! If that soul of a dog can't settle all this business I'm a salamander. James, that dog-hound Glossary beats cock-fighting. He could nose out an earwig and he could kill a bison beast, Glossary could. You go to your rest, James.'

And James went, but not to rest – never again under heaven. The huntsman's plan must have failed, for horrors thickened upon him; the image of his niece, vision, hallucination, or mirage, was fraught with unending torture.

The vicar spoke to the doctor, the doctor told the squire, the squire revealed that Old Martin's retirement from sea had been adroitly hastened by the shipowners on account of certain delusions held by the captain; quite simple, harmless delusions, but seamen were superstitious, uneasy men, and the owners could not afford to take any risks. Besides, their old trusted servant had done exceedingly well; he had amassed a modest little fortune which they supplemented with a pension. And so on.

Barnover began to watch him, but no one came near him any more; even the faithful huntsman deserted him. His obsession, however, did not desert him; it ravaged his life and left him peaked and pined.

One day in October, when the last apples were being gathered, a cadaverous Old Martin called once more at the vicarage. The vicar could not see him, he was unwell. A few days later Martin called again; the vicar was ill. In short, the Rev. Coberly Nashe was unable to fulfil his engagement to marry the spinster, for he died.

Behold, he was buried under the pavement of his own church, in the same tomb with his long-departed wife, and not more than twenty feet from the coffin of Ephraim Stinch.

OLD MARTIN

An excellent change was soon observable in the conduct and appearance of Old Martin. It could not be exactly dated, but imperceptibly that haunted look slipped from his visage, the quiet smile came back. Good health overtook him, his ribs began to fatten, his back to unbend, his beard to be clipped again. He became once more the sprightly veteran, not less immersed in his own quiet thoughts, but at least happy in them. Other elderly men chatted to him, complimenting him upon his recovery, and when they did so, 'Ho, my son!' he would say, and exchange amiable views with them about the affability of the weather, the price of crops, or the shortening days, as is the custom of amiable, affable persons in Barnover – and possibly elsewhere. Little Pollys, Janes, Arabellas, and Rachels, who had lived as many months as he had years, again became his 'Old Girls,' receiving also a largesse which led to such an increase of trade at the lollypop shop that its ancient dame, Miss Phipps, threw up her hands and recklessly ordered a whole seven pounds of butterscotch where she had previously contracted for four.

When the hounds met at the end of Barnover High Lane just before Christmas, Old Martin, too, walked along to the assembly of hounds and hunters. Every one was jolly, and George sat on a big sandy-coloured gelding in the midst of the hounds, a grand figure in his scarlet coat. A good sixpennyworth of cochineal had been exhausted in cleaning that coat from stain; the pipeclay on his breeches, the gloss upon his hunting cap, the lustre of his boots, the sparkle of his spurs! Wonderful! George kept cracking his whip and roaring at the dogs. 'You . . . Waterford! Nora, girl! Come back, Glossary!' Glossary, indeed, was particularly tiresome. People from miles around, important people, too, who had come in to the meet, walked up to George and shook hands with him, while he cracked a joke or cracked his whip or swore lustily at a slinking hound. 'You, Glossary!'

'Why, James!' he cried, when he saw Old Martin. Martin stepped among the hounds to his friend and shook hands heartily with him. George retained the old sailor's hand in his clasp and, bending down, whispered confidentially, 'Old friend, how is it with you?' and Martin replied that he was never so well in his life before. George released his hand after another earnest pressure and sat upright in the saddle. 'Good 'ealth,' said the huntsman with a sigh – though why that figure of prime and radiant existence should exude a sigh when joy was surely chippering in his birdlike breast is a matter beyond explanation – 'Good 'ealth's a wonderful thing!'

Then he leaned down once more, while for a space the hounds roamed unreproved. 'How is that sad business? Do you see anything o' nights now?'

Old Martin smiled sweetly: 'My poor girl is at rest at last.'

'Good!' murmured the huntsman fervently. 'What did I tell you! That dog I killed – that . . . that Bolingbroke – he was the masterpiece of this earth! A masterpiece!' He repeated it again and again, much louder. 'A masterpiece!'

'Three weeks since, though,' Old Martin said, 'I saw a thing that would have interested you.' He smiled up at George. 'I saw, on my soul, I saw Ephraim Stinch!'

The huntsman sat up and surveyed his friend with stern, puckered eyes. Martin beckoned with his finger and the huntsman bent down to him again. 'There were two of them, though. I saw those two ghosts as clear as I see you, Bartlett. He was arm-in-arm with Parson Nashe. I never saw a living man so drunk as that dead parson was.'

George perked himself upright with a shout of laughter. 'Don't tell me! God above, would you believe it, James! Good for you, James,' he roared. 'Damned if ever I heard tell of a boozy ghost afore! Never on my life, ho, ho! ha, ha!'

At that moment, Barnover clock struck eleven. The master called out, 'Hounds, please, gentlemen!' and they all moved off to the top of the hills.

THE LITTLE MISTRESS

I

SMALL AS IT WAS, AND AMPLY SHADED BY MAPLE trees, the little villa was hidden in a garden wholly enclosed by a high wall of brick. There was a bright green door with a latch in one corner of the wall, its lintel and sill painted white: near the top of the door was a white word *Sackville*, and in the middle of the door was a brass plate.

Curious travellers on the tops of passing omnibuses could just glance into the two lower rooms of the house; they had no time to observe much, but they could see in the first room a fireplace framed with marble in the back wall, with a tall mirror upon the mantel and a gilt clock under a glass dome. In the second room they could see the same features meticulously repeated, nothing but fireplace, white mantel, large mirror, gilt clock. Once inside the garden you felt that the modest little house took on, or seemed to take on, a watching self-conscious air, an impression not at all lessened by the dark door which confronted you with a large knocker of very conscious brass, three separate bell-pulls — one marked NIGHT, one marked DAY, the third not marked at all, but possibly for use in time of an eclipse — a brass-mouthed letter-box, a brass speaking-tube, and a new glistening name-plate of much brass inscribed *HUGH HARPER, Physician*. Visiting consultants would be ushered into the right-hand room — all marbled and gilt-clocked and mirrored — by a more or less spruce maidservant, and chronic patients, not too far lapsed from the arts of observation, might have remarked a changing succession of these domestics. The Harpers never had more than one; they came, they served, they departed; they did not continue to serve at *Sackville*. After a month or two of the discomposure induced by each of them the young doctor would say to his wife in a soft meditative voice: 'Francesca, I shall discharge her.'

In contrast to his wife Harper was of quite distinctive avoirdupois, almost a colossus, with crisp hair, brown moustache growing tightly on a round fresh face, and a lot of pleasant teeth. He always dressed in grey, and a watchguard of gold and black silk always stretched from pocket to pocket of his vest in a broad grin. His hands lived in the pockets of his trousers like rabbits in a burrow; he was never seen to stretch himself. Harper and his wife Francesca might be defined typographically, the one a capital O and the other an asterisk: there was always an implied footnote about Francesca, who was small and dusky and lovely.

'Yes, I shall discharge her now.'

Harper always discharged the servant, quietly, after a few weeks. He had no liking for such an office, it was disagreeable to him, but somehow or other, sooner or later, like a domestic Henry the Eighth he discharged everybody — even his friends — and he always had a reason for that course. Maggie Taproe committed unmentionable indiscretions, Eva Lodden developed incurable boils, Lena Hughes would spill oil into the bath and neglect that business of the cat: they were discharged without a gramme of compunction or gratitude; service was service, and if you paid for it it should be worth paying for. Each departing menial was a vicious unspeakable hag, while her successor — for how brief a date! — was a peerless angel. But the doctor's antipathies, though vast, were superficial; his sympathy and kindness in their narrower range were deep and prodigious.

In the fullness of time and dissatisfaction he prepared to discharge Fanny Hackbut, who had been engaged by him without a recommendation of any sort, human, devilish, or divine. It appeared that her last mistress had indulged in a most scandalous affair with a fascinating gentleman, a Perugian from South America. Miss Hackbut's moral pride had revolted and demanded recognition; she had prudently left. That was good enough for Harper, who admired (amongst a heap of other things) conscience and character; he engaged her: 'She's a howling prude, but I think she'll do.'

And she didn't do at all. He met her more than once descending the stairs. There was nothing more unendurable to him than the sight of a woman wearing a man's boots — and they were his own boots. 'I shall discharge her,' he told Francesca.

'What has she done?' asked his gentle wife, who was as delightful as an antelope.

'Oh, curse the girl, she's a great female elephant!'

Fanny Hackbut had features — God made them, it is true, but you could not think of that, said Francesca — which were too improbable for description, and she had a mind like a devitalized fowl — God inscrutably made that, too. In times gone by she had been engaged (Providentially engaged, Francesca couldn't help thinking) to the thin youth with the physique of a hairdresser who came round upon a bicycle carrying a large tin that had once (according to Francesca) contained pounds and pounds of jam, and was now used to convey pints and pints of milk. That was all over. So few virtues and so few vices had she that the whole lot might have been collected like half a dozen buttons, black and white ones, left unnoticed on the corner of a large dark table: there might once have been more of them, but they had dropped off. The rest of the large dark table was the rest of Fanny.

Meals were late, or if not late were badly served, or if not badly served were poorly conceived. Everything was left to Fanny, for Francesca — the doctor confided it to himself — though dainty and adorable was, oh, capricious: she was all brains and apprehension, but she hadn't any sense; they might talk of a thing for a week and she would forget it in five minutes. Piles of unclean dishes languished in the kitchen sink from morn to eve. Those brooms on the dark places of the stairs, those pails in the passage corners — they were man-traps, deliberate traps, diabolical! Fanny's one grace was a devotion to her little mistress who, unlike the huge master, had the tiniest of shoes, of hats, of gloves, indeed of everything. Those personal belongings delighted Fanny in the way that a doll's things delight a child. Francesca's room was always a pattern of brightness and discretion, the buckles on her shoes most perspiringly shone, hose and linen had the perfect sequence and spontaneity of a packet of new envelopes; brushes and combs never lost their pristine order; while the silver trinkets of the dressing-table, sconces and caskets and phials, beamed as in the days when they adorned some jeweller's window. But as for the young doctor, it appeared that not a thing was ever in place, or rightly done, or punctually performed. A clean shirt was as rare as a gift from the King! Socks! He had no socks, once there had been millions! She was a squab, a fœtus, a sprout!

Like the servant, he too adored the little mistress and could deny her nothing, not even the lover whose blue-grey letters strangely inscribed so often appeared in the letter-box. Even Fanny had noticed their impressive caligraphy, a battalion of half-dressed letters flung boldly across the solitude of the envelope and left at astonished attention.

After the usual couple of months Fanny had become insupportable to Harper. On a warm September eve he and Francesca had concluded a disillusioning dinner. Windows and doors were open, the thrush in the garden was trying to recapture its old gamut, lamps were yet unlit, though it was growing a little dim.

'I shall give her notice now, I think,' he mumbled. At the door which led to the kitchen he stood for a moment, listening.

'She's singing, Frances, singing to herself, the fool!'

36

Playfully Francesca grimaced at him.

'Can't sack a person who is singing,' he growled. 'But why not?'

'Well, I dunno, you can't somehow.' He lumbered about the room and grinned apologetically at Francesca. He shook his fist at the door.

'Minx, elephant! Stop it, will you!' he chuckled. 'Dash it, she'll stop soon.' He grew very serious. 'I'll tell her then, presently. If not – to-morrow. Go she must, the Kaffir!'

He sat down and began to play a game of dominoes with his wife.

'Now she's not singing,' remarked Francesca presently.

'No, she's stopped, hasn't she?' Harper gazed at his wife. 'Yes, she's stopped, but let's finish this game and then I'll sack her. Presently will do, or to-morrow. You know, she's *so* ugly; I didn't notice that at first, did you?'

'Oh, Lord, yes,' replied Francesca.

'You did! You didn't tell me! I thought she was going to be so good. She was good at first, damn her, wasn't she?'

'Oh, I think she does rather well; she dotes on doing things for me,' Francesca said. 'My room is immaculate, I'm almost pained to touch anything, and when I tell her to get my bath ready she's enchanted; I have to shove her out of the room while I undress, for I can't take off so much as a shoe while she's there, she gloats so.'

'Yes, she would,' cried Hugh, 'just gloat and gloat.

That's good of her though, I'll give her one more chance. You talk to her, look after her, and be firm with her, Frances, will you?'

'Yes, Hugh.' Francesca's eyes dropped under their lids. 'But do you know what I've heard — she's got a baby.'

'Baby! A baby!' The doctor was incredulous, 'How?'

'She keeps it at Tappingham and goes over to see it whenever she can.'

'At Tappingham! Does she know?'

'Know?' Frances was puzzled.

'I mean does she know that *you* know?'

'She thinks we don't know.'

'What a devil! How *did* you come to know?'

'The grocer's wife told me. Oh, such a fool I am! That grocer muddled me up about the candles I ordered; the beast has sent packets and packets, there are 432 candles in the kitchen and Fanny can't find anywhere to put them. What can we do with them all, Hugh?'

'Burn 'em,' said the doctor. 'How old is this kid?'

'Only a few months. I like her much better now, don't you? I'm rather pleased, aren't you? She's not our fool of a Fanny, now. It's such an enlightening surprise, Hugh; I'm rather pleased.'

'Pleased! And all that pious reason of hers for leaving her last situation was just bunkum. What a libellous cat! She was thrown out because of this.'

'Oh, Hugh, do you think so? How shameful! I'd rather liked what she told me about that mistress.

Good Lord, Hugh, our Fanny was too good for such people!'

'I shall discharge her now, certainly.'

'No, Hugh, not now! What difference does it make?'

'On the spot!' he cried, rising and approaching the door leading to the kitchen. 'She's a liar, a baggage, an immoral fool!' But he paused, doubtfully. 'Shall I? Shall I sack her? Now?'

After a moment or two he turned back with a tortured grin. 'She's singing again!' He meditated. 'Well, at any rate, I can tell her to stop that, and if she don't stop it I'll sack her on the spot. And if she does stop it – well, I can sack her presently. Do you know, I *like* the word sack.' He went and sat down by Francesca. 'It's such a satisfactory word, it's like a funnel; you pour your feeling into it – sack – and it swirls and swishes down through the pipe – sack – such a beautiful jolt.'

'Hm! Sack, sack, sack, sack – yes,' said Francesca, 'but I think the loveliest word of all is cotton.'

'Cotton!' he cried.

'No, say it cot'n: the "cot" hard, mute the next "t" and then gulp the "n."'

'Cot'n, cot'n, cot'n, cot'n. Oh my, yes, isn't it delicious!' cried the doctor. 'Cot'n, cot'n, cot'n!'

2

For a few days longer some baffling protector seemed to ward from Fanny the menace of dismissal – Harper's tremors, his absences, or the servant's temporary disappearances. It was a task the young doctor would not delegate to his wife, for whom he strove to maintain an atmosphere of congruity and peace, with no disturbing elements crossing her apprehension of what life meant to her. Whether that was much or little mattered not at all so long as the mild air of its enchantments engrossed and sustained her. Francesca was moulded less by her acts than by her intentions; her will was so much less strong than her desires that life was coloured more by the intensity of her moods than by its misuse of her aims.

But even Francesca, indifferent, forbearing, pounced with anger one morning just as she had pounced, like a cat, into her own room, for there she beheld the execrable Fanny perusing with eminent delight a bundle of those blue-grey letters which usually reposed in a locked drawer. So engrossed was the culprit that she did not hear her mistress until, venting a sigh of appreciation, she suddenly realized that she was observed. Guilty Fanny dropped the letters to the table and turned briskly to her broom and bushes. Francesca closed the door behind her and said very disgustedly, 'Yes, Fanny?' The servant with pained innocence murmured, 'What, ma'am?'

Francesca directed at her a gaze that mutely fulminated. 'I suspected this: you read my private letters! You do read them,' insisted the trembling Francesca. 'You've read them all, I know you.'

There was no answer; there were just the broom, the brushes, and Fanny, and as Francesca scuffled the letters back into their drawer and turned the key Fanny went towards the door.

'Where are you going?' hissed Francesca.

'Downstairs, ma'am,' the lost sheep whispered.

'You abominable thing! What have you to say?'

'Oh, for sure, I'd never say anything, ma'am,' said the astonishing culprit, 'never anything to anybody I shouldn't say, not to anyone, ma'am.'

'What do you mean – what is there to say? You wicked eavesdropping girl! It's the wickedest thing in the world to do, the most wicked.'

'I didn't mean to, ma'am . . .'

'Of course not, of course you didn't – they bit you, I suppose.'

'I saw them lying about.'

'Where? Where did you see them?'

'Just there on the table.'

'When?' Francesca had to repeat it. 'When were they lying on the table?'

'When I came here, the first week.'

'So you read them before, all of them! I guessed that! How horrible and vulgar! When did you read them since?'

'Every day, ma'am, I think.'

'But it's impossible; I lock them up.'

'You leave the key in the drawer, ma'am. (You have now, ma'am.) But I didn't do it sneakily . . .'

'No?'

'I didn't, ma'am; you leave 'em lying about. And you see he calls you by the name of Dear Fan, and that's my name – it's the same as me.'

'Absurd devil!' commented Francesca. 'You've read them all?'

41

'That's no harm, ma'am. I shan't make any trouble, ma'am,' wailed unhappy Fanny. 'I like you too much, I do, and him too.'

The women gazed at each other curiously for a few moments until Fanny was moved to say: 'It's rather . . . it's so . . . so . . .' The ghost of a smile seemed to chase the ghost of a word from the girl's lips.

'So what?' snapped the little mistress.

Fanny let it surprisingly fall at last. 'Funny!' she said, and the indignant flush on Francesca's cheeks deepened as the domestic continued. 'His name is just like my friend's, who I used to walk out with; he used to write to me, just like that. It was rude of me to read your letters, ma'am, and me so fond of you, but my name's Fan, too, and it didn't seem rude, not with the same names. I'm stupid, ma'am, I don't know everything sometimes, ma'am.'

Fanny's eyes glimmered ruefully in her yellow face, and her small nose exhibited a perfect stupidity of pink that almost disarmed Francesca.

'Oh, I don't mind your having read them, though of course I don't like it really; it's loutish. But it's the beastly furtiveness you've imported into my private affairs which I resent. If my private affairs aren't safe from this . . . Oh, you cursed devil, you've spoiled everything now, you've made everything ridiculous, you beastly clammy Hackbut! I suppose' — she gleamed ironically at the stricken servant — 'you spied on your last mistress, just the same? And then you left her, didn't you, proper Hackbut? I shall never call you Fanny again, never;

never anything but Hackbut until you go, for of
course you would not dream of stopping here now,
would you?'

'I don't want to leave you, ma'am.'

'Oh,' raged Francesca, 'I must tell Dr. Harper at
once.' And she ran angrily out of the room.

Fanny returned to the kitchen, full of musing tremors, but with just one gleam of confidence: her
mistress couldn't tell the doctor. God's body, she
would not dare! Why, the letters . . . Oh, but they
were so . . . so . . . they were like what you read
about, like the Bible, they were like plays. If she
only had a lover like that she'd go with him and do
things and things, all sorts of things. She would do
whatever she liked, and he would do what he wanted,
and they'd go all over the world together – the Isle
of Wight and Tappingham Woods, Tappingham,
Tap . . .' Hackbut drooped forlornly upon the
kitchen table and broke into tears. There her mistress found her again.

'Why, what's the matter? Don't be such a fool,
Fanny! I'm going out to tea this afternoon and I
want you to . . .'

'It's my afternoon off,' Fanny interjected with
sullen promptitude, through her tears.

'Oh,' exclaimed Francesca, sullenly too, 'dear me,
yes.'

'I've got an appointment,' explained Fanny.

'I see. All right then,' agreed her mistress.

Having prepared lunch, Fanny hurried from the
house, dressed in her brown jacket and the flaunting

hat with green bow as large as a lampshade. Francesca hated it; she always wore small hats herself, like the socket of an acorn.

After lunch the little mistress cycled away to a country friend, five miles off. You couldn't help staring at Francesca, always, and now she was dressed in white she was more beguiling than ever – all white from head to foot except the gold ring on her finger and the strip of crimson ribbon hanging from her hat. The hat was not quite white, perhaps; shaped like the moon in its first quarter it curved round her dark fringed hair as if it loved her, and the points almost brushed her pink cheeks. You couldn't help staring at Francesca.

Stopping at the Tappingham café on the way, for a cup of coffee, she sat at a table opposite a nun who was eating three sausages. Three! But Francesca did not stare at the nun; no, she only sipped her coffee and glanced out of the window at the passers-by, or looked at the other customers. There were two ladies with a youngish man who took snuff frequently. Disgusting! Presently the ladies retired to the lavatory and left the youngish man alone at the table. He did not look very merry: small squeezed eyes he had, thin mouse-coloured hair, and was painfully shaven. Francesca could see in the mirror behind him that a bald patch as large as a teacup had already established itself upon his oily skull. And what a squab nose! But it must have smelt money, Francesca thought, for he looked, indefinably, quite rich. He took the small box again from his fob,

44

tapped it, opened it, took a pinch between finger and thumb, shook the surplus to the floor (how filthy!), pressed the thumb into his right nostril, the forefinger into the left, replaced the box and drew out his handkerchief. There followed a mild dexterous convulsion.

But oh, how happy little Francesca was! There was nothing in life so exciting as one's interest in one's self, and she had nothing to do but sit and see her own life glide sweetly by, like — like a yacht. Indeed it was she herself that seemed to glide and glide, with infinite gentleness, like a little white yawl sliding to its moorings in a green crystal bay, with a yard-long burgee of crimson galloon. She could rest apart, as it were, and behold herself living and acting as something beautifully strange. Some day, soon, she was to go on a cruise with a friend whose yacht was called *The Francesca*.

Well, she must get on, so on she goes. She pays for her coffee, and as she steps into the street a clergyman crosses the road towards her, dressed in his cassock, and hatless. In his arms he carries a pile of six or seven money-boxes for missionaries, and as he is about to enter the ironmonger's shop next door to the café one of the boxes tumbles from his arms and clutters along the pavement to Francesca's feet. Francesca picks it up for him. 'Thank you,' he intones solemnly, but as he replaces it another box falls. Francesca with a gleam of gaiety restores this too; the clerical gentleman says solemnly, 'I am much obliged to you,' and then dives into the doorway.

'Fop!' mutters Francesca, turning to her bicycle. But again she is interrupted, she almost bumps into two passing women, one old and one young. Francesca draws sharply back, for the young one, in black attire, carries in her arms before her a little white coffin. She does not wear the appearance of grief, indeed she seems secretly to enjoy the surprise of the staring people. The older woman is weeping. With a little chilling shock Francesca recognizes the girl with the coffin; it is Fanny Hackbut, in a borrowed black hat and cloak. The two mourning women pass along the pavement for some distance and then cross the road into the churchyard at the end of the street. The clergyman comes out of the ironmonger's shop and hurries after them.

Francesca rode away to her friend, a little quenched in spirit.

'So miserable I am,' she wailed to Goneril Stroove, 'I passed a funeral, and I hate funerals.'

Miss Stroove dwelt in a village that was but a higgledy-piggledy street with an inn at each end. One, *The Crown*, had lost the sign from its tall white pole: the other was *The King's Head*. Her tiny house was higgledy-piggledy too. It had a rather large bakery on one side, a rather small post office on the other, and behind was a blacksmith's yard — she could hear the anvil chiming all day long. Her front door, painted deeply blue, had a disc of glass as large as a coal plate above the black knocker. The ground floor was a little below the level of the street and visitors had accordingly to descend two stone steps and crank themselves through the doorway straight into a room where the ceiling was altogether too low for the lofty thoughts encouraged there. Its two front windows each had six bulbous panes that defeated inquisitive scrutineers, and left even the dweller herself in a state of hapless speculation about passing identities. A clear window at the back revealed the yard of the smith.

Goneril was a plump grey lady, spruce as a crested lark, with wavery eyes the colour of zinc. She dabbled a little in occultism and other sidereal quackery, but her ideas, good or bad, were never indifferent, were pungently expressed, and her pathetic belief in human brotherhood – as if the whole of mankind might be turned into a joint stock soul company with herself as private secretary – infected her hearers with the charm of her sincerity. For some years now she had been compiling a History of History.

While Goneril went into her kitchen to prepare tea Francesca sat and listened to the ching of the anvil. The smith was shoeing a horse, and the smell of its burning hoofs came unpleasantly through the open window. Neither men nor horses could be seen, but gruff voices of the smith and a carter in charge of the horse carried on a conversation much broken by violent admonitions to the animal. Pit, pit, pit, went the hammer on the new shoe.

'Whuppah!' yelled the smith. It startled Francesca at first; she thought the horse must have bitten somebody, but it was not so. 'Git over, Dragon.

Doh-wee-yock, boy,' cried the very affable carter.
Pit, pit, pit, went the hammer again.

'How much they give for this hoss, Archie?' puffed
the smith.

'Sixty pounds,' replied Archie. 'He cost sixty golden
(Whoa!) sovrins, Ted.'

'Too much, that,' gurgled the smith. 'Whoa, Dragon!
Whoa, boy!'

'Bought him from a man as had the whooping-
cough or summat.'

'Git up there!' roared the smith. To Francesca his
voice sounded fearfully brutal.

Over some rather intense muffins and cups of China
tea Goneril discoursed to Francesca for some time
upon universal space, of the way to raise sunken
ships, and lastly of dual personality.

'Yes, Goneril,' said Francesca at length, 'there
is nothing in life so exciting to me as my own interest
in myself. I suppose I am an egoist.'

'I dare say — if one only knew them — the things other
people think about you would be quite as exciting.'

'Oh, but . . .' objected Francesca.

'Almost everything one person *thinks* of another,'
persisted Goneril, 'is likely to be bad rather than
good. We are all of us at once delicate and brutal,
wise and wanton, courageous and procrastinating.
But well, then, our virtues are taken for granted, or
what is pleasanter, they are generally known; but it
is what is unknown in others that offers itself to our
crooked furtive speculations. Fortunately these inde-

48

cencies are seldom expressed. It's a sublime reticence.'

'Aren't we foul!' ejaculated Francesca. 'And yet I was thinking only as I came along that there is nothing in life so fascinating as one's own view of oneself. Do you ever stand apart, as it were, and observe yourself, living and acting as some enchanting thing, beautifully strange?'

The zinc eyes wavered about the visitor's visible daintiness. 'I never see myself in that way, no, but sometimes I do feel my being as a kind of labyrinth, with my spirit wandering in it lost and sighing, in search of something. I don't know what — I wish I did. Yes, take that piece of muffin, please. I'm not a romantic, you see; I can only probe into myself, make dissections of my tendencies, my impulses.' Francesca had a fleeting vision of numberless rashers of bacon. 'It is very hopeless, though, disillusioning,' continued Goneril. 'The person I really am is the person I understand least of all. I never do see myself. No, Nimrod, no; you are a filthy cat!'

Nimrod's stiff upstanding tabby tail reminded her — Miss Stroove said — of the Tower of Babel: she was debarred for ever from understanding even with him. Whenever it ceased to prowl the tabby imp continued to lift its paws in apparent trepidation, as though it could feel the fire which is said to lie in the heart of the earth. Silently for a few moments they watched him do this; then the voices from the smithy broke upon them again.

'He's a queer hoss, Ted,' the carter was saying. 'If

he've bin in mud and his fetlocks be all mired up he'll stand to the brush and let a child groom him; but if you went to lay a finger on him when he was clean he'd kick a fly's eye out. Now then, Dragon! What be at? Git over!'

'Yes,' Francesca resumed, 'I suppose the average person is romantic?'

'The average person!' said Goneril, with a whimsical frown. 'What is that? There was once an Average Man, and his good and bad deeds were mingled in such equal proportions, so absolutely balanced, that no one could determine whether he had any goodness at all. In consequence everybody believed him to be bad. When he was swayed by his bad desires they called him Sinner and Monster. When he had his good ones, they could not believe the evidence of their senses, it was too good to be true: they called him Hypocrite, Impostor, Liar. When he did things neither good nor bad they said he was trivial – and wished him dead.'

She was interrupted by renewed uproar from the smithy.

'What a hubbub!' cried Francesca, 'it must annoy you dreadfully.'

'No, no,' cried Goneril, 'I like it, I like it. I expect it's a difficult horse to shoe.'

'Git over, Dragon!' shouted Archie, 'you lolloping badger, you! I'll gie you a drench to-morrow.' The silent women peered a little apprehensively at the back window.

'He's not up to much,' the smith growled and

puffed, 'what you been feeding him on — unction?'
'Oh, they has to be fed, we know. Horses have to be fed, Ted, we knows that. He's too fat, now, but not so bloody . . .'
'Whoa up, there! Gee whoa, Dragon!' roared the smith, 'gee whoa!'
Pit, pit, pit, went the hammer again.
'He ain't — whoa, Dragon, good boy,' said Archie, 'he ain't so bloody . . .'
'Yah, whuppah!' the smith again momentarily raged. The horse subsided, it was bearing its ordeal with fortitude, the hammer resumed its pit, pit, pit.
'What was that you was a-going to say, Archie?'
'To say, Ted?' the carter questioned, 'to say? What *was* I a-going to say?'
'Ah, I can't tell you, Archie. Only God Almighty could do that, but it were summat about this 'ere hoss, I believe.'
'Oh, ah, I know!' Archie crowed. 'I was only going to say as how he a'n't so fat as he was, not near.'
The smith made no reply, the shoeing was finished. 'So long, Ted.'
'So long, Archie.' A great horse, with a man on its back, clumped past Goneril's little window.
'I am romantic, you know,' continued Francesca at last, 'I am too romantic, such a fool I am!'
'No, no, don't say too romantic,' protested Goneril; 'all romantic souls have compassion. One of the most beautiful things in life is mankind's pity for its own sinfulness.'
'Do you think so?' Francesca said. 'It sounds rather

maudlin to me. But it is you who are compassionate, Goneril. Nobody could be more compassionate than you. And you're not a *bit* romantic! Too, too compassionate you are, you never find fault with the world, the flesh, or the devil, or anything else – if there is anything else!'

'If there are faults to find, Francesca,' Goneril's gaze seemed to pierce her visitor's, 'it is not my business to find them, and I don't want to find them. True, this is an entirely inexplicable existence: we may be living in a fool's paradise, but it *is* paradise. You see,' she went on as Francesca did not speak, 'romance is a bridge between mysticism and reality. To the mystic nothing is impossible save reality, which is vanity and vexation of spirit; while to the realist all things are possible, except mysticism. You are neither, dear little Francesca, you are like love itself, and love's only duty is to be delightful.'

'Dear Goneril,' protested the other, 'you rush over me like a cataract, terrifying! And I don't understand your axioms one bit – I never do, though I like them enormously – they seem to me to be just sufficiently comprehensive to be either true or untrue. So puzzled I am! Surely love now should be faithful, that is its duty, surely?'

'Faithful to what?'

'To what it loves.'

'It can only be faithful or unfaithful to itself, Francesca, to its own genius of delight. Yes, yes, and to that faith I know we all prove false: men are ungrateful and women are unwise. Blessed are the pure in heart, for they shall see God: but isn't that just too hard a price to pay — even for heaven?'

'Ah, yes,' said Francesca, 'we always know what we can do until we try!'

Goneril had brought their talk to an altitude at which (as happened with the Tower of Babel) neither knew what to do with it. It stood there, tempting time, until Francesca put on her yellow gloves and Goneril declared that it — the weather — was blowing up for rain.

So Francesca departed: she kissed her friend in the sunken doorway.

'Good-bye, Goneril, you will come in to tea soon?'

'Yes, I will. Have you got rid of your tiresome servant yet?'

'No,' Francesca deliberated, with one leg over the cycle saddle, 'we've not, no. She's begun to be satisfactory. We are keeping her on.'

'Indeed!'

'Oh, she's quite a friend of the family now — she reads our letters! Good-bye!'

'Dear me! Good-bye, Francesca.'

Francesca cycled away quite swiftly, for she was exhilarated. 'What a curious day it keeps on being!' she breathlessly mused. Goneril always excited her. She felt like a tiny plant, recently parched, that had just been cheered by soft copious streams from a pot that had a brass sprayer, very large and shiny, with very little holes in it.

'And it's not half over yet. Oh, all sorts of things I've got to tell Hugh.'

She came to the railway crossing and abated her speed.

'I'm sure it is not going to rain, it is only splendidly dull. I think that railway station is perfectly beautiful, too. Railway stations can be, and they are. Oh, isn't it! It must be charming to live there.'

It was a very, very small station – there were only two advertisements even: one that promised soft white hands and a good complexion (Francesca had both), the other a gall cure for horses. One bench, one window, one lamp, and one fox-terrier dog that dashed from the booking office six times a day to bark at a train coming almost silently from the tunnel in the green hills and then sliding through the lime works that sprawled in a white pit with six black cupolas and a high pink chimney.

'Goneril's talk is so stimulating. And yet that's strange, too, for it's no more like real life than a topic of conversation in a train. I don't know, I can't think she can have been in love many times; perhaps not more than once – everybody has loved once. In men it is an art – she says – and in women it is a gift. That's very true, only, how can one keep on giving one's gift away? As one does?'

Back through Tappingham she rode with undiminished spirit. The ironmonger's shop was closing; the baths and shovels had been taken down so that she could now see the name above the window, *Kitchen, late Kettle*. The churchyard was very still. Francesca glanced over the wall as she sped by, but she could see nothing disquieting. She was glad. It would be nice when one died to have a very beautiful quotation on one's grave, something quite distinctive that no one else had ever thought of; she determined to make notes of suitable mottoes.

In the park under Tappingham woods scores of deer were browsing under the trellising trees, and close to the metal palings there was a small but emphatic lake, its ambulant swan covering the beholder with the shrewd eye of a strumpet.

'Goneril doesn't help me in the least, really. She makes everything one hopes for seem impossible. And one always longs for the impossible – there's nothing else to wish for. Oh, but I love days like this, they are so exciting!'

On reaching home Francesca ran first to peep in the kitchen. Nobody there, but it smelled of dinner – divinely. Stuffed hare, force-meat balls, fried whiting – lovely! How pathetic the fishes would look under their little sprigs of parsley! How delicious! How tantalizing! Oh, hunger was quite the most heavenly thing in the world! Nobody in the dining-room either, no letters by the afternoon post, the gilt clock had stopped at twenty-five minutes past six. It often stopped between six and seven – so stupid of it. Then, through an open doorway that led into the garden, she could see and hear her husband talking to Fanny, a very quenched Fanny standing with a bowl of corn in her hands. Hugh had the appearance of a virtuous man about to convict a despicable scoundrel of some misdemeanour.

'Stupid,' he said softly, but disagreeably, 'you needn't

do that, I've already fed them; besides, some of them are broody and mustn't be fed at all. You are a fool, you know nothing about chickens, do you? No, you know nothing about chickens!'

'Hugh, Hugh,' cried Francesca from the doorway, 'come in quickly, please, I want you.'

'Hello, hello!' He came at once, and Francesca closed the door.

'You mustn't do it, Hugh, not now. You mustn't do it at all.'

'Do what?'

'Mustn't discharge her, her baby is dead.'

'Oh!' he said blankly. 'Well, they always do die. I'm rather glad.'

'But, Hugh, you mustn't discharge her at all now. She only buried it to-day, this afternoon. I saw her carrying the coffin in her arms, in the street, Hugh.'

They sat down side by side and she told him all about it. Later on, after dinner, as they sat in the gathering dusk still harping upon Fanny, Francesca said: 'She's been reading my letters.'

Hugh made no comment.

'My private ones,' Francesca proceeded. 'I caught her at them, all of them!'

'Your private letters? From . . . him?'

Francesca nodded with a playful grimace.

'Well,' said he slowly, ' that's a reason the more for getting rid of her, isn't it? Not that we want any more, when there are already 999, the slut.'

'Reasons? Yes, but perhaps . . . we must let this

blow over. You mustn't do it now, Hugh, at least, you mustn't do it yet, must you?'

'Oh, because of the letters! I see, I see, yes, I see. Darn her,' he added softly, but after a few seconds he burst out petulantly: 'I wish you'd give up this confounded flirtation. You've let yourself in for something now, if she goes tattling – as of course she will!'

'But you said I could.'

'Could?' he snapped.

'Have a friend.'

'O God! You say that as if I had said that you might have a cake.'

'Well,' Francesca said, a little hardly, and it seemed the only thing to say, 'what about it?'

'About it! I did say so, yes, I did say it, yes, certainly; but if he writes you letters which horrify our scullion . . .

'Oh, but they don't, Hugh; she revels in them, she's in love with them, her imbecility is quite touching.'

'He's a philanderer,' replied her husband severely, 'a posturer, a scandal-maker and a liar. Besides, I don't approve of him. I liked him once, but I loathe him now. I warn you, he has a crooked bawdy mind, and is not to be trusted or believed.'

'Does all that matter, Hugh?'

'Doesn't it?'

'No, his only duty is to be delightful.'

'And is he?'

She nodded again. 'It's so odd, Hugh, I'm fond of him.' Her small white hands groped their way

57

into the doctor's large fist. 'I shall be seeing him
again . . . soon.'

'When?'

Francesca did not reply.

'Well,' he said, releasing her, 'he's not in love
with me, nor I with him. I don't like him. His
clothes always look too large for him, and his hats too
small.'

'Oh, Hugh, Hugh!' Francesca shuddered.

'I used to like him once, very much, but he hasn't
a scrap of conscience, not a scrap. Everybody has
some sort of conscience, but he has none; I couldn't
exist without it. One forgets it, it's true, same as one
forgets the collar stud at the back of one's neck — but
it's *there*! When are you going to see him?'

He gleamed at her with all his pleasant teeth.

'To-morrow, Hugh.'

Again she groped her way into his unresponsive
hands. He could enjoy the perfume of her dark
fine hair, carelessly combed, but never dishevelled.
Ah, she was most lovely, most discerning, and yet
still most fantastic.

They were silent for a very long time. He could
hear the maple trees in their garden swishing and
sighing. He thought Francesca had gone to sleep,
she fell asleep so easily; he got up, groping his way
towards the door, and put on a hat. Her voice at
last broke drowsily into the darkness that had grown
chill about them.

'Good night, Hugh,' she said; and he said 'Good
night' and went out to walk in the dark streets. The

58

wind had roughened and he tramped in freshened airs as far as the borders of the town where there were no public lights, only a few scattered villas with long hedged gardens and lines of trees. There seemed to be light as well as sound in the windy sky, but earth remained all one streaming blackness, and he stepped along timidly. His soul was full of doubt, mournful as the dark seething trees. The gates in the gardens rattled their loose latches, dim lights shone through most of the upper windows, each casting the shadow of a looking-glass upon its drawn blind — symbol of curiosity and care, vanity and love. What a world it would be without looking-glasses, wherein we see ourselves as others do *not* see us! The wind blows; upon its unknown course rolls this vast surprising world; how idle is sorrow, how vain is faith, how slight a thing is love. Nothing, nothing (his mind chattered) but a little fervid dust peering into a mirror that reflects only its own gazing face.

'It's beginning to rain,' sighed Harper, 'I must go back home,' and he returned home to find an urgent summons from an old colleague desiring his assistance in a critical case some fifteen miles away.

On several nights he was away from home, it was the desperate case of an unimportant but wealthy woman, and for many days he scarcely saw Francesca at all, except that always on his tired return she would meet him, beautifully sympathetic, and minister to him.

But she made no further confidences, his almost frenzied desire to be assured of her romantic infidel-

59

ity was never satisfied. As to that the absurdest inhibition possessed him, he could not muster the will to ask her and discover. He knew Francesca too well to be hopeful, she had a curious ruthlessness. Yet he was puzzled, and he kept the puzzle lying in his hands like some useless intricate ingenuity that he could neither conquer nor discard. And there was some sort of solace in mere doubt – doubt and hope were just two sides of the same coin – it left him a margin on which he could still precariously, though so intolerably, live. How serious Francesca intended this affair to be he did not know, he could only guess. She had opportunity for anything, every-thing, but opportunity was nothing unless time, or chance, or the devil himself, transfigured it.

'Why, oh, why,' he groaned, 'doesn't she go and see him? Or does she? She ought to go, it's the thing to do. She is fond of him. I wish it were not true. What a thing love is! Well, well, but if it's got to be borne! O God, I wish it were not true!'

If he could only be certain of something, good or bad! He would feel better, even if it were bad; he would indeed welcome the ignominy of that relief. But he dared not for the peace of his soul ask the simple question of Francesca. Let sleeping dogs lie – he remembered the adage, only he wanted to be sure that they *were* sleeping and not shamming for some infernal purpose. Francesca was quite blameless; he envisioned her always, always as a tender flower; but she had to grow in the way God made her. 'All brains and apprehension – but she hasn't any sense,' he confided to himself, and in that state of mind he moodily waited, and only frigidly fingered the distractions of duty, of scene, of appetite.

One afternoon, three weeks having gone by, he came home and found her kneeling in front of the fire with a pile of blue-grey letters in her lap.

'Hello!' He squatted down beside her. 'What's all this?'

'Junk!' said Francesca. 'Do you see, Hugh?' She smiled at him and continued idly throwing the letters by twos and threes into the flames. 'Junk!' Francesca repeated, 'throw some on, Hugh, quickly.'

He began to throw letters upon the fire.

'Do you think I'm faithless, Hugh?'

'Well, he hasn't much to congratulate himself upon; how long did it last?'

'Oh, I don't mean faithless to him. Besides, it doesn't matter how long, does it?'

'Not as long as it was long enough,' said he.

'Enough for what?' Francesca shot a glance at him, but he was not looking at her.

'Enough to get tired of,' he rejoined.

She seized some of the remaining letters and began to peruse them silently, even sullenly.

'These will do,' at last she cried, throwing the rest away, 'they are not too wicked, they won't corrupt her, they couldn't demoralize anyone, even me; they wouldn't agitate a nun. I'm keeping these for Fanny, she explained, 'I shall leave them about on purpose for her to read.'

'Humph!' grinned the doctor. 'Tell me what happened.'

'Oh, it was too silly! She read them all, and revelled in them.'

'Fanny?'

'Yes, it spoilt everything and made it ridiculous. I could see myself in such an absurd light, like a housemaid! Do you ever see yourself, Hugh, living and acting very strangely apart from your real self? No? I suppose I am too sensitive, but it seemed as if Fanny and I had changed places, that the letters were more hers than mine – she liked them better than I did – and that *he* was, too. Preposterous situation! Have you ever felt like that, Hugh?'

'Yes,' murmured the doctor, gazing at his wife, 'I think, yes.'

'Too preposterous, isn't it? But it was you who were so right, Hugh. It's incredible – but you are always so incredibly right. You aren't ever right in the ordinary way. You are really rather wrong about him generally: he is just like Goneril's average man, so very balanced that he's just trivial. But what I do see so absurdly now – I can see nothing else and it's horribly ridiculous – is that his clothes *are* too big, and his hats *are* too small!'

The doctor grinned as generously as his somewhat strained apprehension allowed. Francesca clasped her white hands and gazed at the paper ashes; the doctor gathered her tiny fists into his own.

'Hugh, am I a faithless being?'

'Well,' he replied, 'isn't that just what I want to know?'

'Dear Hugh!' and then Francesca irrelevantly said: 'Fanny's such an impossible fool!'

'Now, isn't she?' the doctor softly groaned. 'I shall sack her at once.'

'Hugh,' Francesca murmured, ' why don't you ever want to sack me?'

ON A FINE AFTERNOON IN APRIL A MAN IS SITTING at the foot of an ash-tree beside the pool of water on Peck Common. Twelve tiny ducklings on the water belong to him, and he is admiring them. There are four ash-trees there, growing out of the tenderest turf and spreading over the pool; the bright air seems to swim visibly around their bare grey limbs. A carrier this man is, a little man with an old conical hat, his coat sleeves coming down over his knuckles, his hat coming down over his ears, and he is the masterpiece of the whole district for trapping a mole. Beside him a sallow bush, richly embowered, also stretches out above the pool, every twig of it bearing a ball of blossom covered with yellow dust, whereon fat bees are mumbling and clinging. But the day's air comes coldly from the east, and at intervals the bees, so chilled, tumble into the pool. The man takes a branch he has broken from the palm tree and drags them to earth again, where they dry their wings and crawl into the grass for comfort. 'Lend us your saw, Willie Waugh,' said Peter Finch, coming suddenly upon him.

'Good evening,' said the man in the funny hat, without looking up. He had not noticed Peter's approach, for the grass was quiet under his footfall, and then his ducklings had just paddled to the shore and one of them was behaving queerly. It would not follow its friends, it just kept turning round and turning round, squealing all the time.

Peter Finch asked again: 'Will you lend me your saw for a few nights, Willie?'

'Look at that duckling,' Waugh indicated the creature with his pipe ; 'do you know what the matter is with that duckling?'

'I only waunts to borrow it for a few nights,' continued Peter Finch, a tall man, a thin man, who shaved in vain so blue was his sharp chin. 'The old keeper asked me to fell some trees arter I done my daily work, so it's for a bit of overtime, you see. Your big saw, if you're not a-using of it.'

'It's blind, that duckling is,' explained the other, 'blind.'

'I ain't got a saw of my own, Willie, or I wouldn't ask ye.' — Peter was not to be diverted — 'I'll take care of it, you knows that, I'll take care of it well.'

'I shan't kill it for a day or two, not yet I shan't. I'll see how it gets on. It eats like a blam young tiger,' commented Waugh.

'Dan'l Gunn,' pursued Peter, 'ask me and Hoppy Marlow to fell they trees. We'em a-going to do it between us, overtime work. It 'ull put three or four pounds apiece in our pockets. If so be as you'd lend us your big saw.'

'Blind as a bat,' Willie Waugh continued, 'that's why he keeps on turning round. It ain't got no tail now, neither.'

'I thought Hoppy nad got one, but he ain't. He used to have a big saw, I thought; I quite thought that, but he says as how he didn't.'

'That foal in Casby's paddock,' cried Waugh,

'picked it up in its mouth last night and started chawing of it like a wisp hay. That little duck! That's a fine caper, an' it? I collared that duckling away from it just in time, but his tail was gone.' As disgust and indignation mounted within him Willie turned and looked Peter Finch fiercely in the eyes. 'An' I gin him a kick in the stomach as cured him o' duck hunting, I warrant!'

'So I'll send my young Tommy,' said Peter, 'round for it to-morrow, after tea-time. Right-o.' And off went Peter.

Next evening little Tom Finch came to the carrier's door to fetch the saw for his father to fell the trees along of Hoppy Marlow.

'I've changed my mind,' declared Willie Waugh. 'I can't lend him, tell your father.'

'Our father sent me for the saw, please,' repeated the child.

'And I tell you I ain't a-going to lend him. Can't you hear? I told you once and now I tell you twice. Tell your father I've changed my mind.'

Away went little Tom, and soon afterwards Peter Finch appeared at the door of Waugh's cottage, which was No. 93 Peck Common, although if you took a spyglass, even, you would not, and could not, see more than ten or a dozen cottages there. Willie had crept away to the pool, but Peter saw him and went after him.

'Lend us your saw, Willie Waugh,' begged Peter, 'I've a job of overtime to do.'

'I can't lend you,' Willie said.

'Why can't you lend me your big saw?' There was a sharpish note in Peter's voice.

'I've changed my mind.'

'And for why have you changed your mind?'

Willie meditated, stared at his interrogator's chest, removed his pipe with his right hand, and with the forefinger of his left he tapped the arm of Peter Finch, and began:

'I'll tell you for why, I'll diagonize it for you. You're a man in full heart of work, from Monday morning to Saturday arternoon; a full week's work, and a full week's pay you draws.'

'Ah?'

'Well, there's a-plenty men roundabout here's not doing more than two or three days' work instead of a week, and they's the ones as ought to be set to do this overtime job. When you be in full heart o' work and they be not, you to go and work overtime for another man does them out of the chance.'

'Ho, that's how it runs, is it?' commented Peter.

'That's it an' all. Several there be. Two of 'em I knows for certain at Creevey Lane – Moby Colfax for one – and there's Topper Oakes over at Fire-brass Hill, and some more I knows. And that's why I shan't a-lend 'ee my saw.'

'Topper Oakes! He couldn't fell a nut tree! Look here, did I ever do you a bad turn, Willie Waugh?'

Willie began to fill his pipe. 'No, not to my knowledge, I can't say you ever did that.'

'Treat me as a neighbour, then, as a neighbour

67

should. Do me no harm. Do me no harm, and I'll do none. Only man I ever harmed is myself. Full work and full pay, says you; but you knows you can put that thirty shillings in your eye and sneeze on it — and *then* it wouldn't choke you.'

'I understands all that. . . .'

'Eight young uns I got, and a wife, and a cripple mother. . . .'

'Well, that's your look out, it's your luck. I understands all that. But if you doos this overtime job you're depriving another man of his just dues, and if I lends you my saw I be just as bad.'

'How d'ye make that out?'

'Stands to reason. You be a-taking the bread out of a man's mouth. That's truth and sound sense.'

Peter Finch stared at him as if he were an absurd phenomenon — an ox with a hat on, perhaps, or a pig with a toothbrush. 'You're chattering as if you was the lord mayor of this parish.'

'Sound truth and sound sense,' repeated Willie, 'sound as a bell.'

'Ah, and hard as a ram's horn,' quoth Peter. 'There's many a man as wouldn't ever speak to you again for this, Willie Waugh. You talk of robbing men of their bread: tell me this — Would you lend e'er a one of 'em your big saw?'

'If they asked me,' replied Waugh imperturbably, 'I might.'

'Then wouldn't you be a-robbing me and mine, and Hoppy Marlow and his'n?'

'No!'

'Course you would. Come on, I'll pay you a crown for the use of that saw.'

'I couldn't take it,' said Waugh, 'my conscience wouldn't let me.'

'Bah! If I harboured a thing like that I wouldn't call it a conscience! You're a sour neighbour, Willie Waugh, sour as varjuice. I've done a good deed to you, more than once I have, and known you all my life.'

'The same to you, many a time!' ejaculated Willie. Then he lit his pipe that he always smoked with the bowl upside down.

'When the wheel of your cart come off on Cadmer Hill,' continued Finch, 'and we had to unempty it 'cause of a storm coming on . . .'

'I unemptied it myself,' cried the carrier.

'Didn't I carry four sacks of meal home for you? On my back? Half a mile each time, and rain and sweat sopping me through!'

'Who was it drove your missus to the 'firmary when she had her breast off for cancer, eh? A day's journey, that were, free and for nothing!'

'Well, and when you and your wife was down with fever, and no one come near you for fear of catching it, not even the parson, eh? Said he never knew about it . . .'

'Ah, the Peter!'

'Who looked after you then, Willie Waugh, and your stock, Willie Waugh, and emptied your slops, Willie Waugh?'

'And who collected a subscription for you when

your sow died?' rejoined the carrier. 'Seven pounds fourteen shillin's and ninepence ha'penny for a pig as warn't worth half that money.'

'That's right enough,' Peter agreed. 'You been a good neighbour, good as a man ever knowed. But why do you round on me now?'

'I've not rounded on you, I'm only telling you.'

'A neighbour,' Peter Finch observed, 'should stand *by* his neighbour, turn and turn about. I've lived next or nigh you all my life. You riz in the world, you've prospered, but I haven't.'

'God bless me,' cried Waugh, 'when I started out to work I got three and six a week and a pound at Michaelmas. My old dad would give me a penny out of that on Saturdays.'

'Oh, I knows. I knowed you, Willie Waugh, ever since you was a nipper; I knowed you when you put the tadpoles in the font at Farmer Fescot's christening.'

'Five o'clock we had to get up then, and work till dark. None of this 'ere starting at seven and leaving off at five, and football, and crickets, and God knows what all! They *was* some farmers in those days, but if their old corpses could come out of their holes and see what goes on now, why, they . . . they . . . they'd go mad – it 'ud kill 'em!'

Peter was unmoved, a very unfeeling, unprincipled man.

'Too many holidays in this country,' Willie rambled moodily on, 'that's what there is. I'd sooner work seven days a week than six, for I don't know what to be at a' Sundays.'

'We was at school then,' mused Peter. 'I caught the tadpoles, a tin-full, and you tipped 'em in the font water. There was a racket about that.'

'Ah,' commented Willie, 'you was afraid to do it of yourself.'

'I bet you once as you couldn't swallow a butter-fly . . .'

'Ah, and I ate four of 'em at once,' interrupted Willie.

'But you was sick arterwards.'

'Nor you didn't pay up, by dam.' Waugh, leaning against one of the ash-trees, smiled into the pool. 'That Farmer Fescot was a good old farmer as ever was, a thoroughbred 'un.'

'Thoroughly thoroughbred,' granted Peter. 'We cooked the liver of his piebald nag when it died, you and me!'

'His wife warn't much,' declared Willie.

'No. She ought to have had her head shook. Do you recollect that circus as come by here one even-ing? Going out west somewheres. They pasted up bills on the barns and walls as they went along, and we dogged 'em and turned their bills all upsy down. Miles we followed that circus, and it wasn't half late when we got home!'

'Ah,' chortled Willie, 'I 'members you falling over the elephant's dung in the dark.'

'That's a few years ago,' sighed Peter, 'a few years ago, thirty, forty. Ah!' He turned and sauntered

71

away, plucking as he did so a blade of grass and chewing it as he went.

Willie called after him. 'Arn't you going to take that saw?'

'If you like, Willie,' Peter turned, 'if you don't mind obliging me for a few nights.'

'Well, take the blam saw,' said Willie gruffly. 'Think I'm going to run about arter you with it!'

So they went back to the cottage, and Peter got the saw and took it home. When he had gone Willie Waugh came and leaned over his garden gate, staring across the common at the four ash-trees by the pond where the grass was so very geen. The trees were budding; the sky beyond them was glassy blue, with a cusp of new white moon, and clouds with fiery fringes hovering on the borders of everywhere. Long shadows slanted from the ash-trees, and long smoke twirled from the village chimneys. Tir-a-loo sang the birds, and the eyes of the playing children shone with a golden light.

'I never see,' grumbled Willie to himself, 'never in all my days — such a pack of fools — as there be in this world. And,' he added, 'they be all alike.'

THE HIGGLER

I

ON A COLD APRIL AFTERNOON A HIGGLER WAS driving across Shag Moor in a two-wheeled cart.

H. WITLOW
Dealer in Poultry
DINNOP

was painted on the hood; the horse was of mean appearance but notorious ancestry. A high upland common was this moor, two miles from end to end, and full of furze and bracken. There were no trees and not a house, nothing but a line of telegraph poles following the road, sweeping with rigidity from north to south; nailed upon one of them a small scarlet notice to stonethrowers was prominent as a wound. On so high and wide a region as Shag Moor the wind always blew, or if it did not quite blow there was a cool activity in the air. The furze was always green and growing, and, taking no account of seasons, often golden. Here in summer solitude lounged and snoozed; at other times, as now, it shivered and looked sinister.

Higglers in general are ugly and shrewd, old and hard, crafty and callous, but Harvey Witlow, though shrewd, was not ugly; he was hard but not old, crafty but not at all unkind. If you had eggs to sell he would buy them, by the score he would, or by the long hundred. Other odds and ends he would buy or do, paying good bright silver, bartering a bag of apples, carrying your little pig to market, or fetching a tree from the nurseries. But the season was backward, eggs were scarce, trade was bad — by crumps, it was indeed! — and as he crossed the moor Harvey could not help discussing the situation with himself. 'If things don't change, and change for the better, and change soon, I can't last and I can't endure it; I'll be damned and done, and I'll have to sell,' he said, prodding the animal with the butt of his whip, 'this cob. And,' he said, as if in afterthought, prodding the footboard, 'this cart, and go back to the land. And I'll have lost my fifty pounds. Well, that's what war does for you. It does it for you, sir,' he announced sharply to the vacant moor, 'and it does it for me. Fifty pounds! I was better off in the war. I was better off working for farmers — much. But it's no good chattering about it, it's the trick of life; when you get so far, then you can go and order your funeral. Get along, Dodger!'

The horse responded briskly for a few moments. 'I tell ye,' said Harvey adjuring the ambient air, 'you can go and order your funeral. Get along, Dodger!'

Again Dodger got along.

'Then there's Sophy, what about Sophy and me?'

He was not engaged to Sophy Daws, not exactly, but he was keeping company with her. He was not pledged or affianced, he was just keeping company with her. But Sophy, as he knew, not only desired a marriage with Mr. Witlow, she expected it, and expected it soon. So did her parents, her friends, and

74

everybody in the village, including the postman who didn't live in it but wished he did, and the parson who did live in it but wished he didn't.

'Well, that's damned and done, fair damned and done now, unless things take a turn, and soon, so it's no good chattering about it.'

And just then and there things did take a turn. He had never been across the moor before; he was prospecting for trade. At the end of Shag Moor he saw standing back on the common, fifty yards from the road, a neat square house set in a little farm. Twenty acres, perhaps. The house was girded by some white palings; beside it was a snug orchard in a hedge covered with blackthorn bloom. It was very green and pleasant in front of the house. The turf was cleared and closely cropped, some ewes were grazing and under the blackthorn, out of the wind, lay half a dozen lambs, but what chiefly moved the imagination of Harvey Witlow was a field on the far side of the house. It had a small rickyard with a few small stacks in it; everything here seemed on the small scale, but snug, very snug; and in that field and yard were hundreds of fowls, hundreds, of good breed, and mostly white. Leaving his horse to sniff the greensward, the higgler entered a white wicket gateway and passed to the back of the house, noting as he did so a yellow wagon inscribed *Elizabeth Sadgrove. Prattle Corner.*

At the kitchen door he was confronted by a tall gaunt woman of middle age with a teapot in her hands.

'Afternoon, ma'am. Have you anything to sell?' began Harvey Witlow, tilting his hat with a confident affable air. The tall woman was cleanly dressed, a superior person; her hair was grey. She gazed at him.

'It's cold,' he continued. She looked at him as uncomprehendingly as a mouse might look at a gravestone.

'I'll buy any mottal thing, ma'am. Except trouble; I'm full up wi' that already. Eggs? Fowls?'

'I've not seen you before,' commented Mrs. Sadgrove a little bleakly, in a deep husky voice.

'No, 'tis the first time as ever I drove in this part. To tell you the truth, ma'am, I'm new to the business. Six months. I was in the war a year ago. Now I'm trying to knock up a connection. Difficult work. Things are very quiet.'

Mrs. Sadgrove silently removed the lid of the teapot, inspected the interior of the pot with an intent glance, and then replaced the lid as if she had seen a blackbeetle there.

'Ah, well,' sighed the higgler. 'You've a neat little farm here, ma'am.'

'It's quiet enough,' said she.

'Sure it is, ma'am. Very lonely.'

'And it's difficult work, too.' Mrs. Sadgrove almost smiled.

'Sure it is, ma'am; but you does it well, I can see. Oh, you've some nice little ricks of corn, eh! I does well enough at the dealing now and again, but it's teasy work, and mostly I don't earn enough to keep my horse in shoe leather.'

'I've a few eggs, perhaps,' said she.

'I could do with a score or two, ma'am, if you could let me have 'em.'

'You'll have to come all my way if I do.'

'Name your own price, ma'am, if you don't mind trading with me.'

'Mind! Your money's as good as my own, isn't it?'

'It must be, ma'am. That's meaning no disrespects to you,' the young higgler assured her hastily, and was thereupon invited to enter the kitchen.

A stone floor with two or three mats; open hearth with burning logs; a big dresser painted brown, carrying a row of white cups on brass hooks and shelves of plates overlapping each other like the scales of fish. A dark settle half hid a flight of stairs with a small gate at the top. Under the window a black sofa, deeply indented, invited you a little repellingly, and in the middle of the room stood a large table, exquisitely scrubbed, with one end of it laid for tea. Evidently a living-room as well as kitchen. A girl, making toast at the fire, turned as the higgler entered. Beautiful she was: red hair, a complexion like the inside of a nut, blue eyes, and the hands of a lady. He saw it all at once, jacket of bright green wool, black dress, grey stockings and shoes, and forgot his errand, her mother, his fifty pounds, Sophy — momentarily he forgot everything. The girl stared strangely at him. He was tall, clean-

77

shaven, with a loop of black hair curling handsomely over one side of his brow.

'Good afternoon,' said Harvey Witlow, as softly as if he had entered a church.

'Some eggs, Mary,' Mrs. Sadgrove explained. The girl laid down her toasting-fork. She was less tall than her mother, who she resembled only enough for the relationship to be noted. Silently she crossed the kitchen and opened a door that led into a dairy. Two pans of milk were creaming on a bench there, and on the flags were two great baskets filled with eggs.

'How many are there?' asked Mrs. Sadgrove, and the girl replied: 'Fifteen score, I think.'

'Take the lot, higgler?'

'Yes, ma'am,' he cried eagerly, and ran out to his cart and fetched a number of trays. In them he packed the eggs as the girl handed them to him from the baskets. Mrs. Sadgrove left them together. For a time the higgler was silent.

'No,' at length he murmured, 'I've never been this road before.'

There was no reply from Mary. Sometimes their fingers touched, and often, as they bent over the eggs, her bright hair almost brushed his face.

'It is a loneish spot,' he ventured again.

'Yes,' said Mary Sadgrove.

When the eggs were all transferred her mother came in again.

'Would you buy a few pullets, higgler?'

'Any number, ma'am,' he declared quickly. Any number; by crumps, the tide was turning! He followed the mother into the yard, and there again she left him, waiting. He mused about the girl and wondered about the trade. If they offered him ten thousand chickens, he'd buy them, somehow, he would! She had stopped in the kitchen. Just in there she was, just behind him, a few feet away. Over the low wall of the yard a fat black pony was strolling in a field of bright greensward. In the yard, watching him, was a young gander, and on a stone staddle beside it lay a dead thrush on its back, its legs stiff in the air. The girl stayed in the kitchen; she was moving about, though, he could hear her; perhaps she was spying at him through the window. Twenty million eggs he would buy if Mrs. Sadgrove had got them. She was gone a long time. It was very quiet. The gander began to comb its white breast with its beak. Its three-toed feet were a most tender pink, shaped like wide diamonds, and at each of the three forward points there was a toe like a small blanched nut. It lifted one foot, folding the webs, and hid it under its wing and sank into a resigned meditation on one leg. It had a blue eye that was meek – it had two, but you could only see one at a time – a meek blue eye, set in a pink rim that gave it a dissolute air, and its beak had raw red nostrils as if it suffered from the damp. Altogether a beautiful bird. And in some absurd way it resembled Mrs. Sadgrove.

'Would you sell that young gollan, ma'am?' Harvey inquired when the mother returned.

Yes, she would sell him, and she also sold him two

dozen pullets. Harvey packed the fowls in a crate.
'Come on,' he cried cuddling the squawking gander
in his arms, 'you needn't be afeard of me, I never
kills anything afore Saturdays.'

He roped it by its leg to a hook inside his cart.
Then he took out his bag of money, paid Mrs. Sadgrove her dues, said 'Good day, ma'am, good day,'
and drove off without seeing another sign or stitch
of that fine young girl.

'Get along, Dodger, get along wi' you.' They went
bowling along for nearly an hour, and then he could
see the landmark on Dan'el Green's Hill, a windmill
that never turned though it looked a fine competent
piece of architecture, just beyond Dinnop.

Soon he reached his cottage and was chaffing his
mother, a hearty buxom dame, who stayed at home
and higgled with any chance callers. At this business
she was perhaps more enlightened than her son.
It was almost a misfortune to get into her clutches.
'How much you give for this?' he cried, eyeing
with humorous contempt an object in a coop that
was neither flesh nor rude red herring.

'Oh crumps,' he declared, when she told him, 'I
am damned and done!'

'Go on with you, that's a good bird, I tell you, with
a full heart, as will lay in a month.'

'I doubt it's a hen at all,' he protested. 'Oh, what a
ravenous beak! Damned and done I am.'

Mrs. Witlow's voice began indignantly to rise.
'Oh, well,' mused her son, 'it's thrifty perhaps. It
ain't quite right, but it's not so wrong as to make a

fuss about, especially as I be pretty sharp set. And if it's hens you want,' he continued triumphantly, dropping the crate of huddled fowls before her, 'there's hens for you; and a gander! There's a gander for you, if it's a gander you want.'

Leaving them all in his cottage yard he went and stalled the horse and cart at the inn, for he had no stable of his own. After supper he told his mother about the Sadgroves of Prattle Corner. 'Prettiest girl you ever seen, but the shyest mottal alive. Hair like a squirrel, lovely.'

'An't you got to go over and see Sophy to-night?' inquired his mother, lighting the lamp.

'Oh lord, if I an't clean forgot that! Well, I'm tired, shan't go to-night. See her to-morrow.'

2

Mrs. Sadgrove had been a widow for ten years — and she was glad of it. Prattle Corner was her property, she owned it and farmed it with the aid of a little old man and a large lad. The older this old man grew, and the less wages he received (for Elizabeth Sadgrove was reputed a 'grinder'), the more ardently he worked; the older the lad grew the less he laboured and the more he swore. She was thriving. She was worth money was Mrs. Sadgrove. Ah! And her daughter Mary, it was clear, had received an education fit for a lord's lady; she had been at a seminary for gentlefolk's females until she was seventeen. Well, whether or no, a clock must run as you time it; but it wronged her for the work of a

farm, it spoiled her, it completely deranged her for
the work of a farm; and this was a pity and foolish,
because some day the farm was coming to her as
didn't know hay from a bull's foot.

All this, and more, the young higgler quickly
learned, and plenty more he soon divined. Business
began to flourish with him now; his despair was
gone, he was established, he could look forward, to
whatever it was he wanted to look forward, with
equanimity and such pleasurable anticipation as the
chances and charges of life might engender. Every
week, and twice a week, he would call at the farm,
and though these occasions had their superior business inducements they often borrowed a less formal
tone and intention.

'Take a cup of tea, higgler?' Mrs. Sadgrove would
abruptly invite him; and he would drink tea and
discourse with her for half an hour on barndoor
ornithology, on harness, and markets, the treatment
of swine, the wear and tear of gear. Mary, always
present, was always silent, seldom uttering a word
to the higgler; yet a certain grace emanated from
her to him, an interest, a light, a favour, circum-
scribed indeed by some modesty, shyness, some inhibition, that neither of them had the wit or the
opportunity to overcome.

One evening he pulled up at the white palings of
Prattle Corner. It was a calm evening in May, the
sun was on its downgoing, chaffinches and wrens
sung ceaselessly. Mary in the orchard was heavily
veiled; he could see her over the hedge, holding a

brush in her gloved hands, and a bee skep. A swarm
was clustered like a great gnarl on the limb of an
apple tree. Bloom was thickly covering the twigs.
She made several timid attempts to brush the bees
into the skep, but they resented this.

'They knows if you be afraid of 'em,' bawled Harvey; 'I better come and give you a hand.'

When he took the skep and brush from her she
stood like one helpless, released by fate from a task
ill-understood and gracelessly waived. But he liked
her shyness, her almost uncouth immobility.

'Never mind about that,' said Harvey, as she unfastened her veil, scattering the white petals that had
collected upon it; 'when they kicks they hurts, but
I've been stung so often that I'm 'nocolated against
'em. They knows if you be afraid of 'em.'

Wearing neither veil nor gloves he went confidently
to the tree, and collected the swarm without mishap.

'Don't want to show no fear of them,' said Harvey.
'Nor of anything else, come to that,' he added with a
guffaw, 'nor anybody.'

At that she blushed and thanked him very softly,
and she did look straight and clearly at him.

Never anything beyond a blush and a thank-you.
When, in the kitchen or the parlour, Mrs. Sadgrove
sometimes left them alone together Harvey would
try a lot of talk, blarneying talk or sensible talk, or
talk about events in the world that was neither the
one nor the other. No good. The girl's responses
were ever brief and confused. Why was this? Again
and again he asked himself that question. Was

there anything the matter with her? Nothing that you could see; she was a bright and beautiful being. And it was not contempt, either, for despite her fright, her voicelessness, her timid eyes, he divined her friendly feeling for himself; and he would discourse to his own mother about her and her mother: 'They are well-up people, you know, well off, plenty of money and nothing to do with it. The farm's their own, freehold. A whole row of cottages she's got, too, in Smoorton Comfrey, so I heard; good cottages, well let. She's worth a few thousands, I warrant. Mary's beautiful. I took a fancy to that girl the first moment I see her. But she's very highly cultivated – and, of course, there's Sophy.'

To this enigmatic statement Mrs. Witlow offered no response; but mothers are inscrutable beings to their sons, always.

Once he bought some trees of cherries from Mrs. Sadgrove, and went on a July morning to pick the fruit. Under the trees Mary was walking slowly to and fro, twirling a clapper to scare away the birds. He stood watching her from the gateway. Among the bejewelled trees she passed, turning the rattle with a listless air, as if beating time to a sad music that only she could hear. The man knew that he was deeply fond of her. He passed into the orchard, bade her Good morning, and, lifting his ladder into one of the trees nearest the hedge, began to pluck cherries. Mary moved slimly in her white frock up and down a shady avenue in the orchard waving the clapper. The brightness of sun and sky was almost harsh; there was a little wind that feebly lifted the despondent leaves. He had doffed his coat; his shirt was white and clean. The lock of dark hair drooped over one side of his forehead; his face was brown and pleasant, his bare arms brown and powerful. From his high perch among the leaves Witlow watched for the girl to draw near to him in her perambulation. Knavish birds would scatter at her approach, only to drop again into the trees she had passed. His soul had an immensity of longing for her, but she never spoke a word to him. She would come from the shade of the little avenue, through the dumb trees that could only bend to greet her, into the sunlight whose dazzle gilded her own triumphant bloom. Fine! Fine! And always as she passed his mind refused to register a single thought he could offer her, or else his tongue would refuse to utter it. But his glance never left her face until she had passed out of sight again, and then he would lean against the ladder in the tree, staring down at the ground, seeing nothing or less than nothing, except a field mouse climbing to the top of a coventry bush in the hedge below him, nipping off one thick leaf and descending with the leaf in its mouth. Sometimes Mary rested at the other end of the avenue; the clapper would be silent and she would not appear for—oh, hours! She never rested near the trees Witlow was denuding. The mouse went on ascending and descending, and Witlow filled his basket, and shifted his stand, and wondered.

At noon he got down and sat on the hedge bank to

eat a snack of lunch. Mary had gone indoors for
hers, and he was alone for awhile. Capriciously
enough, his thoughts dwelt upon Sophy Daws.
Sophy was a fine girl, too; not such a lady as Mary
Sadgrove — oh lord, no! her father was a gamekeeper!
— but she was jolly and ample. She had been a little
captious lately, said he was neglecting her. That
wasn't true; hadn't he been busy? Besides, he
wasn't bound to her in any sort of way, and of course
he couldn't afford any marriage yet awhile. Sophy
hadn't got any money, never had any. What she
did with her wages — she was a parlourmaid — was a
teaser! Harvey grunted a little, and said 'Well!'
And that is all he said, and all he thought, about
Sophy Daws, then, for he could hear Mary's clapper
begin again in a corner of the orchard. He went
back to his work. There at the foot of the tree were
the baskets full of cherries, and those yet to be filled.
'Phew, but that's hot!' commented the man, 'I'm as
dry as a rattle.'

A few cherries had spilled from one basket and
lay on the ground. The little furry mouse had
found them and was industriously nibbling at one.
The higgler nonchalantly stamped his foot upon it,
and kept it so for a moment or two. Then he looked
at the dead mouse. A tangle of entrails had gushed
from its whiskered muzzle.

He resumed his work and the clapper rattled on
throughout the afternoon, for there were other
cherry trees that other buyers would come to strip in
a day or two. At four o'clock he was finished. Never

a word had he spoken with Mary, or she with him. When he went over to the house to pay Mrs. Sadgrove Mary stopped in the orchard scaring the birds.

'Take a cup of tea, Mr. Witlow,' said Mrs. Sadgrove; and then she surprisingly added, 'Where's Mary?'

'Still a-frightening the birds, and pretty well tired of that, I should think, ma'am.'

The mother had poured out three cups of tea.

'Shall I go and call her in?' he asked, rising.

'You might,' said she.

In the orchard the clappering had ceased. He walked all round, and in among the trees, but saw no sign of Mary; nor on the common, nor in the yard. But when he went back to the house Mary was there already, chatting at the table with her mother. She did not greet him, though she ceased talking to her mother as he sat down. After drinking his tea he went off briskly to load the baskets into the cart. As he climbed up to drive off Mrs. Sadgrove came out and stood beside the horse.

'You're off now?' said she.

'Yes, ma'am; all loaded, and thank you.'

She glanced vaguely along the road he had to travel. The afternoon was as clear as wine, the greensward itself dazzled him; lonely Shag Moor stretched away, humped with sweet yellow furze and pilastered with its telegraph poles. No life there, no life at all. Harvey sat on his driving board.

musingly brushing the flank of his horse with the
trailing whip.

'Ever round this way on Sundays?' inquired the
woman, peering up at him.

'Well, not in a manner of speaking, I'm not, ma'am,'
he answered her.

The widow laid her hand on the horse's back,
patting vaguely. The horse pricked up its ears, as if
it were listening.

'If you are, at all, ever, you must look in and have a
bit of dinner with us.'

'I will, ma'am, I will.'

'Next Sunday?' she went on.

'I will, ma'am, yes, I will,' he repeated, 'and thank
you.'

'One o'clock?' The widow smiled up at him.

'At one o'clock, ma'am; next Sunday; I will, and
thank you,' he said.

She stood away from the horse and waved her hand.
The first tangible thought that floated mutely out of
the higgler's mind as he drove away was: 'I'm
damned if I ain't a-going it, Sophy!'

He told his mother of Mrs. Sadgrove's invitation
with an air of curbed triumph. 'Come round – she
says. Yes – I says – I 'ull. That's right – she says –
so do.'

3

On the Sunday morn he dressed himself gallantly.
It was again a sweet unclouded day. The church
bell at Dinnop had begun to ring. From his win-

dow, as he fastened his most ornate tie, Harvey could observe his neighbour's two small children in the next garden, a boy and girl clad for church-going and each carrying a clerical book. The tiny boy placed his sister in front of a hen-roost and, opening his book, began to pace to and fro before her, shrilly intoning: 'Jesus is the shepherd, ring the bell. Oh lord, ring the bell, am I a good boy? Amen. Oh lord, ring the bell.' The little girl bowed her head piously over her book. The lad then picked up from the ground a dish which had contained the dog's food, and presented it momentarily before the lilac bush, the rabbit in a hutch, the axe fixed in a chopping block, and then before his sister. Without lifting her peering gaze from her book she meekly dropped two pebbles in the plate, and the boy passed on, lightly moaning, to the clothes-line post and a cock scooping in some dust.

'Ah, the little impets!' cried Harvey Witlow. 'Here, Toby! Here, Margaret!' He took two pennies from his pocket and lobbed them from the window to the astonished children. As they stooped to pick up the coins Harvey heard the hoarse voice of neighbour Nathan, their father, bawl from his kitchen: 'Come on in, and shut that bloody door, d'y'ear!'

Harnessing his moody horse to the gig Harvey was soon bowling away to Shag Moor, and as he drove along he sung loudly. He had a pink rose in his buttonhole. Mrs. Sadgrove received him almost affably, and though Mary was more shy than ever before, Harvey had determined to make an impression. During the dinner he fired off his bucolic jokes, and pleasant tattle of a more respectful and sober nature; but after dinner Mary sat like Patience, not upon a monument, but as if upon a rocking-horse, shy and fearful, and her mother made no effort to inspire her as the higgler did, unsuccessful though he was. They went to the pens to look at the pigs, and as they leaned against the low walls and poked the maudlin inhabitants, Harvey began: 'Reminds me, when I was in the war. . . .'

'Were you in the war!' interrupted Mrs. Sadgrove.

'Oh, yes, I was in that war, ah, and there was a pig. . . . Danger? Oh lord, bless me, it was a bit dangerous, but you never knew where it was or what it 'ud be at next; it was like the sword of Damockels. There was a bullet once come 'ithin a foot of my head, and it went through a board an inch thick, slap through that board.' Both women gazed at him apprehendingly. 'Why, I might 'a been killed, you know,' said Harvey, cocking his eye musingly at the weather-vane on the barn. 'We was in billets at St. Gratien, and one day a chasseur came up – a French yoossar, you know – and he began talking to our sergeant. That was Hubert Luxter, the butcher: died a month or two ago of measles. But this yoossar couldn't speak English at all, and none of us chaps could make sense of him. I never could understand that lingo somehow, never; and though there was half a dozen of us chaps there, none of us were man enough for it neither. 'Nil compree,' we

says, 'non compos.' I told him straight: 'you ought
to learn English,' I said, 'it's much easier than your
kind of bally chatter.' So he kept shaping up as if he
was holding a rifle, and then he'd say 'Fusee —
bang!' and then he'd say 'cushion' — kept on saying
'cushion.' Then he gets a bit of chalk and draws on
the wall something that looks like a horrible dog,
and says 'cushion' again.

'Pig,' interjected Mary Sadgrove softly.

'Yes, yes!' ejaculated Harvey, 'so 'twas! Do you
know any French lingo?'

'Oh, yes,' declared her mother, 'Mary knows it very
well.'

'Ah,' sighed the higgler, 'I don't, although I been
to France. And I couldn't do it now, not for luck
nor love. You learnt it, I suppose. Well, this
yoossar wants to borrow my rifle, but of course I
can't lend him. So he taps on this horrible pig he'd
drawn, and then he taps on his own head, and rolls
his eyes about dreadful! "Mad?" I says. And that
was it, that was it. He'd got a pig on his little farm
there what had gone mad, and he wanted us to come
and shoot it; he was on leave and he hadn't got any
ammunition. So Hubert Luxter he says, "Come on,
some of you," and we all goes with the yoossar and
shot the pig for him. Ah, that was a pig! And
when it died it jumped a somersault just like a
rabbit. It had got the mange, and was mad as anything I ever see in my life; it was full of madness.
Couldn't hit him at all at first, and it kicked up bobs-
a-dying. "Ready, present, fire!" Hubert Luxter

says, and bang goes the six of us, and every time we missed him he spotted us and we had to run for our lives.'

As Harvey looked up he caught a glance of the girl fixed on him. She dropped her gaze at once and, turning away, walked off to the house.

'Come and take a look at the meadow,' said Mrs. Sadgrove to him, and they went into the soft smooth meadow where the black pony was grazing. Very bright and green it was, and very blue the sky. He sniffed at the pink rose in his buttonhole, and determined that come what might he would give it to Mary if he could get a nice quiet chance to offer it. And just then, while he and Mrs. Sadgrove were strolling alone in the soft smooth meadow, quite alone, she suddenly, startlingly, asked him: 'Are you courting anybody?'

'Beg pardon, ma'am?' he exclaimed.

'You haven't got a sweetheart, have you?' she asked, most deliberately.

Harvey grinned sheepishly: 'Ha, ha, ha,' and then he said, 'No.'

'I want to see my daughter married,' the widow went on significantly.

'Miss Mary!' he cried.

'Yes,' said she; and something in the higgler's veins began to pound rapidly. His breast might have been a revolving cage and his heart a demon squirrel. 'I can't live for ever,' said Mrs. Sadgrove, almost with levity, 'in fact, not for long, and so I'd like to see her settled soon with some decent understanding young man, one that could carry on here, and not make a mess of things.'

'But, but,' stuttered the understanding young man, 'I'm no scholar, and she's a lady. I'm a poor chap, rough, and no scholar, ma'am. But mind you . . .'

'That doesn't matter at all,' the widow interrupted, 'not as things are. You want a scholar for learning, but for the land . . .'

'Ah, that's right, Mrs. Sadgrove, but . . .'

'I want to see her settled. This farm, you know, with the stock and things are worth nigh upon three thousand pounds.'

'You want a farmer for farming, that's true, Mrs. Sadgrove, but when you come to marriage, well, with her learning and French and all that . . .'

'A sensible woman will take a man rather than a box of tricks any day of the week,' the widow retorted. 'Education may be a fine thing, but it often costs a lot of foolish money.'

'It do, it do. You want to see her settled?'

'I want to see her settled and secure. When she is twenty-five she comes into five hundred pounds of her own right.'

The distracted higgler hummed and haa-ed in his bewilderment as if he had just been offered the purchase of a dubious duck. 'How old is she, ma'am?' he at last huskily inquired.

'Two-and-twenty nearly. She's a good healthy girl, for I've never spent a pound on a doctor for her, and very quiet she is, and very sensible; but she's got a

93

strong will of her own, though you might not think
it or believe it.'

'She's a fine creature, Mrs. Sadgrove, and I'm very
fond of her. I don't mind owning up to that, very
fond of her I am.'

'Well, think it over, take your time, and see what
you think. There's no hurry, I hope, please God.'

'I shan't want much time,' he declared with a laugh,
'but I doubt I'm the fair right sort for her.'

'Oh, fair days, fair doings!' said she inscrutably,
'I'm not a long liver, I'm afraid.'

'God forbid, ma'am!' His ejaculation was intoned
with deep gravity.

'No, I'm not a long-living woman.' She surveyed
him with her calm eyes, and he returned her gaze.
Hers was a long sallow face, with heavy lips. Sometimes she would stretch her features (as if to keep
them from petrifying) in an elastic grin, and display
her dazzling teeth; the lips would curl thickly, no
longer crimson, but blue. He wondered if there
were any sign of a doom registered upon her gaunt
face. She might die, and die soon.

'You couldn't do better than think it over, then,
eh?' she had a queer frown as she regarded him.

'I couldn't do worse than not, Mrs. Sadgrove,' he
said gaily.

They left it at that. He had no reason for hurrying
away, and he couldn't have explained his desire to
do so, but he hurried away. Driving along past the
end of the moor, and peering back at the lonely farm
where they dwelled amid the thick furze snoozing in

the heat, he remembered that he had not asked if
Mary was willing to marry him! Perhaps the widow
took her agreement for granted. That would be
good fortune, for otherwise how the devil was he to
get round a girl who had never spoken half a dozen
words to him! And never would! She was a lady, a
girl of fortune, knew her French; but there it was,
the girl's own mother was asking him to wed her.
Strange, very strange! He dimly feared something,
but he did not know what it was he feared. He had
still got the pink rose in his buttonhole.

4

At first his mother was incredulous; when he told
her of the astonishing proposal she declared he was
a joker; but she was soon as convinced of his sincerity
as she was amazed at his hesitation. And even
vexed: 'Was there anything the matter with this
Mary?'

'No, no, no! She's quiet, very quiet indeed, I tell
you, but a fine young woman, and a beautiful young
woman. Oh, she's all right, right as rain, right as a
trivet, right as ninepence. But there's a catch in it
somewheres, I fear. I can't see through it yet, but
I shall afore long, or I'd have the girl, like a shot I
would. 'Tain't the girl, mother, it's the money, if
you understand me.'

'Well, I don't understand you, certainly I don't.
What about Sophy?'

'Oh lord!' He scratched his head ruefully.

'You wouldn't think of giving this the go-by for

Sophy, Harvey, would you? A girl as you ain't even engaged to, Harvey, would you?'

'We don't want to chatter about that,' declared her son. 'I got to think it over, and it's going to tie my wool, I can tell you, for there's a bit of craft some-wheres, I'll take my oath. If there ain't, there ought to be!'

Over the alluring project his decision wavered for days, until his mother became mortified at his in-explicable vacillation.

'I tell you,' he cried, 'I can't make tops or bottoms of it all. I like the girl well enough, but I like Sophy, too, and it's no good beating about the bush. I like Sophy, she's the girl I love; but Mary's a fine crea-ture, and money like that wants looking at before you throw it away, love or no love. Three thousand pounds! I'd be a made man.'

And as if in sheer spite to his mother; as if a bushel of money lay on the doorstep for him to kick over whenever the fancy seized him; in short (as Mrs. Witlow very clearly intimated) as if in contempt of Providence he began to pursue Sophy Daws with a new fervour, and walked with that young girl more than he was accustomed to, more than ever before; in fact, as his mother bemoaned, more than he had need to. It was unreasonable, it was a shame, a foolishness; it wasn't decent and it wasn't safe.

On his weekly visits to the farm his mind still wavered. Mrs. Sadgrove let him alone; she was very good, she did not pester him with questions and entreaties. There was Mary with her white dress and her red hair and her silence; a girl with a great fortune, walking about the yard, or sitting in the room, and casting not a glance upon him. Not that he would have known it if she did, for now he was just as shy of her. Mrs. Sadgrove often left them alone, but when they were alone he could not dish up a word for the pretty maid; he was dumb as a statue. If either she or her mother had lifted so much as a finger then there would have been an end to his hesitations or suspicions, for in Mary's presence the fine glory of the girl seized him incontinently; he was again full of a longing to press her lips, to lay down his doubts, to touch her bosom — though he could not think she would ever allow that! Not an atom of doubt about *her* ever visited him; she was unaware of her mother's queer project. Rather, if she became aware he was sure it would be the end of him. Too beautiful she was, too learned, and too rich. Decidedly it was his native cunning, and no want of love, that inhibited him. Folks with property did not often come along and bid you help yourself. Not very often! And throw in a grand bright girl, just for good measure as you might say. Not very often!

For weeks the higgler made his customary calls, and each time the outcome was the same; no more, no less. 'Some dodge,' he mused, 'something the girl don't know and the mother does.' Were they going bankrupt, or were they mortgaged up to the neck, or was there anything the matter with the girl, or was it just the mother wanted to get hold of him?

He knew his own value if he didn't know his own mind, and his value couldn't match that girl any more than his mind could. So what *did* they want him for? Whatever it was Harvey Witlow was ready for it whenever he was in Mary's presence, but once away from her his own craftiness asserted itself: it was a snare, they were trying to make a mock of him!

But nothing could prevent his own mother mocking him, and her treatment of Sophy was so unbearable that if the heart of that dusky beauty had not been proof against all impediments, Harvey might have had to whistle for her favour. But whenever he was with Sophy he had only one heart, undivided and true, and certain as time itself.

'I love Sophy best. It's true enough I love Mary, too, but I love Sophy better. I know it; Sophy's the girl I must wed. It might not be so if I weren't all dashed and doddered about the money; I don't know. But I do know that Mary's innocent of all this craftiness; it's her mother trying to mogue me into it.'

Later he would be wishing he could only forget Sophy and do it. Without the hindrance of conscience he could do it, catch or no catch.

He went on calling at the farm, with nothing said or settled, until October. Then Harvey made up his mind, and without a word to the Sadgroves he went and married Sophy Daws and gave up calling at the farm altogether. This gave him some feeling of dishonesty, some qualm, and a vague unhap-

piness; likewise he feared the cold hostility of Mrs.
Sadgrove. She would be terribly vexed. As for
Mary, he was nothing to her, poor girl; it was a
shame. The last time he drove that way he did not
call at the farm. Autumn was advancing, and the
apples were down, the bracken dying, the furze out
of bloom, and the farm on the moor looked more
and more lonely, and most cold, though it lodged a
flame-haired silent woman, fit for a nobleman, whom
they wanted to mate with a common higgler. Crafty,
you know, too crafty!

5

The marriage was a gay little occasion, but they
did not go away for a honeymoon. Sophy's grandmother from a distant village, Cassandra Fundy,
who had a deafness and a speckled skin, brought
her third husband, Amos, whom the family had
never seen before. Not a very wise man, indeed he
was a common man, stooping like a decayed tree,
he was so old. But he shaved every day and his hair-
less skull was yellow. Cassandra, who was yellow
too, had long since turned into a fool; she did not
shave, though she ought to have done. She was
like to die soon, but everybody said old Amos would
live to be a hundred; it was expected of him, and he,
too, was determined.

The guests declared that a storm was threatening,
but Amos Fundy denied it and scorned it.

'Thunder p'raps, but 'twill clear; 'tis only de pride
o' der morning.'

'Don't you be a fool,' remarked his wife enigmatically, 'you'll die soon enough.'

'You must behold der moon,' continued the octogenarian; 'de closer it is to der wheel, de closer der rain; de furder away it is, de furder der rain.'

'You could pour that man's brains into a thimble,' declared Cassandra of her spouse, 'and they wouldn't fill it – he's deaf.'

Fundy was right; the day did clear. The marriage was made and the guests returned with the man and his bride to their home. But Fundy was also wrong, for storm came soon after and rain set in. The guests stayed on for tea, and then, as it was no better, they feasted and stayed till night. And Harvey began to think they never would go, but of course they couldn't and so there they were. Sophy was looking wonderful in white stockings and shiny shoes and a red frock with a tiny white apron. A big girl she seemed, with her shaken dark hair and flushed face. Grandmother Fundy spoke seriously, but not secretly to her.

'I've had my fourteen touch of children,' said Grandmother Fundy. 'Yes, they were flung on the mercy of God – poor little devils. I've followed most of 'em to the churchyard. You go slow, Sophia.'

'Yes, granny.'

'Why,' continued Cassandra, embracing the whole company, as it were, with her disclosure, 'my mother had me by some gentleman!'

The announcement aroused no response except

sympathetic, and perhaps encouraging, nods from the women.

'She had me by some gentleman – she ought to ha' had a twal' month, she did!'

'Wasn't she ever married?' Sophy inquired of her grandmother.

'Married? Yes, course she was,' replied the old dame, 'of course. But marriage ain't everything. Twice she was, but not to he, she wasn't.'

'Not to the gentleman?'

'No! Oh, no! He'd got money – bushels! Marriage ain't much, not with these gentry.'

'Ho, ho, that's a tidy come-up!' laughed Harvey.

'Who was that gentleman?' Sophia's interest was deeply engaged. But Cassandra Fundy was silent, pondering like a china image. Her gaze was towards the mantelpiece, where there were four lamps – but only one usable – and two clocks – but only one going – and a coloured greeting card a foot long with large letters KEEP SMILING adorned with lithographic honeysuckle.

'She's hard of hearing,' interpolated grandfather Amos, 'very hard, gets worse. She've a horn at home, big as that . . .' His eyes roved the room for an object of comparison, and he seized upon the fire shovel that lay in the fender. 'Big as that shovel. Crown silver it is, and solid, a beautiful horn, but' – he brandished the shovel before them – 'her won't use 'en.'

'Granny, who was that gentleman?' shouted Sophy. 'Did you know him?'

'No! no!' declared the indignant dame. 'I dunno ever his name, nor I don't want to. He took hisself off to Ameriky, and now he's in the land of heaven. I never seen him. If I had, I'd a given it to him properly; oh, my dear, not blay-guarding him, you know, but just plain language! Where's your seven commandments?'

At last the rain abated. Peeping into the dark garden you could see the fugitive moonlight hung in a million raindrops in the black twigs of all sorts of bushes and trees, while along the cantle of the porch a line of raindrops hung, even and regular, as if they were nailheads made of glass. So all the guests departed, in one long staggering, struggling, giggling and guffawing body, into the village street. The bride and her man stood in the porch, watching and waving hands. Sophy was momentarily grieving: what a lot of trouble and fuss when you announced that henceforward you were going to sleep with a man because you loved him true! She had said good-bye to her grandmother Cassandra, to her father and her little sister. She had hung on her mother's breast, sighing an almost intolerable farewell to innocence – never treasured until it is gone, and thenceforward a pretty sorrow cherished more deeply than wilder joys.

Into Harvey's mind, as they stood there at last alone, momentarily stole an image of a bright-haired girl, lovely, silent, sad, whom he felt he had deeply wronged. And he was sorry. He had escaped the snare, but if there had been no snare he might

this night have been sleeping with a different bride.
And it would have been just as well. Sophy looked
but a girl with her blown hair and wet face. She
was wiping her tears on the tiny apron. But she had
the breasts of a woman and decoying eyes.

'Sophy, Sophy!' breathed Harvey, wooing her in
the darkness.

'It blows and it rains, and it rains and it blows,'
chattered the crumpled bride, 'and I'm all so be-
scambled I can't tell wet from windy.'

'Come, my love,' whispered the bridegroom, 'come
in, to home.'

6

Four or five months later the higgler's affairs had
again taken a rude turn. Marriage, alas, was not all
it might be; his wife and his mother quarrelled
unendingly. Sometimes he sided with the one and
sometimes with the other. He could not yet afford
to instal his mother in a separate cottage, and therefore even Sophy had to admit that her mother-in-law
had a right to be living there with them, the home
being hers. Harvey hadn't bought much of it; and
though he was welcome to it all now, and it would
be exclusively his as soon as she died, still, it was her
furniture, and you couldn't drive any woman (even
your mother) off her own property. Sophy, who
wanted a home of her own, was vexed and moody,
and antagonistic to her man. Business, too, had
gone down sadly of late. He had thrown up the
Shag Moor round months ago; he could not bring

himself to go there again, and he had not been able
to square up the loss by any substantial new con-
nections. On top of it all his horse died. It stumbled on a hill one day and fell, and it couldn't get
up, or it wouldn't — at any rate, it didn't. Harvey
thrashed it and coaxed it, then he cursed it and
kicked it; after that he sent for a veterinary man,
and the veterinary man ordered it to be shot. And it
was shot. A great blow to Harvey Witlow was that.
He had no money to buy another horse; money
was tight with him, very tight; and so he had to hire
at fabulous cost a decrepit nag that ate like a good
one. It ate — well, it would have astonished you to
see what that creature disposed of, with hay the price
it was, and corn gone up to heaven nearly. In fact
Harvey found that he couldn't stand the racket
much longer, and as he could not possibly buy
another it looked very much as if he was in queer
street once more, unless he could borrow the money
from some friendly person. Of course there were
plenty of friendly persons, but they had no money,
just as there were many persons who had the money
but were not what you might call friendly; and so
the higgler began to reiterate twenty times a day,
and forty times a day, that he was entirely and absolutely damned and done. Things were thus very
bad with him, they were at their worst — for he had a
wife to keep now, as well as a mother, and a horse
that ate like Satan, and worked like a gnat — when it
suddenly came into his mind that Mrs. Sadgrove
was reputed to have a lot of money, and had no call

to be unfriendly to him. He had his grave doubts
about the size of her purse, but there could be no
harm in trying so long as you approached her in a
right reasonable manner.

For a week or two he held off from this appeal, but
the grim spectre of destitution gave him no rest,
and so, near the close of a wild March day he took
his desperate courage and his cart and the decrepit
nag to Shag Moor. Wild it was, though dry, and
the wind against them, a vast turmoil of icy air
strident and baffling. The nag threw up its head
and declined to trot. Evening was but an hour away,
the fury of the wind did not retard it, nor the clouds
hasten it. Low down the sun was quitting the
wrack of storm, exposing a jolly orb of magnifying
fire that shone flush under eaves and through the
casements of cottages, casting a pattern of lattice and
tossing boughs upon the interior walls, lovelier than
dreamed-of pictures. The heads of mothers and
old dames were also imaged there, recognizable in
their black shadows; and little children held up
their hands between window and wall to make five-
fingered shapes upon the golden screen. To drive
on the moor then was to drive into blasts more dire.
Darkness began to fall, and bitter cold it was. No
birds to be seen, neither beast nor man; empty of
everything it was except sound and a marvel of dying
light, and Harvey Witlow of Dinnop with a sour
old nag driving from end to end of it. At Prattle
Corner dusk was already abroad: there was just one
shaft of light that broached a sharp-angled stack in

the rickyard, an ark of darkness, along whose top the gads and wooden pins and tilted straws were miraculously fringed in the last glare. Hitching his nag to the palings he knocked at the door, and knew in the gloom that it was Mary who opened it and stood peering forth at him.

'Good evening,' he said, touching his hat.

'Oh!' the girl uttered a cry, 'Higgler! What do you come for?' It was the longest sentence she had ever spoken to him; a sad frightened voice.

'I thought,' he began, 'I'd call – and see Mrs. Sadgrove. I wondered . . .'

'Mother's dead,' said the girl. She drew the door farther back, as if inviting him, and he entered. The door was shut behind him, and they were alone in darkness, together. The girl was deeply grieving. Trembling, he asked the question: 'What is it you tell me, Mary?'

'Mother's dead,' repeated the girl, 'all day, all day, all day.' They were close to each other, but he could not see her. All round the house the wind roved lamentingly, shuddering at doors and windows. 'She died in the night. The doctor was to have come, but he has not come all day,' Mary whispered, 'all day, all day. I don't understand; I have waited for him, and he has not come. She died, she was dead in her bed this morning, and I've been alone all day, all day, and I don't know what is to be done.'

'I'll go for the doctor,' he said hastily, but she took him by the hand and drew him into the kitchen. There was no candle lit; a fire was burning there, richly glowing embers, that laid a gaunt shadow of the table across a corner of the ceiling. Every dish on the dresser gleamed, the stone floor was rosy, and each smooth curve on the dark settle was shining like ice. Without invitation he sat down.

'No,' said the girl, in a tremulous voice, 'you must help me.' She lit a candle: her face was white as the moon, her lips were sharply red, and her eyes were wild. 'Come,' she said, and he followed her behind the settle and up the stairs to a room where there was a disordered bed, and what might be a body lying under the quilt. The higgler stood still staring at the form under the quilt. The girl, too, was still and staring. Wind dashed upon the ivy at the window and hallooed like a grieving multitude. A crumpled gown hid the body's head, but thrust from under it, almost as if to greet him, was her naked lean arm, the palm of the hand lying uppermost. At the foot of the bed was a large washing bowl, with sponge and towels.

'You've been laying her out! Yourself!' exclaimed Witlow. The pale girl set down the candle on a chest of drawers. 'Help me now,' she said, and moving to the bed she lifted the crumpled gown from off the face of the dead woman, at the same time smoothing the quilt closely up to the body's chin. 'I cannot put the gown on, because of her arm, it has gone stiff.' She shuddered, and stood holding the gown as if offering it to the man. He lifted that dead naked arm and tried to place it down at the body's side, but it resisted and he let go his hold.

The arm swung back to its former outstretched
position, as if it still lived and resented that pressure.
The girl retreated from the bed with a timorous cry.
'Get me a bandage,' he said, 'or something we can
tear up.'

She gave him some pieces of linen.

'I'll finish this for you,' he brusquely whispered,
'you get along downstairs and take a swig of brandy.
Got any brandy?'

She did not move. He put his arm around her and
gently urged her to the door.

'Brandy,' he repeated, 'and light your candles.'

He watched her go heavily down the stairs before
he shut the door. Returning to the bed he lifted
the quilt. The dead body was naked and smelt of
soap. Dropping the quilt he lifted the outstretched
arm again, like cold wax to the touch and unpliant as
a sturdy sapling, and tried once more to bend it to
the body's side. As he did so the bedroom door
blew open· with a crash. It was only a draught of
the wind, and a loose latch — Mary had opened a
door downstairs, perhaps — but it awed him, as if
some invisible looker were there resenting his presence. He went and closed the door, the latch had a
loose hasp, and tiptoeing nervously back he seized
the dreadful arm with a sudden brutal energy, and
bent it by thrusting his knee violently into the
hollow of the elbow. Hurriedly he slipped the
gown over the head and inserted the arm in the
sleeve. A strange impulse of modesty stayed him
for a moment: should he call the girl and let her

complete the robing of the naked body under the quilt? That preposterous pause seemed to add a new anger to the wind, and again the door sprang open. He delayed no longer, but letting it remain open, he uncovered the dead woman. As he lifted the chill body the long outstretched arm moved and tilted like the boom of a sail, but crushing it to its side he bound the limb fast with the strips of linen. So Mrs. Sadgrove was made ready for her coffin. Drawing the quilt back to her neck, with a gush of relief he glanced about the room. It was a very ordinary bedroom: bed, washstand, chest of drawers, chair, and two pictures — one of deeply religious import, and the other a little pink print, in a gilded frame, of a bouncing nude nymph recumbent upon a cloud. It was queer: a lot of people, people whom you wouldn't think it of, had that sort of picture in their bedrooms.

Mary was now coming up the stairs again, with a glass half full of liquid. She brought it to him. 'No, you drink it,' he urged, and Mary sipped the brandy.

'I've finished — I've finished,' he said as he watched her, 'she's quite comfortable now.'

The girl looked her silent thanks at him, again holding out the glass. 'No, sup it yourself,' he said; but as she stood in the dim light, regarding him with her strange gaze, and still offering the drink, he took it from her, drained it at a gulp and put the glass upon the chest, beside the candle. 'She's quite comfortable now. I'm very grieved, Mary,' he said with awkward kindness, 'about all this trouble that's come on you.'

She was motionless as a wax image, as if she had died in her steps, her hand still extended as when he took the glass from it. So piercing was her gaze that his own drifted from her face and took in again the objects in the room: the washstand, the candle on the chest, the little pink picture. The wind beat upon the ivy outside the window as if a monstrous whip were lashing its slaves.

'You must notify the registrar,' he began again, 'but you must see the doctor first.'

'I've waited for him all day,' Mary whispered, 'all day. The nurse will come again soon. She went home to rest in the night.' She turned towards the bed. 'She has only been ill a week.'

'Yes?' he lamely said. 'Dear me, it is sudden.'

'I must see the doctor,' she continued.

'I'll drive you over to him in my gig.' He was eager to do that.

'I don't know,' said Mary slowly.

'Yes, I'll do that, soon's you're ready. Mary,' he fumbled with his speech, 'I'm not wanting to pry into your affairs, or any thing as don't concern me, but how are you going to get along now? Have you got any relations?'

'No,' the girl shook her head, 'No.'

'That's bad. What was you thinking of doing? How has she left you—things were in a baddish way, weren't they?'

'Oh, no,' Mary looked up quickly. 'She has left

me very well off. 'I shall go on with the farm; there's the old man and the boy — they've gone to a wedding to-day; I shall go on with it. She was so thoughtful for me, and I would not care to leave all this, I love it.'

'But you can't do it by yourself, alone?'

'No. I'm to get a man to superintend, a working bailiff,' she said.

'Oh!' And again they were silent. The girl went to the bed and lifted the covering. She saw the bound arm and then drew the quilt tenderly over the dead face. Witlow picked up his hat and found himself staring again at the pink picture. Mary took the candle preparatory to descending the stairs. Suddenly the higgler turned to her and ventured: 'Did you know as she once asked me to marry you?' he blurted.

Her eyes turned from him, but he guessed — he could feel that she *had* known.

'I've often wondered why,' he murmured, 'why she wanted that.'

'She didn't,' said the girl.

That gave pause to the man; he felt stupid at once, and roved his fingers in a silly way along the roughened nap of his hat.

'Well, she asked me to,' he bluntly protested.

'She knew,' Mary's voice was no louder than a sigh, 'that you were courting another girl, the one you married.'

'But, but,' stuttered the honest higgler, 'if she knew that why did she want for me to marry you?'

'She didn't,' said Mary again; and again, in the pause, he did silly things to his hat. How shy this girl was, how lovely in her modesty and grief!
'I can't make tops or bottoms of it,' he said; 'but she asked me, as sure as God's my maker.'
'I know. It was me, I wanted it.'
'You!' he cried, 'you wanted to marry me!'
The girl bowed her head, lovely in her grief and modesty: 'She was against it, but I made her ask you.'
'And I hadn't an idea that you cast a thought on me,' he murmured. 'I feared it was a sort of trick she was playing on me. I didn't understand, I had no idea that you knew about it even. And so I didn't ever ask you.'
'Oh, why not, why not? I was fond of you then,' whispered she. 'Mother tried to persuade me against it, but I was fond of you — then.'
He was in a queer distress and confusion: 'Oh, if you'd only tipped me a word, or given me a sort of look,' he sighed. 'Oh, Mary!'
She said no more, but went downstairs. He followed her and immediately fetched the lamps from his gig. As he lit the candles: 'How strange,' Mary said, 'that you should come back just as I most needed help. I am very grateful.'
'Mary, I'll drive you to the doctor's now.'
She shook her head; she was smiling.
'Then I'll stay till the nurse comes.'
'No, you must go. Go at once.'
He picked up the two lamps, and turning at the

door said: 'I'll come again to-morrow.' Then the
wind rushed into the room: 'Good-bye,' she cried,
shutting the door quickly behind him.

He drove away into deep darkness, the wind howling, his thoughts strange and bitter. He had thrown
away a love, a love that was dumb and hid itself.
By God, he had thrown away a fortune, too! And he
had forgotten all about his real errand until now,
forgotten all about the loan! Well, let it go; give it
up. He would give up higgling; he would take on
some other job; a bailiff, a working bailiff, that was
the job that would suit him, a working bailiff. Of
course there was Sophy; but still — Sophy!

ONE TIME I WAS IN A LITTLE ITALIAN TOWN NOT FAR from Pisa, and in the middle of it was a scrap of waste ground that no one seemed to own or to require. A sweet grove of pollarded sycamores grew along one of its three sides — for it had the shape of a triangle — with two blocks of tall yellow dwellings along the others and a statue of Christopher Columbus in one corner. The triangle was occupied, in a sort of a way, by a caravan, a shooting alley, and a merry-go-round; of course you wouldn't break your neck looking at a fair like that, it was too small, indeed it wasn't big, just the whirligig and the shooting stall.

Well, I lived there in one of those yellow buildings a deuce of a hard time with a man who had fallen in love; a great philosopher fellow, my friend, with no money, not a bean — they never have. And she was a beautiful girl with sandy hair and a sandy face and a necklet of coral beads: an English girl from Scunthorpe. All day long Dapson — that was his name — would be singing a little bit of a song:

> I sat with my love in the ivy tree,
> And hid her coat under the brier.

But I can take my oath that was a thing he never would do, for he was a squirrel itself for shyness, very shy. A person of great mind, though, full of rich thoughts, but he was not fond of exposing them

114

— unless it was to myself. He was like a man who kept his treasures in a dim room — they were dim treasures, too, and you wouldn't understand them — only at odd times he would take up one of these treasures and polish it till it would shine, or tap it and tune it until it rang like a marriage bell. That was his imagination, his ideas. And this girl, she used to hang her stockings out of her window overlooking the roundabout and things. I suppose she hung them there to dry, and not for any token, for when I told her one day that Dapson was pining to a thread for love of her: 'Good sakes!' she said, 'I'd want to marry something a little better than that backward creature.' And then she added, looking very straight at me, 'But not so very much better, neither.'

'His aunt,' I said, 'keeps him short of money, but she has erysipelas and she'll die of it yet.'

'What's the use complaining you're poor?' said the bright girl, 'there's always more money in the world than you can do with!'

'Will you be going to the fair when it opens?' I asked her.

'The fair? What fair?' she says.

'This little bit of a spree.' And I pointed out of her window.

'Oh, that! But it *is* open,' she said.

'Then why don't it begin?'

'It *has* begun.'

'What do you tell me? There's never a soul goes into it!'

'And never will, for nobody wants it, and to tell you the truth it wants nobody either.'

'Then why don't it go away?'

'That I can't tell you, but I've heard that it's been here for years.'

'That's queer,' I said, 'for I seen the master of it, an old man with big moustaches, very gentle he seems, and he's always painting new paint on his attractions, making them very neat and very fetching.'

'Gentle!' she cried.

'Indeed, yes, so it seems.'

'Good sakes! Once he had a pony, but it was half-starved, so they say, and a wife that was three parts dead for the same reason, so I've heard, and some children that ought never to have been alive.'

'And where are they now then — don't they look after him?' I asked her.

'They are in their graves, poor dears, where else could they be?'

'The devil take him!' said I.

When I left her I took a walk into the fair and everything was quiet, even the shooting alley. It was painted like a castle, with clay pipes stuck in every cranny, and bits of shell you'd gather from the shore dangling on threads from the battlements, to be popped at by boys. Just one little gun, and no more. The merry-go-round was not a great contrivance: seven wooden horses there were, painted a white that was very white, with black tails, black manes and eyes, their hoofs black and a red ring round each eye; but their mouths and nostrils were red as dripping blood, and their necks and behinds were dappled with rose spots as big as crab apples. Then there were two lions amongst them, and one dragon, sandy lions with thin rumps but massy heads; the half of them was head, like a John Dory, and very ferocious. That dragon was large as a hog, but more like a fish — saving the legs — and his eyes were gold and his teeth were green and a dreadful conglomeration he was, with a great show of paint on him. To turn it all there was a handle in the middle, and an organ full of brass spouts shining like a doctor's door-knocker, but not a groan or a grunt coming from the lot of it. I couldn't understand it. All spick and span with new paint, saving the caravan that was burst to a ruin that you wouldn't put a crow in. The old man of the fair went by me, going with a pail of water he had drawn from the fountain. He was mumbling to himself, he was always mumbling, and what I heard him say was just this: 'She's better to-day, better to-day, she'll soon be well. Oh, yes, she's much better to-day.' I tell you, I couldn't understand it at all.

Indoors I went and found Dapson, and I told him about the young girl — how she was pining to a thread for love of him. But he said he didn't care now, so I asked him why was that? And he asked me did I happen to notice her stockings hanging out, and did I see anything peculiar about them?

'Peculiar?' I said.

'About the feet of them?' says he.

'No, I did not.'

'Well,' he said, 'I look at them every day, morning and evening, and they affect me curiously, strangely they affect me. Can you understand? – they look ungainly, heavy, they give me a painful impression. In short,' said he, 'they convey to me the disagreeable suggestion that her feet have lumps on them!'

'Lumps!' I thought he was crazy.

'Yes, something rather monstrous. It's quite indescribable, I'm bewitched by it; can you understand?'

'But what sort of lumps?' I thought he was crazy.

'Oh, I can't explain, but it's spoilt everything, and it's quite impossible for me to love her now.' He put his head down between his hands. Sick and sorry he looked. 'I wish I had never seen them.'

'I think,' I said, 'you are too much cooped up here in the summer heat. Come out, now, and sit in the public gardens.' For I knew the young girl would be walking there with her two little feet going sweetly as a deer's.

But he would not do that. 'Summer is good, yes,' he said, ' but if you can't sit in the house the flies in the garden are mad to kill you, and they would kill you if you didn't smoke, and you can't smoke without tobacco,' he said, 'and you can't get tobacco without money, and money simply isn't to be had.'

'Come out, you,' says I again to him then, 'and let's go to the fair!' I told him what I had heard of it and seen of it. He would not do that either, but he sat up and began turning over one of his thoughts, and polishing it, and tapping and tuning it.

'For some reason,' he began, 'no one patronizes that charming institution. Even I, who am full of admiration, have never spent a coin upon it. And this is the reason—it would be sacrilege! Do you follow me? Times are not bad, and the children play, but no one ever seeks to bestride those gallant beasts, or try his skill with the popgun. And it does not seem to cause any concern to the owner, that old man. On the contrary! He cherishes his steeds and lions in a strange way. How delicately dreadful they are with their snarly mouths! Day by day I see him with a pot of white paint, or a pot of blue or red or green, adding a daub of colour to the dragon's eye, the lions' manes, or the horses' hooves. Like an artist he touches here, touches there, and then withdraws to scan the effect with a closed eye, and perhaps an anxious smile curving under his old moustache. Then sometimes he paints the white pipes whiter, or shines the barrel of the little gun — how fearfully it gleams! And I feel that he is dwelling in an absurd world of love of these simple funny things. No longer a means of life to him they have come into life itself, transcendent and for ever young. Some days they actually seem to have grown fatter! He will never suffer a strange hand to touch them now, no one must use them but him alone, for they mean splendid things to him, and he worships them like a monk. Do you understand this?'

'It's queer talking,' I answered.

'Ah,' he went on, 'the heart of man is full of queernesses and strange loves. And yet, after all, it's most full of strange hatreds. Turn and turn about we come to hate most things, even life itself. I'm not sure whether one hates life more for the responsibilities it entails, or for the disappointments it daily brings.'

'Ha, ha! Were you thinking of those stockings again?' I asked him with a playful shout.

'No, no,' he was speaking quietly, turning it over in his mind as he said it, 'I was thinking of my aunt's erysipelas. It is true each responsibility seems to give you a new strength, but that in turn becomes only a new weakness ; whereas disappointments put such a lustre upon your desperate hopes that they become bright landmarks on your road, hostages as it were for the ultimate attainment '

'Meaning the erysipelas, I suppose!'

'No, the stockings I mean,' he cried.

'Mr. Dapson, – I put it to him decently – 'you had better come out in the air and sit in the public gardens.'

THE JEWEL OF JEOPARDY

I

Papa Lanksheer got up from the table and stood in front of the fire clutching the corner of *The Morning Post* at his side between an irritated forefinger and a quite passionate thumb. Emma was removing breakfast things with the reckless tinkling of china and silver that always vexed him.

'Emma! For Heaven's sake!' he exclaimed, shaking his newspaper admonishingly. Then he turned to his beautiful but wretched daughter Helen and said: 'Rubbish! Vanity!'

'Yes, I know, father, but you don't understand vanity; it really is necessary, it isn't a crime. You wouldn't have me hideous, would you?'

'I'd rather have you hideous than blind. Eyesight's a most precious thing, I tell you, Helen. I can remember – but there, I won't go into that. You really must consult an oculist. Why, confound it, you'll be colliding with cabstands, and dashing into nursery maids with perambulators who never look where they are going, never. Yes, you must, I insist, vanity or no vanity, it stands to reason. And what's the matter with glasses? Glasses don't make you hideous, they set off your expression, make you look intellectual. I wear 'em, worn 'em all my life. What's the matter with glasses?'

'I know it's unreasonable, but you don't understand how I shrink from the ugly things; I've never worn them before, I've never had to, and now . . . but

there, after all, one might as well be dead as blind.'
'Why *do* you keep buzzing about ugliness — like
some wretched bee! I tell you a woman with a bee
in her bonnet hasn't any honey in her mind . . . nor
. . . nor . . . nor anything else. Go and see this
man, go this afternoon, go and see him now, before
lunch!'

If Mr. Lanksheer had scope for anxiety about his
daughter he had none for personal vanity. He was
holding his newspaper at his side as a child sometimes holds its pocket-handkerchief; it would not
have surprised you had he picked up another corner
and inserted it between his teeth. He was an
ordinary ageing man who, without being corpulent,
carried some implications of grossness. Yet he was
the mildest of tipplers. You would have had no
scruples about attributing to him a rich, abundant
appetite — until you saw him eat; he dared not
succumb to its temptations for he was the prey of
dyspepsia. Very fat fingers adhered to his plump pink
hands, the lobes of his ears were pendulous as pears
against his unbulging but nevertheless puffy cheeks.
And hooky was his nose; it was on terms of ferocious
intimacy with his moustache. His voice was inelastic
and hard. Helen was not like that at all, and, to be
frank, she did not admire her father.

She visited the ophthalmist after lunch and all her
alarms were confirmed to the uttermost. The ail-
ment was perhaps even worse than she had feared.
Reading, music, sewing, cinemas, all forbidden — for
a time, at least — and glasses to be worn constantly;

really very serious. So judged the delightful young man who had examined her eyes. He was not the actual specialist, he was an Irishman, temporarily from London, deputizing for the great man. He had signed the prescription for her glasses with the name Paul Duhy. He had strange, delicate-looking hands, and he wore glasses himself: otherwise he looked anything but delicate, and he was undeniably handsome. Before the professional consultations ceased — and Mr. Lanksheer began to have apprehensions that they would never cease — Paul and Helen had grown very fond of each other, and there ensued consultations elsewhere upon topics other than ophthalmy, although Helen's eyes — for they were very beautiful — were the subject of most frequent, and the happiest possible, reference.

But Helen Lanksheer was a calamitous girl. She did not inspire or promote calamity, it followed her doggedly as a wolf. She knew it, and she feared the course of her true love would never run smooth. Of delightful presence, of good family, of impeccable virtue, she had yet a fantastic reputation that even as I set it down here seems to contain assumptions that are grotesque, too extravagant for credence by any normal mind. Yet I reflect that as late as the eighteenth century, even in England, women with far less sinister renown were burnt at the stake, and it is certain that though the so-called punishments have ceased, belief in witchcraft and baleful influence has by no means reached its conclusion. Helen brought disaster upon nearly all who foregathered with her. In beauty she was a jewel, but, alas, a jewel of jeopardy. Her mother died in giving her birth. A brother had drowned in saving her at a boating accident. Relatives and intimate friends, those whose affections she cherished, suffered misfortunes to which Helen's fatal destiny had innocently, but none the less irresistibly, drawn them. Perhaps it was entirely fallacious to associate the poor girl with these happenings. After all, *is* it a platitude to insist that the only certainty in life is its uncertainty? Perhaps the arts of coincidence, whatever they may be, excelled in some marvellous way because she was beautiful and striking. Perhaps; but the sequence of misfortune cannot be scorned, these things undoubtedly happened. Her sister, sleeping with her in the same bed, was burned to death in a fire. Her remaining brother was killed in a railway accident while travelling to fetch Helen home from a visit to Scotland. Her cousin, Helen Lanksheer — christened so in her honour — became an idiot. When she alone was left to live with her father his fortunes markedly declined. No, the occasions when her fatal associations could be vividly traced were so numerous, even in minor happenings, so pointed, that her circle of friends dwindled away and at twenty-two the charming girl was a very lonely one. She herself had come to recognize, and to accept tacitly, the vicarious blame; it could not fail to be borne upon a sensitive mind, and Helen was above everything sensitive-minded. She had other graces as well: she was nearly tall but not quite tall, hair not quite golden though it had the glister, eyes more blue than grey but not quite either. Her face, with that pinkness that looks like fragrance itself, and long thin lips, was lovingly shaped even to the slightest of flaws in the dainty nose. Though not even yet fully developed – she was a singularly virginal type – you could have no shadow of doubt that she would be wonderful. And Paul Duhy already found her wonderful, so wonderful indeed that he was quick to negotiate an opportunity to enter into a partnership with his specialist friend, declaring to himself and to Helen that he had no desire to resign that favoured town while she walked its forever-lighted streets! All this, and much besides, he declared to Helen who loved to hear it, and all might have gone well with them, despite her forebodings of that ever-hovering malignity ever seeking to deprive her of her one lover, her only friend, had not the last week of Paul's term in the town coincided with an unexpected visit to London that her father was called upon to make. This threw the lovers together in freedom for a week of delicious days. Paul's absence, before he could return to take up his partnership, might last perhaps for a couple of months, so with all the urgency of new lovers soon to be parted they crowded into those days an abundance of joys, vows, smiles, kisses and tears. And at the end, tears, everlasting tears. For the unbelievable, the unforeseen, happened; not a quarrel, not a tragedy, but an event that drove Paul irrevocably from her side.

2

Mr. Lanksheer returned from London to a sad, dispirited daughter, but her condition failed to impress itself upon him for his own health had become a matter of desperate concern, more vivid than any to which Helen's sorrows, even had he divined them, could have moved him. He was an egotist, almost devoid of the sympathetic sense, and with little wisdom. Knowledge he had, but nature had not given him any art in the common use of it. The letters M.A. — he was a Brasenose man — were just a tiny intellectual seal that he dangled from a rather empty mental fob. So Helen was lonely, and her father was sick. She had lost Paul. Paul was gone, she had no word from him and his silence was charged with more of his contempt than a sheaf of sharp reproaches. She did not complain of that, she could not complain of anything about Paul, they were in it too deeply together. She derived no feeling of triumph from her successful avoidance of — well, whatever it was she had avoided or foregone. On the contrary, she felt guilty, as deeply as she could possibly have been had their swift passionate project been carried out. Her father's sickness made therefore a diversion from her own sad thoughts, and when his physician prescribed an immediate resort to the seaside she was glad to hail her father's eagerness to obey.

You may figure them, then, from the sharp spring onward, at a resort on the south coast, the old man seeking to recover that which he would never have again, his daughter for her part nursing a passion that was equally hopeless. The spring wore into summer, but they stayed on; Mr. Lanksheer's condition shaped to a slow persistent decline, though there were curious improvements in his temper and outlook for which the girl was grateful. Never a cordial man he developed now a whimsical, and on the whole inoffensive, irascibility that was in its way pathetic. The rough crags of his temperament seemed to dissolve as if beaten upon by those waves it was their constant occupation to observe and admire. Her own unhappiness had not been dissolved, and there was renewed anxiety in her mind about her eyes, in which the old alarming symptoms had begun to reassert themselves. But these troubles she never disclosed, and she continued to accompany her father on the daily aimless amble that occupied their rich sunny mornings. Here, for the first time in her life, Helen had taken to calling him ironically 'Papa' because he was so amusing to her. The dignity of fatherhood had left him, he had never been so talkative, so funny, so furious, or so friendly. He was really, in a pathetic way, enjoying himself immensely. Yet they could do nothing except walk along the sea front from one glass shelter to the next, from that glass shelter to the pier, from the pier to the groyne, from the groyne to the bandstand. In his latter days he was dragged about in a Bath chair by a man named Briggs, whom he playfully bullied and poked with his stick. They would move slowly along, staring down upon the crowded beach that her father was too weak to visit now; not that he would have gone down in any case, for he was inveterately arrogant about the merry poor people who did 'that sort of thing.'

'No self-respecting being,' he would rattle on – and he always took the self-respecting being as the exemplar of Christian conduct, thrusting unconsciously a dagger into the heart of secret Helen – 'no self-respecting being would dream of squatting in a mob on that shore.'

'But why not, Papa?'

'Well, look at it, my dear Helen, it's an idiotic place where mobs from other towns resort to lacerate their very bones by squatting on cobbles and hard rocks and the sides of boats; the side of a boat! Did you *ever* sit on anything so profoundly repellent as the side of a boat? And there they go, meditating, with their feet in the water like a lot of herons. I'm glad when the sea's rough, they can't do it. And those unfortunate little girls with buckets and spades. Fatuous buckets they are, always smaller than the spades! Nothing annoys me more. And balloons ! They make me feel giddy, quite giddy.'

But they would continue parading, the old man humming to himself until they reached other manifestations that seldom failed to goad him.

'Where do they come from, these hordes of harpies, where *do* they come from? Blackening their faces for some reason – quite immoral, I've no doubt, unless of course they are very ugly, and they all are: singing wretched songs which I don't want to hear, and pestering me for pennies which I don't want to give. And then they blackguard me, as politely as they dare, because a penny is all I give and all I ever intend to give. Really, I tell you . . .'

They would pass on in a never-ceasing shower of civilized sound: the pat of a thousand footsteps passing them by, rumble of cart, burr of motor, the general clatter of vendors, the blarney of the excursion men, the waves blundering up the beach, the hails of boatmen, fishermen, sailormen, steamermen, the sad hilarity of the minstrels, hoots of steamers, blare of bands, shouts, bangs and chimes that sprang in the air endlessly like hopping fleas.

'But nothing annoys me more,' declared Mr. Lanksheer as he approached them, 'than these hoarse red-faced rascals with rings in their ears, and stinking barrows. There's a green one with red wheels, look, Helen, crowded with dishes. Fearful little animals called cockles, I believe; yes, they *are* cockles. Not, my dear, those that reside traditionally in your heart for the sole purpose of being warmed on precious occasions, ha, ha! but some little piscatorial horrors – look at them, Helen!'

For a moment or two Helen feared that he was going to poke them off the barrow.

'Yes, and people gobble them up, too, they gobble 'em up. Nothing annoys me more. But for the vampires *in excelsis* those are the ones, yes,' he would declare, pointing his malacca cane at the miscreants, 'those old women with baskets of apples that are shrivelled or sour, and oranges that taste like lemons, and nuts that were young when Gladstone was a boy. Are your eyes better to-day, Helen? You are not wearing your glasses. Vanity! Vanity! Helen,' he would drop his voice to a mysterious tone, 'be careful of those scoundrels who try to persuade you to have your photograph taken. They will dish you up, my dear, they will dish you up looking very cross-eyed, I assure you, with a head that is like nothing so much as a misshapen bun. That's how they turn you out. Well, well, it's very pleasant out this morning. How are your eyes?'

'Splendid, Papa, and you, you haven't coughed once this morning!'

At which reminder Papa Lanksheer would develop an irrepressible desire to make good the omission.

In the afternoon he generally slept, and Helen would go out, often into a quiet town enclosure where she could sit alone. She loved to loiter for a while on one of the iron benches in the gravelled walks, her capacities seeming to reverse in the bulky warmth of the afternoons; she could hear the silence and see reflectively things other than objects in her line of sight: though these were dim enough now, those large angular trees, for instance, that turf worn thin as lodging-house carpet, and the iron foot railing that had been painted in some old time darkly blue, or bluely dark, she could not tell which.

And it was then that her unhappiness was prone to descend upon her most intimately. The mood of self-pity is a tempting possession. Her life now was full of stupid futilities; it was like a screen behind which stood possibilities of endless remote happiness, now for ever barred. At such times the hopes of youth and the loveliness of experience made play upon her nature in vain; perplexed with the vagaries of existence she would return to their lodgings tremulous and cast down.

The summer moved exquisitely on, but her father was dying. His pleasant little asperities had disappeared; the balmy heat of the sun became horrible, or the warm crisping breeze was a tempest to him. He could not go out when he most desired, or he had no desire when he was free to go. In short the entire compression of the world fitted down upon him tightly like a steel cap, and at last he quavered and died, perhaps not so much from disease as from total dissatisfaction with the manifold activities of his Maker.

Scarcely had her father's remains been conveyed to a London crematorium, and the last rites done, when a further disaster clapped down upon Helen. The mourning relatives returned again to the seaside to assist and comfort the stricken girl. They did not stay for long, they adjusted her affairs as quickly as they could; none cared to run the risk of her permanent companionship either in their homes or her own. They all confidently urged that her blindness was only temporary, due to the strain of her exceptional situation, though some attributed it to the inexperienced treatment of Paul Duhy. But the girl never recovered her sight.

She spent some agonizing months in various institutions where people were extraordinarily kind to her. She learned to read Braille books and to work in many curious little arts connected with plaiting and weaving. Her life was full of tragedy, her mind brooded upon it, but at length, getting a grip upon her new faculties, she went back to her home and the care of Emma, the old devoted domestic above whom no maleficent influence ever seemed to impend. It was necessary to engage some sort of a helpmate for Emma, and after much cogitation Emma herself lit upon a small boy, a nephew of her own named Frank, who was taken into the household to live with them. It was Frankie's office to attend Helen whenever she went out, to wait upon her generally while she was acquiring the blind's facility of touch and sense of security. He became a charming companion, at first rather shy; he had a pleasant soft voice, and soon established himself not only as her guide but as her philosopher and friend.

Paul Duhy she did not hear of, he seemed out of the range of her approach now; and how could she inflict, even if he desired her in the old, ardent way, a blind lover upon him? There was that other aspect, too, the fate that seemed to cast its shade over her chosen ones. It was a fantastic enemy, but to her a vivid, a real, one. She had scruples strong enough, for a time at least, to put aside any offer to renew the old tie.

The house was a small one of the Georgian age, set in a garden having a small incurious plot of turf surrounded by a frescade of shrubs; there were a few trees, the pleasant haunt of birds, and the house had the deep pent eaves that charm the martin's eye. It was not so pleasant inside; it was dull, rather stridently furnished. Helen spent her days in the room next the kitchen, that had been half parlour, half study in her father's time. Its walls were hung with unpleasant wall-paper which a number of portraits of Papa, all very elaborately framed, partially hid. A large long table stood upon a worn carpet; it had a nice smooth cover of plush-like material that Helen now loved to rove her fingers along. She remembered it was dull green and fringed with balls of worsted wound upon beads of wood. There was a sideboard with large mirrors: everything in that room seemed large, for the leather-lined easy-chair at the fireplace was framed for persons of elephantine proportions. There was a black piano, now never played, and a desk. A bamboo cabinet for china, never opened, occupied one corner, and a camera and stand, never used, another. Under the window was a sofa. Here the blind girl would sit, day in, day out, hour by hour. As the spring ripened and was warm she would go with Frankie into the park where they would mope or converse; but mostly she would sit at home in that room listening and brooding, brooding and listening. Time did not seem to matter now, neither day nor night. The clock was a meaningless instrument to the blind, who had no vanities. If it were not for the dial recording the passage of time, hours, days, weeks,

133

months and years, we should not experience half the unhappiness of growing old, we should age without belief. But the early days in that room, before Frankie came to be her guide, often moved her to hysterics. She felt like the starling in its cage, 'I can't get out, I can't get out.' She thought of the polar bear in the wild beast show, a vivid image, pacing its six steps forward on its zinc floor and six steps back again interminably. She could not even pace the black clinging trap that enmeshed *her*. All her thoughts formed images. She had imaginations unlike those born blind. She remembered reading a tale of a tiger, that, unseen, unheard, crept into the hut of a blind Indian. The terror of that situation one day so wrought upon her that she screamed out in agony until Emma rushed in to comfort her.

One April morning, when earth and sky were so bright and gay that even the melancholy girl could divine their beauty, she was sitting upon the sofa under the window. The window was open behind her; she was listening to the noises of the birds; there was a heavenly thrush, and pleasant sounds seemed to drift in from everywhere. There was a carrier in from the country at the side door, she could hear him talking to Emma about weather.

'Wonderful, wonderful, ma'am, truly,' he was saying, 'yet I met a man only last night, a very old man he was, who remembers sixty-five years ago this very week when you could walk over the tops of the hedges and never see 'em!'

'How's that?' inquired Emma blankly.

'Snow; yes, snow! Did you see that bit in the paper the day afore yesterday then, or was it Wednesday, no, 'twas a' Tuesday?'

'What was that?'

'Nine inches a' snow in Jerusalem!'

'Gracious!'

'Never before knowed in the 'membrance uv man.'

'Did you ever!' said Emma. There was a pause; then she added: 'Ah, well.'

'Beg your pardon, ma'am,' said the carrier.

'I only said 'Ah, well,' Emma explained more loudly.

'Oh, ah, yes, you're right, ma'am, that's true!' he said and departed.

Helen began laughing lightly and cheerfully.

'How absurd they are, but I love them all!'

She put down the book she had been fingering. The air of the world outside was warm and kind, but within the room was a small fire. She sat quite still for a long time recalling every feature of the room, even the electric light pendants. There were two of them, she knew, with odd shades, one in a dim corner that never got any sunlight. The other, just above the table, always had two or three flies flirting beneath it and spotting the glass of the bulb. She rose and moved cautiously to the lamp, holding her hand below it for some moments to see if the flies would rest upon her. But they did not. She returned to the sofa. The marvellous thrush outside sang as if he divined her thoughts, as if they were just the luminous air he breathed. It was simply fancy, of course; she was thinking of Wales, not any special spot; she knew of none, she had never been there. But as an idea, as a locality, its very names stirred secret emotions in her. She could not pore over a map now. All of Wales that she knew or was ever to know was stored in her memory, and what was significantly there now was not the dæmon of Wales but of Paul. The voice of the bird, in her darkness, her loneliness, sang to that undying passion: Paul will cure me! Paul will cure me! But what chiefly moved her soul were images of her lover and his fierce frightening embraces: Paul will love me! Paul will love me! She longed for him without reserve: the fiercer his demands the more she would grant him. What did blind Helen Lanksheer care now for the looks or condemnations of friends she knew but could not see, for the censure of people she did not know and could now never know? Blindness gave her a new moral code, it covered her own longing with a kind of reverent indiscretion and nullified all opprobrium. The consuming regret in her heart concerned her lost lover Paul and their last meeting while her father was absent in London. Even now its desperate significance brought the flame to her cheeks.

The thrush sang on, and Helen lived again those last hours with Paul.

Here in this very room he had been so passionate, so gentle, so persuasive, so kind, but . . . She did not rank herself above reproach, but she was not dreaming of reproaches in what was so strange and exquisite. She too had been passionate, trembling on a cliff of dalliance from which, if she took but one step, she would fly or be borne on wings of enchantment to a world from which there was no return, or from which return was the last thing desired. Paul had proposed to hire a car and take her into Wales for a few days, alone, together. Almost before she was aware she had half consented, and when she clasped him fondly for that good-night she had wholly agreed.

The thrush outside sang madly, distracting her recollections.

What came next? Oh, yes, next morning she had told the astonished but unquestioning Emma to take the remainder of the week for a holiday: she had worked so hard at cleaning during Mr. Lanksheer's absence. At noon next day Emma had gone. Paul was coming for her in the car at seven o'clock when it was dark. At four o'clock she had packed her bag and frittered about with tea. After that she had sat in her cloak in the front room until it grew dark. She did not switch on the light, she preferred the darkness. At seven o'clock the little car glided up to the gate. She was watching behind the drawn blinds. Paul came into the path and rang the bell of the door. It was a sharp impetuous ring. She stood, listening to its vibrations and the low hum of the motor outside. Her heart throbbed, she could not move, she stood transfixed. The bell rang again, two long insistent clangs. She did not go to him. She did not move. Twice again the bell raged, but

Helen was locked in a strange mood, not stupor — she was very much alive — but a stringent fear that possessed her. Paul turned the handle of the door. It was locked. He stood in the garden and surveyed the house. How fine his shape in the gloom! He went to the side door, which he tried without success. At last he went away.

Helen sighed: 'Oh dear, that stupid bird, I wish it would stop. I can't think! I can't think!'

Her thoughts swum back to her.

When Paul departed she had lain coals upon the fire and sunk down, still in her cloak, still in darkness, chilled to the soul with grief. After a long, long time, more than an hour, she heard the motor again glide up to the gate. She half turned in the chair, gripping its padded sides until her nails and fingers were pierced with pain. The bell once more flashed its summons: its idle summons, for she lay cowering until Paul had gone. She sat on in the dark room like a stricken child. At nine o'clock he came yet again, but there was neither fear nor love in her then, neither pride nor passion. She was just empty, dull, weary. She heard him at last go back to the gate. It slammed with a heavy crash. He waited awhile, then just spat into the garden, was gone. She was cold then. She got up and went to her bedroom, carrying the travelling bag with her. She undressed and, lying in her bed, all her love returned. But he would not come again, her dear angry lover. She flung her arms round the vision of him there. Oh, if he would only come again she

138

would unlock the doors and greet him humbly, yes, humbly. Time and again she rose from her bed and peered into the moonlit road, but he was not there, she knew he would never come again. She got up and dressed herself quickly, very, very quickly, and hurried into the empty town, carrying her travelling bag. Where had he gone, where could she look for him, she would never find him again. The night was glorious in beauty, and even the suburban dissonance was vanquished. Yes, there was a soft flush of moonlight from the sharp sky. Bushes, shrubs, and trees in the villas flung grey shades across the road. A clock was chiming twelve. Three dissolute men lay upon a bench, one of them imitating a cock-crow. Tiny gales lifted the boughs, sifted the shadows, and dissolved in them. Sometimes a low-hanging star would trickle behind the moving trees. Ahead lay the shapely heave of a hill, vaguer trees, and the white cheeks of houses. It was cold. A cape of snow cowered in the eastern sky and a cape of snow in the west, but the track of the road was still seen sharply in the moon's light. In her distraction she ran along the great road leading to Wales, following it out into lonely sylvan country, but vainly. She met nobody, and the swift rush of headlights never once gladdened her eager eyes. She never heard from Paul again.

The blinded girl sat up from her daydream as if dazed, intoxicated by her romantic recollections. She began to repeat a sorrowful couplet from an old poem:

Dust hath closed Helen's eye,
I am sick, I must die.

Nothing but darkness, darkness of eye, darkness of mind, of hope, of religion. To her religion offered no solace, no alleviations; most aspects of the religious life left her unmoved.

But the thrush was still singing; trilling a Welsh gamut, it seemed to cry:

My dear, my dear, my dear!
Chirk, chirk, chirk, chirk, chirk, chirk!
Swansea, Swansea!
Poo . . . come along, come along . . .
 Poo . . . Oo . . . Oo . . . flutter Aberdovey!

She could hear the little boy in the kitchen playing with his engine. He had built a toy roundabout, with wheels and rails and cardboard horses and figures that rolled up and down, round and round, as long as he turned a handle. The toy possessed him. She could hear him interminably twisting a handle, its mechanism rattling frenziedly upon the table.

Trevithick! Trevithick!
O-oo, O-oo, O-oo.

Where was Trevithick? Probably near Cardiff.

My dear, my dear!
Chirk-chirk-chirk-chirk.

The thrush went on carolling thus madly.

Helen called out to her boy: 'Frank!' The rattle of the roundabout ceased, the door opened and the little boy came and stood by her. She held out her hands. 'Come here.' They happened to fall upon his thick fluffy hair.

'What is the colour of your hair, Frankie?'

'Brown, miss.'

'Is it dark or light? Is it like chocolate or . . . dead leaves?'

She took the boy into her arms, passing her hands over his strange young face.

'Are you pretty, Frankie? What colour is your hair?'

He appeared to cogitate carefully: 'It's more like seaweed, miss.'

'Dark, then, dark.'

She pressed his head to her bosom. 'Don't call me miss, Frankie, call me Helen, won't you? What colour are your eyes – are they strong eyes?'

'Yes, Miss Helen; I don't know what the colour is.'

'Not know their colour! And you've had them for ten years! Frankie! Why, fetch a looking-glass and tell me what their colour is.'

He obeyed. 'Nearly black, miss.'

'No, no, Frankie!' She put her arms around his neck again with a queer hungering feeling for the child. 'What are you to call me?' she whispered. He, too, lowered his voice as he answered 'Helen.' Thereat she pressed him in both arms again, laying her cheek against his cool small face. Something moved him to touch her cheeks gently with his fingers and kiss her.

The caress enraptured her.

'Frankie, where is Trevithick?'

'He's dead, Helen.'

'Dead? Oh, no . . . I don't mean . . . it's a place . . . in Wales.' Frankie reflected, and declared his belief that Trevithick was the man who made railways first of all, long time ago. Surely that was Stephenson, wasn't it? Frankie explained that it was not so.

'I must have heard it somewhere. Look in the gazetteer, Frankie.'

Frankie was triumphant, for neither gazetteer nor time-table recorded the name.

'Find some notepaper in the desk, Frankie. You are a good writer, aren't you?'

The boy declared that he was.

'Write a letter for me then, Frankie, please, write it in your very best style.'

DEAR PAUL,

Come and see me. I want to speak to you. Come to tea to-day.

Yours,
HELEN.

Frankie stood up and read it over to her. 'You are sure that you have spelt the words all right? And there are no blots?'

'Yes.'

'What else?'

'The envelope.'

'No, I mean what are you to call me?'

Frankie did not reply. He sat down and inscribed the envelope. 'I want you to take it to Fulton Crescent. And wait for an answer. Can you go quickly? How long will you be? Not long, will you, Frankie? Oh, wait, wait! You must open it again, open it, have you opened it? Put P.S. at the bottom. *P.S. I am quite blind, Paul.* Now another envelope, just as you wrote before.'

The envelope was sealed, and the boy departed, promising to return within half an hour. 'Run, Frankie, won't you?' She appealed. She almost counted the beats of the clock until his return. Frankie brought back the letter. Mr. Duhy was not in.

'But, oh, Frankie, how stupid of you! You should have left it. When will he be in?'

'I wanted to leave it,' he replied, 'but she wouldn't let me. She said you take it back where you brought it. He left a year ago and he ain't come back any more . . . Helen!'

'Oh, Frankie, what do you say, not live there?' Her agitation was pitiful. 'Where is he? What does it mean? Run and tell Emma I want my hat and coat. Emma! *Emma!* You must take me there, Frankie, at once, do you hear?'

'Yes, Helen,' he replied. In a few minutes they had left the house together, the boy modestly holding her hand. They walked without speaking, for some dread of that old Malignity, that doom she drew down upon her friends, began to thrust its grim shadow upon her swift intention. But tears rose into her dead eyes; she could not, would not, believe it now. Surely her blindness had expiated all the terrible blame!

'Where are we? Are we nearly there?' she kept asking.

'Yes, nearly . . . Helen.'

They were crossing a road amid a pause in the traffic when an outburst of startled shouting sprang in the air, a vast noise of rushing wagons suddenly boomed upon the street and seemed to swoop at them.

'No! no!' screamed the boy to Helen, 'look . . . !'

He was torn from her grasp, while the clamour of flying horses crashed past her very face and pounded on. There was a shocking silence. Some soft footsteps seemed to assemble near the waiting girl.

'What is it? Frankie! Frankie! Where are you?' she screamed.

But the people, the quite silent people, stooped down just beyond her to gather up the dead boy before they turned to Helen in her doom and her blindness.

ALICE BRADY

BRIGHT? YES, IT WAS BRIGHT. 'THE SUN'S COME up like a fire coal this morning,' said Alice Brady, lying in her room at the *Carpenters' Arms*, a long low room with a little bedstead of brass in a large corner; a stand to wash at, looking very naked, in another; and a lot of cupboards brown and musty. How old she was! Eighty years and more, and every day of those long years she had dwelt and slept at the inn. Father, too. He had died there. For more than a century a Brady had kept the '*Carpenters*.' To-day – it was Old Michaelmas Day – they were thinking to turn her out of it. People pass, they decline and die, the stocks and stones outlast them. Though not so young as she had once been Alice was lasting well, but her landlord had died and the property had been sold to a new brewer; his new tenant was moving in to-day: Old Michaelmas Day.

George's Molly was downstairs cracking sticks for the fire, and, as always, it sounded as if she were in a temper with the faggots. Alice could not bear bad-tempered people. They chilled her, they annoyed, they were exasperating. Cheerful people were the salt of the earth. 'Give me a man as can sing at eight o'clock in the morning, any fool can sing a song at night.' Alice had said it again and again. For years now, George's Molly had come over from her own house and lit Alice's fire and helped her to dress. For years she had done that, but Alice didn't want her to, didn't need her at all, didn't like her, and for those reasons if for no others had never paid her a trifle for her services. She had never spoken to her brother George since his Molly was born, born out of wedlock forty years ago; and George's Molly had always called her Alice, for Miss Brady would never recognize her consanguinity by acknowledging the name of 'aunt.'

Alice began to get up, a long exhausting process, and the pain in her throat hurt her unmercifully, but she would get up by herself. 'They'll find me a bit too young for 'em yet.' She sneezed twice. Then, after dipping her hands in the water bowl and wiping her cheeks with a damp flannel, she knelt down at the bedside: it was more respectful to wash yourself before praying to the Lord.

Peaceful the day was, Old Michaelmas Day. Peering from her window she could see the mild sun airing the wet farms. Winter oats were finger high in Napton's field. Pleasant country to live in, pretty and quiet. But now, what was going to happen to her she didn't know, she didn't care. Only she was not going from her home, not now, at her time of life. You might live to be a hundred – people did – and how could a body go wearing out its days tramping from one end of the world to the other, especially when they had never been married? As she was about to descend the stairs George's Molly came up, humming, with a cup of tea.

'Why, Alice! You up?' And as the old woman made no rejoinder Molly continued: 'The rain's bated, but you can't tell whether it's going to be fine or whether it 'ull be wet.'

'What if it is bated! 'Twill as soon be wet as fine,' declared Alice, 'it's all one to the Lord.'

'Ah, so it ain't, be the look of it,' said her cryptic niece.

Alice drank the tea, and George's Molly helped her to totter downstairs. Then the niece went away home and the old woman was left to grim meditations, arousing old resentments and awakening new fears as she sat by the log fire in her tap-room, the polished feet of the iron firedogs looking like big spurs. It was gloomy there even now, although it had but recently been cleaned with paint and wash that still smelled sourly. Alice had liked it better when the ceiling had been densely blackened with the smoke from the open hearth. A red valance hung along the mantelshelf, on which reposed three brass lamps and two books, a Holy Bible and *Old Moore's Almanac*, while in the darkest corner stood darkly the chain clock that was older even than her father and had never lost an hour; it was true as judgment. A lot of Alice's time was spent in perusing the two books. Her long unsmiling face with its hooky nose and dull glasses sucked consolation from the one and knowledge from the other. But she preferred consolation.

Weeks ago it had been explained to the old woman that the inn was sold. Of course — she said — she was very sorry, but she couldn't help that. And of course she couldn't. What did they expect her to do?

If you were born in a house you'd a right to die in it, hadn't you? No – they said. Not if you had never been married? No – they said again. Then where did they think she was going, or what did they think she would do? She was old, eighty-one, she could go nowhere else, no one had room for an old woman like her, and nothing, nothing in the living world, would ever persuade her to go and live with that George's Molly. Oh, no. They said they would find a place for her to go to. 'Where?' asked Alice. 'Oh, a nice place,' they said, 'neat and comfortable for an old lady.' Alice said she shouldn't go. She would not go if she could, and as of course she couldn't go she wouldn't be able to go at all.

By and by some wretches of men had come and put scaffolding up about the house and taken off the roof tiles, some of them, and laid tarpaulin over the rafters; and while that was doing the weather turned bad. It rained days and it rained nights, and all day long the devils would come in and drink their pints and smoke and swear, but Alice never spoke to them except in the way of custom. At last the roof was repaired and finished, and then the men came into the house and hacked and sawed and painted and swore and spat, but Alice never budged, and when they were finished she didn't know her old home – it was so glaring. People came and told her she was to go out on Old Michaelmas Day, but what could she do, an old woman with no kith nor kin in the world? George's Molly had tried to poison her, often. And there was no call to clatter and smash the house at all. Such a house it had been, too! So steep the roof that the rain swilled from it, it dried in a twinkle of sun. And a tall tower in the middle of the roof, with three chimneypots on it, red, poking from the top of the tower. Four windows on the long sunny front of the house, two up and two down, and a little door in the middle, level with the chimneystack, and two windows at each end, one down and one up. It was all white as a bone, except the roof; so white that when you saw it in the moonlight you would think it a palace built by some good person not too rich to be pleasant. There would be a light, soft and golden, in every lower window. The tower rose up, like a pillar of salt you might think, and the shadow it cast dropped right across the road, black, like a strip of velvet. If a man walked over that shadow on a bright night you could only see the top half of him.

That was the place she'd been born in, and her father had lived in it before then, ever so many years; for over a hundred years a Brady had kept the 'Carpenters,' and no one could remember the 'Carpenters' without ever a Brady in it.

Come midday, it was raining again. The village men came into the tap-room, came crowding into it, Reuben Attwater, Oxlade the farrier, and Toby Daw, a lot of them, tree-fellers, chair bodgers, mole catchers and herds, all having pints and smoking and spitting. What did they all want? They seldom came before evening. They hadn't come to say good-bye; they had come to see her be cast from her house, those men with their pints, and they'd never lift a hand!

And it was true that they had never cared for her — how could they? — an old maid who read her Bible and was punctual as day for closing time, and never had a smile or a good word for a man that drunk beer or was free in his talk. She had even sold her old parrot because it had learnt to swear. And *then* it had died. But they stared at her now, angry and indignant at her misfortunes which they were powerless to prevent. 'Once property is sold, God Almighty Himself can't odds it.' Candour declared it and custom agreed, and they were sullen because they were helpless, subdued by mysterious forces.

'I remember her father, old Jack Brady, . . .' began Reuben Attwater.

'How long's he bin dead and gone?' interrupted Toby Daw in his squeaky voice.

'Forty years . . .' Reuben folded his giant arms and lifted the pipe from his cheerful mouth.

'I 'members him, too,' declared Twit Simmons, 'his missus was a . . .'

'They was a-drawing green beech from the 'ood,' Reuben continued indomitably, 'one stormy day. He'd just stapped under th' 'orse's neck to shoot a trace on the off shaft when a flash o' lightning come and struck th' 'orse dead, but never touched 'e. Dead as a bloody hammer. Killed it.'

'I know. And his wife was a come-by-chance,' pursued Twit Simmons.

'Well,' reflected Attwater, 'you've no call to drag that up agin him.'

'Used to be a lot of chair bodging here in those days,' piped a maker of legs and rungs, Harbottle his name, a man with sore eyes.

'Oh, ah!'

'And a lot o' beer drinked.'

'I dessay.' Reuben nodded and gazed sternly at his pot.

'I *knows* as how there was,' asseverated Harbottle. Oxlade, a morose man, stared out of the window. The rain had ceased to fall, day was brightening again. 'It don't thunder now as it used to years ago, nor lightning now as it used to, and we don't have no winters like there used to be — years ago.'

'It used to thunder *and* lightning,' Toby Daw was moved to enthusiasm, 'four and five days togedder. Wid'out stopping!'

'Lightning is only drawed to ash trees and oak trees,' Oxlade said, 'never strikes no other trees, never,' and the limitation seemed to lie like a canker in his gloomy bosom.

'Here it is,' suddenly said Reuben, and the men all stood up together in a crowd. A man had driven up in a neat pony-chaise, and he sat waiting outside. George's Molly came breathlessly into the tap-room, other women bustling in behind her.

'Come,' said Molly to Alice, 'it's time to go.'

'Go?' quavered Alice, her long hand clutching her Bible, 'where to go?'

'A nice fine house the mister is going to drive you

to,' said Molly. The women glanced at each other and sniffed.

'There's no house like my own.' Alice was proud about it. One of the women took Alice's cloak from a hook and put it round the old woman's shoulders. Another popped a bonnet on her head. Alice snatched them off and threw them on the floor.

'Why, Alice!' exclaimed George's Molly, 'put your bonnet on now!' She picked the things up from the floor and wrapped the old woman in her cloak again. 'The old clock's stopped,' cried Toby Daw. All turned and stared at the dark brass face. In the silence you could hear no tick. The old woman looked at her clock. She walked with weak steps up to the ancient timepiece, peering long and surprisedly at it.

'No,' she mumbled, 'never! Never before! What's up with it? It never stopped before; in all my days, it never stopped before.'

Still clutching her Bible Alice turned to George's Molly, who took her by the arm and led her, unresisting, to the open doorway. They helped the old woman to climb into the trap, and when she had finally settled herself she gave a long look at the village street. The rain had stopped, the sun shone through the clouds and glowed on the breasts of white doves flying high; so miraculous, they were pieces of winged light. And at the end of the street she could see the long down with the mill upon its highest reach, a mill whose arms had not moved these twenty years. It was surrounded by a hedge that lapped over the contour of the down like the fringe of a saddle-cloth. There were no trees, but upon its flank was planted a score of small tods, bushes of whitebeam that in spring were brightly grey.

'God will deal with them,' the old woman was mumbling as the trap moved off. 'God will deal with the rogues and villains of the world. Yes, I know He will, blessed God!'

'Then I wish as how He'd get on with the job,' screamed George's Molly after her, waving her hand.

When they got to the workhouse the first thing they did was to undress Alice and put her into a hot bath. Then they put her to bed, and she never got up again. George's Molly went to her funeral, and when she returned to the village she was full of resentment and full of scorn.

'They said she died of a concert in her throat, but they'd no call to put an old woman into a bath — not all at once. She was too old for that sort of treachery. Wash when you can and when it's wanted, that's what I believe in. I washes up as far as I can, and the next time I washes down as far as I can, but I wouldn't be put in no bath for fifty shillings. If God in heaven meant us to drown'd ourselves in water we'd a bin made like fishes.'

Now, though the inn is whiter and cosier and looks more tall, and on moonlight nights is most grand to view, nobody goes there. There had always been a Brady in *The Carpenters' Arms*, always, for a hundred years. There will never be a Brady there again, and so it is in the other inn that the men forgather, and recall at odd moments what a 'rum old gal' Alice Brady was.

THE WATERCRESS GIRL

I

WHEN MARY MCDOWALL WAS BROUGHT TO THE assize court the place was crowded, Mr. O'Kane said, 'inside out.' It was a serious trial, as everybody – even the prisoner – well knew : twelve tons of straw had been thrown down on the roads outside the hall to deaden the noise of carts passing and suchlike pandemoniums, and when the Judge drove up in his coach with jockeys on the horses, a couple of young trumpeters from the barracks stiffened on the steps and blew a terrible fanfare up into heaven. 'For a sort of a warning, I should think,' said Mr. O'Kane.

The prisoner's father having been kicked by a horse was unable to attend the trial, and so he had enlisted Mr. O'Kane to go and fetch him the news of it; and Mr. O'Kane in obliging his friend suffered annoyances and was abused in the court itself by a great fat geazer of a fellow with a long staff. 'If you remained on your haunches when the judge came in,' complained Mr. O'Kane, 'you were poked up, and if you stood up to get a look at the prisoner when she came in you were poked down. Surely to God we didn't go to look at the judge!'

Short was her trial, for the evidence was clear, and the guilt not denied. Prisoner neither sorrowed for her crime nor bemoaned her fate; passive and casual she stood there to suffer at the willing of the court for a thing she had done, and there were no tears now in

Mary McDowall. Most always she dressed in black, and she was in black then, with masses of black hair; a pale face with a dark mole on the chin, and rich red lips; a big girl of twenty-five, not coarsely big, and you could guess she was strong. A passionate girl, caring nothing or not much for this justice; unimpressed by the solemn court, nor moved to smile at its absurdities; for all that passion concerns with is love – or its absence – love that gives its only gift by giving all. If you could have read her mind, not now but in its calm before the stress of her misfortune, you would have learned this much, although she herself could not have formulated it: I will give to love all it is in me to give; I shall desire of love all I can ever dream of and receive.

And because another woman had taken what Mary McDowall wanted, Mary had flung a corrosive acid in the face of her enemy, and Elizabeth Plantney's good looks were gone, gone for certain and for ever. So here was Mary McDowall and over there was Frank Oppidan; not a very fine one to mislead the handsome girl in the dock, but he had done it, and he too had suffered, and the women in court had pity for him, and the men – envy. Tall, with light oiled hair and pink sleepy features (a pink heart, too, you might think, though you could not see it), he gave evidence against her in a nasal tone with a confident manner, and she did not waste a look on him. A wood-turner he was, and for about four years had 'kept company' with the prisoner, who lived near a village a mile or two away from his home. He had

156

often urged her to marry him, but she would not, so a little while ago he told her he was going to marry Elizabeth Plantney. A few evenings later he had been strolling with Elizabeth Plantney on the road outside the town. It was not yet dark, about eight o'clock, but they had not observed the prisoner, who must have been dogging them, for she came slyly up and passed by them, turned, splashed something in his companion's face and then walked on. She didn't run; at first they thought it was some stupid joke, and he was for going after the prisoner whom he had recognized.

'I was mad angry,' declared Oppidan, 'I could have choked her. But Miss Plantney began to scream that she was blinded and burning, and I had to carry and drag her some ways back along the road until we came to the first house, Mr. Blackfriar's, where they took her in and I ran off for the doctor.' The witness added savagely, 'I wish I *had* choked her.'

There was full corroboration, prisoner had admitted guilt, and the counsel briefed by her father could only plead for a lenient sentence. A big man he was with a drooping yellow moustache and terrific teeth; his cheeks and hands were pink as salmon.

'Accused,' he said, 'is the only child of Fergus McDowall. She lives with her father, a respectable widower, at a somewhat retired cottage in the valley of Trinkel, assisting him in the conduct of his business — a small holding by the river where he cultivates watercress, and keeps bees and hens and things

157

of that kind. The witness Oppidan had been in the habit of cycling from his town to the McDowall's home to buy bunches of watercress, a delicacy of which, in season, he seems to have been — um — inordinately fond, for he would go twice, thrice, and often four times a week. His visits were not confined to the purchase of watercress, and he seems to have made himself agreeable to the daughter of the house; but I am in possession of no information as to the nature of their intercourse beyond that tendered by the witness Oppidan. Against my advice the prisoner, who is a very reticent, even a remarkable, woman, has insisted on pleading guilty and accepting her punishment without any — um — chance of mitigation, in a spirit, I hope, of contrition, which is not — um — entirely inadmirable. My lord, I trust . . .'

While the brutal story was being recounted, prisoner had stood with closed eyes, leaning her hands upon the rail of the dock, stood and dreamed of what she had not revealed:

Of her father Fergus McDowall; his child she was, although he had never married. That much she knew, but who her mother had been he never told her, and it did not seem to matter; she guessed rather than knew that at her birth she had died, or soon afterwards, and the man had fostered her. He and she had always been together, alone, ever since she could remember, always together, always happy, he was so kind; and so splendid in the great boots that drew up to his thighs when he worked in the watercress beds, cutting bunches deftly, or cleaning the weeds from the water. And there were her bee-hives, her flock of hens, the young pigs, and a calf that knelt and rubbed its neck on the rich mead with a lavishing movement just as the ducks did when the grass was dewy. She had seen the young pigs, no bigger than rabbits, race across the patch of greensward to the blue-roan calf standing nodding in the shade; they would prowl beneath the calf, clustering round its feet, and begin to gnaw the calf's hoof until, full of patience, she would gently lift her leg and shake it, but would not move away. Save for a wildness of mood that sometimes flashed through her, Mary was content, and loved the life that she could not know was lonely with her father beside the watercress streams. He was uncommunicative, like Mary, but as he worked he hummed to himself or whistled the soft tunes that at night he played on the clarinet. Tall and strong, a handsome man. Sometimes he would put his arm around her and say, 'Well, my dear.' And she would kiss him. She had vowed to herself that she would never leave him, but then — Frank had come. In this mortal conflict we seek not only that pleasure may not divide us from duty, but that duty may not detach us from life. He was not the first man or youth she could or would have loved, but he was the one who had wooed her; first-love's enlightening delight, in the long summer eves, in those enticing fields! How easily she was won! All his offers of marriage she had put off with the answer: 'No, it would never do for me,' or 'I shall never marry,' but then, if he angrily swore, or accused her of not loving him enough, her fire and freedom would awe him almost as much as it enchanted. And she might have married Frank if she could only have told him of her dubious origin, but whether from some vagrant modesty, loyalty to her father, or some reason whatever, she could not bring herself to do that. Often these steady refusals enraged her lover, and after such occasions he would not seek her again for weeks, but in the end he always returned, although his absences grew longer as their friendship lengthened. Ah, when the way to your lover is long, there's but a short cut to the end. Came a time when he did not return at all and then, soon, Mary found she was going to have a child. 'Oh, I wondered where you were, Frank, and why you were there, wherever it was, instead of where I could find you.' But the fact was portentous enough to depose her grief at his fickleness, and after a while she took no further care or thought for Oppidan, for she feared that like her own mother she would die of her child. Soon these fears left her and she rejoiced. Certainly she need not scruple to tell him of her own origin now, he could never reproach her now. Had he come once more, had he come then, she would have married him. But although he might have been hers for the lifting of a finger, as they say, her pride kept her from calling him into the trouble, and she did not call him, and he never sought her again. When her father realized her condition he merely said 'Frank?' and she nodded. The child was early born, and she was not prepared; it came, and died. Her father took it and buried it in the garden. It was a boy, dead. No one else knew, not even Frank, but when she was recovered her pride wavered and she wrote a loving letter to him, still keeping her secret. Not until she had written three times did she hear from him, and then he only answered that he should not see her any more. He did not tell her why, but she knew. He was going to marry Elizabeth Plantney, whose parents had died and left her £500. To Mary's mind that presented itself as a treachery to their child, the tiny body buried under a beehive in the garden. That Frank was unaware made no difference to the girl's fierce mood; it was treachery. Maternal anger stormed in her breast, it could only be allayed by an injury, a deep admonishing injury to that treacherous man. In her sleepless nights the little crumpled corpse seemed to plead for this much, and her own heart clamoured, just as those bees murmured against him day by day.

So then she got some vitriol. Rushing past her old lover on the night of the crime she turned upon him with the lifted jar, but the sudden confrontation dazed and tormented her; in momentary hesitation she had dashed the acid, not into his faithless eyes, but at the prim creature linked to his arm. Walking away, she heard the crying of the wounded girl. After a while she had turned back to the town and given herself up to the police.

To her mind, as she stood leaning against the dock rail, it was all huddled and contorted, but that was her story set in its order. The trial went droning on beside her remembered grief like a dull stream neighbouring a clear one, two parallel streams that would meet in the end, were meeting now, surely, as the judge began to speak. And at the crisis, as if in exculpation, she suffered a whisper to escape her lips, though none heard it.

"'Twas him made me a parent, but he was never a man himself. He took advantage, it was mean, I love Christianity.' She heard the judge deliver her sentence: for six calendar months she was to be locked in a gaol. 'O Christ!' she breathed, for it was the lovely spring; lilac, laburnum, and father wading the brooks in those boots drawn up to his thighs to rake the dark sprigs and comb out the green scum.

They took her away. 'I wanted to come out then,' said Mr. O'Kane, 'for the next case was only about a contractor defrauding the corporation – Good luck to him, but he got three years – and I tried to get out of it, but if I did that geazer with the stick poked me down and said I'd not to stir out of it till the court rose. I said to him I'd kill him, but there was a lot of peelers about so I suppose he didn't hear it.'

2

Towards the end of the year Oppidan had made up his mind what he would do to Mary McDowall when she came out of prison. Poor Liz was marred for life, spoiled, cut off from the joys they had intended together. Not for all the world would he marry her now; he had tried to bring himself to that issue of chivalry, of decency, but it was impossible; he had failed in the point of grace. No man could love Elizabeth Plantney now, Frank could not visit her without shuddering, and she herself, poor generous wretch, had given him back his promise. Apart from his ruined fondness for her, they had planned to do so much with the £500; it was to have set him up in a secure and easy way of trade, they would have been established in a year or two as solid as a rock. All that chance was gone, no such chance ever came twice in a man's lifetime, and he was left with Liz upon his conscience. He would have to be kind to her for as long as he could stand it. That was a disgust to his mind for he wanted to be faithful. Even the most unstable man wishes he had been faithful – but to which woman he is never quite sure. And then that bitch Mary Mc-Dowall would come out of her prison and be a mockery to him of what he had forgone, of what he had been deprived. Savagely he believed in the balance wrought by an act of vengeance – he, too! – eye for eye, tooth for tooth; it had a threefold charm, simplicity, relief, triumph. The McDowall girl, so his fierce meditations ran, miked in prison for six months and then came out no worse than she went in. It was no punishment at all, they did no hurt to women in prison, the court hadn't set wrong right at all, it never did; and he was a loser whichever way he turned. But there was still a thing he could do (Jove had slumbered, he would steal Jove's light-

ning) and a project lay troubling his mind like a
gnat in the eye, he would have no peace until it was
wiped away.

On an October evening, then, about a week after
Mary McDowall's release, Oppidan set off towards
Trinkel. Through Trinkel he went and a furlong
past it until he came to their lane. Down the lane
too, and then he could hear the water ruttling over
the cataracts of the cress-beds. Not yet in winter, the
year's decline was harbouring splendour everywhere.
Whitebeam was a dissolute tangle of rags covering
ruby drops, the service trees were sallow as lemons,
the oak resisted decay, but most confident of all were
the tender-tressed ashes. The man walked quietly
to a point where, unobserved, he could view the
McDowall dwelling, with its overbowering walnut
tree littering the yard with husks and leaves, its
small adjacent field with banks that stooped in the
glazed water. The house was heavy and small, but
there were signs of grace in the garden, of thrift
in the orderly painted sheds. The conical peak of a
tiny stack was pitched in the afterglow, the elms
sighed like tired old matrons, wisdom and content
lingered here. Oppidan crept along the hedges
until he was in a field at the back of the house, a
hedge still hiding him. He was trembling. There
was a light already in the back window; one leaf of
the window stood open and he saw their black cat
jump down from it into the garden and slink away
under some shrubs. From his standpoint he could
not see into the lighted room, but he knew enough of

Fergus's habits to be sure he was not within; it was his day for driving into the town. Thus it could only be Mary who had lit that lamp. Trembling still! Just beyond him was a heap of dung from the stable, and a cock was standing silent on the dunghill while two hens, a white one and a black, bickered around him over some voided grains. Presently the cock seized the black hen and the white scurried away; but though his grasp was fierce and he bit at her red comb, the black hen went on gobbling morsels from the manure heap, and when at last he released her she did not intermit her steady pecking. Then Oppidan was startled by a flock of starlings that slid across the evening with the steady movement of a cloud; the noise of their wings was like showers of rain upon trees.

'Wait till it's darker,' he muttered, and skulking back to the lane he walked sharply for half a mile. Then, slowly, he returned. Unseen he reached the grass that grew under the lighted window, and stooped warily against the wall; one hand rested on the wall, the other in his pocket. For some time he hesitated, but he knew what he had to do, and what did it matter! He stepped in front of the window.

In a moment, and for several moments longer, he was rigid with surprise. It was Mary all right (the bitch!), washing her hair, drying it in front of the kitchen fire, the thick locks pouring over her face as she knelt with her hands resting in her thighs. So long was their black flow that the ends lay in a small heap inside the fender. Her bodice hung on the back of a chair beside her, and her only upper clothing was a loose and disarrayed chemise that did not hide her bosom. Then, gathering the hair in her hands, she held the tresses closer to the fire, her face peeped through, and to herself she was smiling. Dazzling fair were her arms and the one breast he astonishingly saw. It was Mary; but not the Mary, dull ugly creature, whom his long rancour had conjured for him. Lord, what had he forgotten! Absence and resentment had pared away her loveliness from his recollection, but this was the old Mary of their passionate days, transfigured and marvellous.

Stepping back from the window into shadow again, he could feel his heart pound like a frantic hammer; every pulse was hurrying at the summons. In those breathless moments Oppidan gazed as it were at himself, or at his mad intention, gazed wonderingly, ashamed and awed. Fingering the thing in his pocket, turning it over as a coin whose toss has deceived him, he was aware of a revulsion: gone revenge, gone rancour, gone all thought of Elizabeth, and there was left in his soul what had not gone, and could never go. A brute she had been — it was bloody cruelty — but, but . . . but what? Seen thus, in her innocent occupation, the grim fact of her crime had somehow thrown a conquering glamour over her hair, the pale pride of her face, the intimacy of her bosom. Her very punishment was a triumph; on what account had she suffered if not for love of him? He could feel that chastening distinction meltingly now: she had suffered for his love.

There and then shrill cries burst upon them. The cat leaped from the garden to the window-sill; there was a thrush in its mouth, shrieking. The cat paused on the sill, furtive and hesitant. Without a thought Oppidan plunged forward, seized the cat and with his free hand clutched what he could of the thrush. In a second the cat released it and dropped into the room, while the crushed bird fluttered away to the darkened shrubs, leaving its tail feathers in the hand of the man.

Mary sprang up and rushed to the window. 'Is it you?' was all she said. Hastily she left the window, and Oppidan with a grin saw her shuffling into her bodice. One hand fumbled at the buttons, the other unlatched the door. 'Frank.' There was neither surprise nor elation. He walked in. Only then did he open his fist, and the thrush's feathers floated in the air and idled to the floor. Neither of them remembered any more of the cat or the bird.

In silence they stood, not looking at each other. 'What do you want?' at length she asked, 'you're hindering me.'

'Am I?' he grinned. His face was pink and shaven, his hair was almost as smooth as a brass bowl. 'Well, I'll tell you.' His hat was cumbering his hands, so he put it carefully on the table. 'I come here wanting to do a bad thing, I own up to that. I had it in my mind to serve you same as you served her — you know who I mean. Directly I knew you had come home, that's what I meant to do. I been waiting about out there a good while until I saw you.

And then I saw you. I hadn't seen you for a long, long time, and somehow, I dunno, when I saw you. . .'

Mary was standing with her hands on her hips; the black cascades of her hair rolled over her arms; some of the strands were gathered under her fingers, looped to her waist, dark weeping hair.

'I didn't mean to harm her!' she burst out. 'I never meant that for her, not what I did. Something happened to me that I'd not told you of then, and it doesn't matter now, and I shall never tell you. It was you I wanted to put a mark on, but directly I was in front of you I went all swavy, and I couldn't. But I had to throw it, I had to throw it.'

He sat down on a chair, and she stared at him across the table: 'All along it was meant for you, and that's God's truth.'

'Why?' he asked. She did not give him an answer then, but stood rubbing the fingers of one hand on the finely scrubbed boards of the table, tracing circles and watching them vacantly. At last she put a question:

'Did you get married soon?'

'No,' he said.

'Arn't you? But of course it's no business of mine.'

'I'm not going to marry her.'

'Not?'

'No, I tell you I wouldn't marry her for five thousand pounds, nor for fifty thousand, I wouldn't.' He got up and walked up and down before the fire. 'She's — aw! You don't know, you don't know what you done to her! She'd frighten you. It's rotten, like a leper. A veil on indoors and out, has to wear it always. She don't often go out, but whether or no, she must wear it. Ah, it's cruel.'

There was a shock of horror as well as the throb of tears in her passionate compunction. 'And you're not marrying her!'

'No,' he said bluntly, 'I'm not marrying her.'

Mary covered her face with her hands, and stood quivering under her dark weeping hair.

'God forgive me, how pitiful I'm shamed!' Her voice rose in a sharp cry. 'Marry her, Frank! Oh, you marry her now, you must!'

'Not for a million, I'd sooner be in my grave.'

'Frank Oppidan, you're no man, no man at all. You never had the courage to be strong, nor the courage to be evil; you've only the strength to be mean.'

'Oh, dry up!' he said testily; but something overpowered her and she went leaning her head sobbing against the chimneypiece.

'Come on, girl!' he was instantly tender, his arms were around her, he had kissed her.

'Go your ways!' She was loudly resentful. 'I want no more of you.'

'It's all right, Mary. Mary, I'm coming to you again, just as I used to.'

'You . . .' She swung out of his embrace. 'What for? D'ye think I want you now? Go off to Elizabeth Plantney . . .' She faltered. 'Poor thing, poor thing, it shames me pitiful; I'd sooner have done it to myself; oh, I wish I had.'

With a meek grin Oppidan took from his pocket a bottle with a glass stopper. 'Do you know what that is?' It looked like a flask of scent. Mary did not answer. 'Sulphuric,' continued he, 'same as you threw at her.'

The girl silently stared while he moved his hand as if he were weighing the bottle. 'When I saw what a mess you'd made of her, I reckoned you'd got off too light, it ought to have been seven years for you. I only saw it once, and my inside turned right over, you've no idea. And I thought: there's she — done for. Nobody could marry her, less he was blind. And there's you, just a six months and out you come right as ever. That's how I thought and I wanted to get even with you then, for her sake, not for mine, so I got this, the same stuff, and I came thinking to give you a touch of it.'

Mary drew herself up with a sharp breath. 'You mean — throw it at me?'

'That's what I meant, honour bright, but I couldn't — not now.' He went on weighing the bottle in his hand.

'Oh, throw it, throw it!' she cried in bitter grief, but covering her face with her hands — perhaps in shame, perhaps fear.

'No, no, no, no.' He slipped the bottle back into his pocket. 'But why did you do it? She wouldn't hurt a fly. What good could it do you?'

'Throw it,' she screamed, 'throw it, Frank, let it blast me!'

'Easy, easy now. I wouldn't even throw it at a rat.

170

See!' he cried. The bottle was in his hand again as he went to the open window and withdrew the stopper. He held it outside while the fluid bubbled to the grass; the empty bottle he tossed into the shrubs.

He sat down, his head bowed in his hands, and for some time neither spoke. Then he was aware that she had come to him, was standing there, waiting. 'Frank,' she said softly, 'there's something I got to tell you.' And she told him all about the babe.

At first he was incredulous. No, no, that was too much for him to stomach! Very stupid and ironical he was until the girl's pale sincerity glowed through the darkness of his unbelief: 'You don't believe! How could it not be true!'

'But I can't make heads or tails of it yet, Mary. You a mother, and I were a father!' Eagerly and yet mournfully he brooded. 'If I'd a known — I can't hardly believe it, Mary — so help me God, if I'd 'a known . . .'

'You could done nothing, Frank.'

'Ah, but I'd 'a known! A man's never a man till that's come to him.'

'Nor a woman's a woman, neither; that's true, I'm different now.'

'I'd 'a been his father, I tell you. Now I'm nothing. I didn't know of his coming, I never see, and I didn't know of his going, so I'm nothing still.'

'You kept away from me. I was afraid at first and I wanted you, but you was no help to me, you kept away.'

171

'I'd a right to know, didn't I? You could 'a wrote and told me.'

'I did write to you.'

'But you didn't tell me nothing.'

'You could 'a come and see me,' she returned austerely, 'then you'd known. How could I write down a thing like that in a letter as anybody might open? Any dog or devil could play tricks with it when you was boozed, or something.'

'I ought 'a bin told, I ought 'a bin told.' Stubbornly he maintained it. ''Twasn't fair, you.'

''Twasn't kind, you. You ought to 'a come; I asked you, but you was sick o' me, Frank, sick o' me and mine. I didn't want any help neither, 'twasn't that I wanted.'

'Would you 'a married me then?' Sharply but persuasively he probed for what she neither admitted nor denied. 'Yes, yes, you would, Mary. 'Twould 'a bin a scandal, if I'd gone and married someone else.'

When at last the truth about her own birth came out between them, oh, how ironically protestant he was! 'God a' mighty, girl, what did you take me for! There's no sense in you. I'll marry you now, for good and all (this minute if we could), honour bright, and you know it, for I love you always and always. You were his mother, Mary, and I were his father! What was he like, that little son?'

Sadly the girl mused. 'It was very small.'

'Light hair?'

'No, like mine, dark it was.'

'What colour eyes?'

She drew her fingers down through the long streams of hair. 'It never opened its eyes.' And her voice moved him so that he cried out: 'My love, my love, life's before us; there's a' many good fish in the sea. When shall us marry?'

'I couldn't ever. No, Frank, no.'

'When shall us marry?'

'I couldn't ever go with you, Frank. What you did to me was cruel, but it's gone now – like my reputation: a dog wouldn't pick that up. But nothing can alter what I did to her, and nothing can't mend it. She's ruined. If it weren't for that – but how could I ever forgive myself!'

'When shall us marry?'

'Let me go, Frank. And you'd better go now, you're hindering me, and father will be coming in, and . . . and . . . the cakes are burning!'

Snatching up a cloth she opened the oven door and an odour of caraway rushed into the air. Inside the oven was a shelf full of little cakes in pans.

'Give us one,' he begged, 'and then I'll be off.'

'You shall have two,' she said, kneeling down by the oven. 'One for you – mind, it's hot!' He seized it from the cloth and quickly dropped it into his pocket. 'And another, from me,' continued Mary. Taking the second cake, he knelt down and embraced the huddled girl.

'I wants another one,' he whispered.

A quick intelligence swam in her eyes: 'For?'

'Ah, for what's between us, dear Mary.'

The third cake was given him, and they stood up. They moved towards the door. She lifted the latch. 'Good night, my love.' Passively she received his kiss. 'I'll come again to-morrow.'

'No, Frank, don't ever come any more.'

'Aw, I'm coming right enough,' he cried cheerily and confidently as he stepped away.

And I suppose we must conclude that he did.

AT LABAN'S WELL

ARTON HAD COLLECTED HIS SHEEP FROM DIFFER-
ent fields into the large common that led to the
road.

'A fine day,' said I.

'Too fine,' Barton's wife replied; 'too fine, it will
breed a bad 'un.'

We breakfasted in a room that was full of milk-
pails, harness, guns, and children that were not
washed and had small prospect of being washed for
hours.

Only one sheep was left at home, a ewe that had
lambed since dawn. A fox had already stolen the
lamb – that is why there were guns in the breakfast-
room.

We drove the sheep to a dipping well on a neighbouring farm. Four hundred of them flowed in a
long stream down the lanes, and the odour of the
fleece left a powerful pleasant tang in the air.

There was one jolly little brown rascal of a lamb
with a thick tail. He was of no great age – as yet
only six weeks old – but a few days before he had
travelled quite nimbly here from a market fifteen
miles away. The sound of all the trotting feet was
like a passing shower and, pressed together in a
solid phalanx as they galloped, nothing else could
be distinguished except the black ears of sheep
dancing like dark waves on a rushing river of milk.

Amid vast confusion caused by an encounter with
a team of playful plough-horses who ambled and

gambolled through our flock; the advent of a passionate young terrier who developed a fondness for legs
of mutton; and the fall of two tegs over a bank into
a duck-pond where their inexplicable appearance
harried the souls of a brood of young goslings who
were bathing in defiance of the injunctions of their
Buff Orpington mother; the whole flock was hoicked
and hustled and prodded into the great yard of the
neighbour's farm. Here we were joined by Laban,
a morose lobcock of a man who might have been
twenty-five, or just as possibly fifty, years old. He
was fresh-coloured and he wore a clean shirt. He
had, of course, another name: Jones.

To dip the sheep we ushered thirty or forty at a
time into small pens. A sheep is not a simple thing
to deal with, not an obedient creature, not easy to
circumvent. I infinitely prefer a snake. You may
open forty gates, but no sheep worthy of its flock
will pass through one of them unless accompanied
by its mates. They wedge themselves together between the gate-posts, standing mutely, or perhaps
benignantly baaing, and when, under cover of
stroking one kindly, you attempt to push the whole
mob through the gateway, they skip back around
you with a contemptuous flirt of the hindlegs, and
quite conceivably a wink of the bland bright eye.
When finally penned they huddle in corners and
bury their heads like the youthful ostrich. We catch
one by a leg, its head is put in chancery, our hands
join under its neck and under its stomach, and poor
sheep is toppled backwards into the deep end of a

sloping tank sunk in the earth. There it wallows or is pushed and floundered by Laban Jones with a long pole until, finding bottom, it staggers from the disgusting fluid and wanders away.

But the sky overcast, rain began to fall, and though time passed this did not pass over, it increased; the firmamental buckets were mercilessly tilted until the yard became a wretched stabbled quagmire, a purgatory of slime that turned men from kindly beings into savage swearing tyrants.

At noon we ate and rested in a dry cartshed, but we did not speak, Barton and I, we were silent with discomfort, exhaustion and anger. Laban Jones unfastened a shoulder-basket and drew forth cheese, onion, loaf, and a wedge of meat. It seemed not in his power to munch a casual bite, his habit being to thrust into his jaws a store of provender and then compress and harrow it into the pit of his stomach, an operation that induced protuberation of eye, the distension of his Adam's apple, and meditative gazes. Two others were sheltering in the shed, an old ploughman and an old gipsy man. They were talking together. The ploughman as he ate peered over a sheet of newspaper, and to assist his sight he used a magnifying glass made from the bullseye of a lantern.

'When I was a boy feller,' the gipsy was saying in a husky voice, 'I dwelled over in the forest country beyant W . . .'

'Good sheep country!' interjected the ploughman.

'It is, sir, it is,' cried the gipsy.

'Lord J's place.'

'True, sir, Lord J, a good man as ever druv carriage in this world.'

'Know him?'

'Sir, I worked for him years, I knew Lord J. A nobleman, sir; they said he'd a weak heart, but 'twas in the right place. Always a gentleman, none better, a great loss when he died, God bless him, God bless him.'

'Ah, we must all come to it,' said the ploughman, closely scanning his piece of news.

'Aye, aye, sir, sure, life's very varied, you never understand what's overhanging, misfortune afflicts you, but death reduces you.'

'That's what they be for,' commented the plough-man.

'True, sir, true, there are afflictions and varieties throughout everywhere, like the rain at a marriage or an onion to the eye, God help us all. My wife and me were thrown out of a pony-trap together. I broke my leg in two places. I lay in the infirmary for six months. When I came out my wife was dying.'

'Dear me,' said the ploughman, 'how old was she?'

'Sixty-three, sir, when she died, sixty-three.'

'Ah,' said the old ploughman, planting his reading glass so close against his eye that it looked as large as a hard-boiled egg, 'quite young, quite young.'

'She was a good woman, faithful, but you wouldn't notice her, no. Why, I don't even remember the colour of her eyes. She had twenty children in thirty-one years. Ah, goodness bless me, seventeen of 'em still living, yes; at least they should be. I don't know where they are and I don't want to know. Better keep to yourself quiet-like, for misfortune stalks you like the Almighty hunter, yes. I remember when I was a boy feller, a man, a very wealthy man, who had a couple of sons. Well, after many years the sons collared all his property, they did, those two sons, every rap of it, and he became a poor man. I was astonished at the change in him, sir; he was a good man, yes. Surprising! Very pitiful indeed, a good man. Very varied is life, sir.'

He was silent. We could hear only the pelt of the rain or the sad bleat of sheep. Two pigeons came with bewildered flight through the downpour and perched upon the roof of the barn opposite. They shook the water impatiently from their feathers and sat on exposed to the unslackening fall, hunched like owls. Presently the gipsy got up and left us saying, 'Good day, and a good 'un, gentlemen!'

He returned almost immediately to tell us that the dipped sheep had broken fence and were traversing our neighbour's field of beans. Oh, how difficult it was! Their recovery was attended by every symptom of human mortification. The Old Imp was in them, and they were in the beans. They roved that beanfield as cunningly as a tiger roves the jungle. They triumphed in its coverts and baaed derisively. Each tender plant, too, was a reservoir of accumulated rain that swabbed us with unction. The heavens poured upon us, and the drovers poured upon the sheep the futilities of a deep fund of blasphemy.

When the truants were again locked in the yards we angry unfortunate men turned to the last hundred of the undipped and swept them through their ordeal with the passion of demons. We rushed the shrinking ewes much as the cohorts stormed the Sabine women, and flung them into that infernal trough like the bodies of malefactors cast in to limbo.

But all things come to an end save endlessness, which is infinity — and sheep are only mutton. Yet we had even then perforce to stroll back to our own farm behind a pack of hungry devils who dawdled to crop the hedge-banks while the rain, undiminished, was swept from the trees in gusts that delighted to wreathe us with their veils of lashing water. And on the way we discovered that the little brown rascal was missing. He was never found, and I believe he still prowls in the groves of that Elysium of beans, seeking whom or what he may devour.

A WILDGOOSE CHASE

I

MARTIN BEAMISH IN ANGUISH OF SOUL WANDERED dejectedly up and down their drawing-room, a large apartment almost lavish in its comfort. The autumn night was freezing, but whenever he did approach the fire it was only to stir the blazing fuel to newer fury. Off again then, up and down, hands clasped behind back, and head bent sideways like a listening bird. In extreme anguish, it might be said, for his wife Athalie, so inconsiderate but so handsome, sat by the fire not speaking, and how could he converse with a woman who was shedding tears? It was provoking!

Beamish was a plain man — even his friends said so — and safe. He, too, boasted of it — there is nothing else to be done when you are thirty-five and married. In politics, religion, and morals, he was plain as the Bank of England, and safe as time and tide. He had inherited an income of six or seven hundred a year, and he understood men. Certainly his clothes were plain, and they never seemed to wear out. As for his features they, like his clothes and his morals and the other things, were almost too plain to be nice, so shaven, so sallow, with a Jew nose shaped like a bean, and tough hair, of a colour that you couldn't lay a name to, clasping his skull with the tenacity of a limpet sticking to its rock — at least, that was the impression it gave. Conjugally Athalie knew him to be plain, and she had thought

him safe, but here he was — just listen to him!
'I mean in a friendly way, perfectly friendly, for a
while, a little while, say a month or two. People
do live apart and so might we. Oh, I tell you we
might, you to go your way and I mine.' He urged
this demand upon her with a beguiling reasonable-
ness that touched with the balm of favourable conjecture her wounded pride.

'But what have you against me?' She mused mournfully. 'If I could see that, if I could only fathom it!'
'Nothing, nothing, my dear girl. Beautiful you are,
and — er — and always have been; you are only thirty-
one — or thirty-two is it? — affectionate and intelligent; but' — he paraded on his heel — 'I cannot live
with you. I cannot. I mean to say you are the most
excellent wife and we've had seven years of ideal
bliss. No, I am not teasing, it is absolutely true,
but I will tell you: at thirty-five a man's life — at
least mine does — it seems to shape up suddenly in a
different way. Perhaps I'm different from most men,
I can't say, but there seems to be no further outlet,
I am all closed in; I'm in a great globe of emptiness, and I want to smash it, to get out and realize.'

To live in such emptiness — he explained to baffled
Athalie — was not to live at all; it was even a complicated death, indeed it was, for the spirit kept
dying and only the body lived on; only the appetite
for beef and bread and such disgusting things
remained. How trivial it was, but how hideous, she
would never be able to comprehend, but he had
suffered, he could tell her that. Sorrow and such-like

things were sweeping over his life. Nothing tragic really, he supposed; just dull, dull, but wasn't that worse than any tragedy?

'Do put that poker down,' said she.

'It will be best for both of us. Do believe that, Athalie; can't you see it?' And he held out the little brass poker to Athalie.

'Put it down,' she said.

Bah! That was just like her, *that* was his curse! An intention as open and direct as the free air she had, and even a certain nobility of mind, but it was coupled with an infirmity of purpose which . . . well, her mind was really like a little silk purse that when you opened it disclosed immensely important trifles like buttons, hooks and eyes – and pokers. Damn the thing; he threw it on the hearth. *That* was what he wanted to get away from.

'Far better separate happily for a while,' he repeated, 'better for both of us.'

'Best for you, perhaps.' Sadly she said it. 'But my life so clings to yours.'

No, no, that was not so at all. It would be just as good for her, he was positive. Nothing would be changed except that he would go away for a while. She could keep the house and stay on – no difficulty about money. He might travel a little, stay in lodgings and so on, and sometimes he would come back and stay with her; in fact, quite often, if she would have him. 'You'd be glad to see me,' he queried gaily, 'wouldn't you?' And as she did not answer he continued, 'Why, of course you would. It would be splendid, terrific!'

'I should like to travel, too,' Athalie said, looking up at him.

'Certainly, certainly, why not!'

'Couldn't I come with you?'

'Why, no.' He was soft and deliberate about that. As her head drooped again he begged her not to think of him, she was to think only of herself, her own freedom. She would be free, quite free, to do as she liked, just as she liked.

'And you? You will be free, too?'

'Yes, that's what I mean, Athalie. You can trust me, of course, and I've the most perfect trust in you. We need not talk of restrictions, they are not necessary. No restrictions. You can trust me, you know that, Athalie?'

'I've been faithful to you, too faithful, I suppose,' she remarked bitterly.

Grave and insistent he was, with the sort of dignity that a superintendent of police might wear when about to enter the kingdom of heaven upon some professional inquiry: 'You can trust *me*, Athalie; that you know, right well.'

She rose up, uttering a shocking scream, and stumbling towards the couch flung herself upon it in a passion of tears. Beamish was horrified. He hesitated for a moment or two, but her tears were awful, awful. With a shrug of his shoulders he went to her, took her into his arms and begged her to calm herself, she was his darling, his sweetheart. Awful, awful tears!

'Oh, damnation, this is dreadful!' he moaned.

'Athalie! Listen! Suppose the servant was to come in! Good heavens!'

The door of the room was shut. He slipped away to it — for some reason he went on tiptoe — and turned the key in the lock gently. There he stood listening for a few seconds, and when he turned round Athalie was sitting up. Somehow she had achieved pacification, she was smiling through her tears! He sat by her side, and chatted and smoked and very charmingly forgave her for the injury she had not done him; and though she would not agree — she could not, and never, never would — it was somehow settled that he was to go away for a while, and go soon.

In a few days his trunks were packed and his arrangements made. The last morning arrived, cold but bright, and the passers-by in the street seemed full of cheer; men were humming as they went to their work, lads were whistling, and the trot of the horses had such a gay sound. But Beamish had lain in dread all night, and when he rose he did not even peep into her room, he breakfasted alone. There would be those awful tears again, Athalie was so hysterical, and the anticipation made him sweat. Then the cab came, and so he went up to her room, cheerfully like the men going to their work, two steps at a time. And Athalie was sitting up in her bed, smoking a cigarette.

'Oh, time to go?'

'Yes,' he said, but he could not look her in the eyes, indeed he could hardly speak; strange pangs seemed to surge into his throat; and those marvellous white arms – perhaps he would never see them again! 'Well,' she went on, puffing with astounding deliberation, 'make the most of your freedom, and smash your globe; it was a globe, wasn't it? I wish you joy.'

'Yes, yes,' he quavered, almost dumb, 'you too.'

'You'll write sometimes, Martin?'

He nodded, and then bent over Athalie, but she held her hand against his breast and, smiling, puffed a whiff of smoke into his face. 'Don't forget – no restrictions!' were her last words.

2

But now when his destiny fairly confronted him Beamish was found (though he did not find himself) a little inadequate. Exulting in his escape – how simple it was! – and retrieving so whatever it was he had wanted to retrieve, he made only a modest use of the occasion because he had no clear idea of what he wanted to be at except to be going, going, going – and now he was gone! No feasible hope need have been unrealized; his tastes were simple, his desires plain, even if not plain to his mind. Although the soul kept dying and the body lived on, one's appetite was easily assuaged; and Beamish had no more definite ambition than would trouble a cat in a fender. Would you believe it, then, that he fled from the arms of his wife and buried himself in the British Museum? Well, that is what he did. What is more, the incentive to this strange course arose only during his train journey from Wiltshire to Paddington.

The seclusion of the third-class carriage in which he had been installed by his porter was disturbed two stations later by the advent of a hairy vivacious terrier, dragging at the end of its strap a nurse with a markedly fresh, intolerably healthy, complexion and massive haunches. The nurse immediately leaned out of the window and remarked to a young lady who had accompanied her to the platform: 'And then, of course, the body gives off its waste products.'

'Oh, I see,' returned the young lady, nodding with a gravity that was powerless to dissipate any of her abundant charm. 'Darling doggie! He's a good guard, isn't he?' she inquired, eyeing Beamish with a placid gaze.

'A precious!' nurse exclaimed. 'Last night we met three awful, awful cats, three! Of course he can't bear cats. The first ran up a tree, and the second, do you know, he couldn't quite get at it; but the third one he almost killed. I believe he would have — if he had only caught it. But they are so cunning.'

'Isn't he sweet!' commented the houri. 'But I shall never . . . Oh, you are off now. Good-bye, Miss Tonks.'

'Good-bye,' chanted the nurse. 'And don't forget. Come as soon as you can. We are two doors from the station and five miles from the river.'

'That's nice!'

'It is, yes.'

'Very nice indeed. Good-bye.'

Nurse sat down heavily as the train moved off, and bade her dog go to sleep, which he immediately and miraculously did. Then she must have bidden herself to do likewise, for she soon massively slumbered and left Beamish to his contemplation of the pleasant twirling country.

Landscapes – he mused – are like women: there are some that excite, some that soothe, some that annoy. Neither category quite fitted the one just here, with its tangled spaces of cropped field, dark trees with shadows under them, and soft-inclining hills with the sky's brightness over them, and clouds travelling from thence to here and yet not moving. It was something different. Perhaps it was the wave of autumn, for although the fields new-ploughed, the ricks new-thatched, the leaves new-toned, gave pleasure to the eye an air of melancholy hovered over the spirit. But what is this he sees over upon the hills? On their green bulk is scratched the vast white outline of a horse in canter, monument of battle, birth, or bridal, some event momentous in a history that itself has died. Often he had heard of this; he is in the Vale of the White Horse. At once the imagination of Beamish was engaged, as if his mind, having severed its familiar links, had begun moth-like to gesture at once and admiringly in the brightness of the first new flame. What was there to be learnt about such things, earthworks, monoliths, trackways, Stonehenge, the giants, and the White Horse? Some of them, the Long Man of

Wilmington and the Cerne Giant, he had known in boyhood. Their origins were so remote that you peered into history as in a reversed telescope, where conjecture roved with bears over the English downs and hobnobbed even with elephants. Marvellous, marvellous! He longed to know it all. The fit lasted until he reached London, and for long afterwards. In a few days he had procured lodgings near the Temple, and thereafter we may perceive him in the British Museum, pondering tomes of archæology as bulky as ledgers or as lean as tracts, immured under the dome of the great library like a placid carp glimmering among its weeds. So engrossed did he become that he would have forgotten Athalie had she not written regularly to him, so scrupulous of his welfare, or begging him to return, or anon sending him a knitted tie. All her letters concluded with the admonition, 'No restrictions.' At which Martin would smile and send her an affectionate reply, but without ever touching upon her desire for their reunion.

Several months passed in this way and Beamish was still teasing the dust of this extinguished history, occasionally paying visits to the more prominent remains, when he had the good fortune to light upon the tradition of a remarkable figure on a Cotswold hill-side, long since overgrown or obliterated, but which it seemed might yet yield some possibility of reconstruction. It was variously described by aged gaffers who had heard tell of it as the figure of 'a deer with harns like a prop,' a flying duck, 'a pig with frills along his back like a porkapus,' and a 'wild 'ooman wid no clothes on.' Just at that time Athalie wrote to him that she was shutting up the house for a while and going off to Italy with some friends. Owing to his absence in the Cotswolds the letter lay awaiting him several days, and by the time he returned and opened it Athalie was gone. It was a startling moment; it was as if someone had suddenly planted on his head a hat full of snow. The Cotswold expedition had been fruitless; the deer, the duck, the woman, or the pig – and Beamish's private hope had been for the woman – were either tremendously interred, or a tremendous hoax, and in the bitter chill of a rather conspicuous failure his thoughts had warmed to Athalie, he had intended to visit her. Now she was gone, and the usual taunt at the bottom of her letter, '*No restrictions, mind!*' affected him like a leer. He felt he had been abandoned, yes, abandoned at a juncture when he most desired comfort and solace. Thereupon, what with the check to his hopes in the Cotswolds, and the check to his pride occasioned by Athalie's departure, his archæological fevers underwent some abatement. For a while a pang at his domestic loss filled their place. It culminated, in brief, by Beamish's return to their home in Wilts. Recalling the servants he settled down to resume his studies there. Of course he had joined various societies, and had corresponded with curators and scientific pundits to his heart's content; he was in, deeply in, and his enthusiasm had been boundless. But now the novel brightness of his theme had suffered some diminution. Gone was the magic that had inspired him, perhaps shut up in those tiny lodgings near the Temple, or packed away in the British Museum. He found himself languishing in a discontent that affected even him with a vague surprise until one afternoon, while stalking about the room, his glance happened to take in a photograph hanging on the wall. It had hung there since their marriage, but he had not noticed it for years. Staring at it with new vision, as it were, he felt that she was still as beautiful as in her bridal days, that she had hardly changed, that her face still wore the impress of an intellect he had never sufficiently regarded. And yet, no, it was misleading; she was not a woman of intellect. Ah, but she was calm and certain and sufficient. Her thought was as steady and direct as a man ploughing; it may have been as slow, but it turned over a fair neat clod and its furrow was straight. Something came wandering into his heart, tremulous joy, soft as the summer air that moves a curtain in a quiet room.

3

Athalie, it appeared, was enchanted with life in Italy. Her letters, prompt and voluminous, were full of the sweet Ligurian air, orange trees and violet bays. Friends seemed to spring up wherever she went along the coast of the Gulf of Genoa, she was picking up the language, and her days were full of the happiest incident. That Beamish was home again gave her a pleasure she never tired of expressing; in each letter the 'hope everything is all right' was as invariable as the stamp on the envelope; and always there was her familiar postscript, '*No restrictions*.' And he would reply that everything was all right, but he could not bring himself to inquire about her return. No, that must be left to her; he had taken his own step, the next must come from her; she would know that he waited, and she would come soon.

So three months passed by, and then he was deeply perturbed to hear that although her friends had returned Athalie had stayed behind. Beamish was so vexed that he did not write to her for nearly a month, although her letters came to him with the usual regularity. She did not complain of his silence, she did not ask him to go to her, she did not touch upon the question of her own return. Beamish explained his silence by saying that he had had nothing to write about, buried as he was in Wilts; that her life was so full and varied that of course it was easy for her to write long charming frequent letters. And Athalie, unperturbed, continued to write little accounts of visits to monasteries and mountains and the devil knows what, and she described the little flat she had taken, of two rooms, where she 'did' for herself except for some cleaning assistance by the *padrona*, until Beamish could stand it no longer; he suddenly became perfectly definite, if not peremptory, and asked her when she was coming home? He had wasted all the summer for her, he said. At the last moment, though, he altered the word 'wasted' and turned it into 'waited.'

Her answer was shocking to him. About their mutual freedom — she wrote — she hoped he had been serious and wouldn't mind, but she had taken him at his word. There was a man she had met, he had become a very great friend; she had not thought of coming home just yet — was it *absolutely* necessary: and so on and so on.

Lord God above! what did she mean? It surely could not mean . . . He read the letter again. 'Struth! Damnably vague it was. And that was just like her, always, always, always. You could never tell what it was she was wanting; not one clear cut solid statement did he ever get from her, never, never, never. The most incoherent, inchoate woman he had ever known. Monstrous, monstrous it was that she did not want to come home, for *any* reason; but if it meant that this man . . . He rushed to get her previous letters, and found that for some two months past she had omitted her tag of *No restrictions*! He scrutinized her photograph again and was reassured, it was so morally faultless. But what is this? Upon the nail from which the photograph hung a ring also was hanging, unnoticed before. He took it down, a plain gold ring it was that slipped out of his fingers. Dropping to the floor it went rolling slowly across the room until it came to rest with a sharp click against the leg of a chair. That meant nothing, he was certain it meant nothing; there was nothing of the wanton in the pictured face.

But the bad idea would not leave him, it embraced

him as a grave may clasp a corpse, and in an hour he had packed his bag and caught a train to London. Crossing to Calais by the night boat, he was in Paris at early morn, feeling sick as he passed the time tramping to and fro a great bridge. The Seine was a river of mud; the blunt façades lining it were mud-coloured, without the sheen that even the filthy river managed to receive. There was haze, enough haze to keep the sun from glittering, just as the sun had enough brightness to keep the haze from utter gloom.

From Paris Beamish travelled for twenty hours in the same compartment as an Irish quack doctor and an Italian waiter from Edinburgh. He did not care much for the bulky and blatant Irishman whose intellect seemed to flower in large patterns of obscure meaning (it reminded Beamish of chintz) and he could not agree with him upon anything at all. Beamish hated to differ from anyone — although he was bound to differ — because it always gave him a sense of menace, of personal danger. Why wouldn't people agree with *him*? He was always reasonable enough. But the Italian was a delightful companion, genial and gracious to Beamish; he even showed him a set of indecent photographs. Beamish gurgled and flushed at these, but the quack doctor dismissed them as very tame, nothing, he had seen much better. Then the little Italian said to Beamish that he would give him an address, could recommend it, if he cared for that sort of thing; and Beamish astonishingly found himself noting down the address in his

pocket-book, wishing as he did so that he had had
the courage to reject the friendly offer. And it *is*
unpleasant when the imperfections of a friend are of
the kind particularly distasteful to you: let them be
the ones *you* can enjoy, that is good; or let them sin
your sins, though it is important that they do them in
a different way; one likes to be heeded, not aped.

'Twenty years I am married,' said the little waiter,
'and I was not on the loose more times than twice a
year.'

Nobody commented.

'That's good, isn't it?' queried the Italian.

'Good!' yelled the Irishman, 'with forty fornications
on your conscience! O God . . . bah!' Such a wave
of indignation seemed to pound in his chest that he
lolled back in his corner and gazed out of the window. Then he began to whistle a lively lovely tune,
only to break off suddenly and lean forward to
shout:

'How many women?'

The little Italian looked blankly at Beamish, then
at the other. 'Beg pardon?' he asked mildly.

'How many women have you seduced?' sternly
inquired the quack doctor. Beamish listened in-
tently.

'Oh!' said the culprit. He wore whipcord riding
breeches with brown leather gaiters — and he rubbed
his knees reflectively with his hands. 'It was not me
that accomplished any . . . any of that. Not much,
not many.'

'Were they prostitutes?'

'Oh, no!' exclaimed he, with a deprecatory smile.
'Well, then, what?' demanded the investigator.
'Young or old?'

The Italian rubbed his knees more gaily and
emitted a smiling cackle. 'They wasn't very old, no,
not old.'

'Single women?'

'Some was single, yes.'

'And some married, I suppose?'

'Oh, all sorts, they was all sorts.'

Again a great ninth wave rolled over the doctor.
He toppled back and gazed out at a mountain that
had a cone of snow, beyond a lake crumpled and
blue. On a road near the railway track some fawn
bullocks were drawing a wagon full of barrels, and a
giant of a man in wooden shoes walked beside them
carrying a long wand. For some minutes the doctor
was whistling shrilly, but at length he shifted nearer
to the Italian and said:

'Come, tell us all about them.'

Then for an hour or two Beamish listened to
scandalous relations that fascinated but unnerved
him, though the doctor seemed a little disappointed.

4

At Genoa his fellow-travellers left the carriage, bidding Beamish farewell, and an hour later, in the
afternoon, the train reached Athalie's town.

Her villa was not far off, so he walked to it. The
piazza was planted with palm trees, their trunks
like vast pineapples, loaded with bright saffron

trusses – as large as wheat sheaves – of dates. And there was the very blue sea that he had watched all the way from Genoa. Nothing else he noted, for he was enchantingly thrilled by the sense of Athalie's nearness. She did not know of his intention, he had not wired or written; how surprised she would be! Forgotten, or almost forgotten, were those doubts, those insane fancies, the cause of this flying visit. In two or three minutes she would be in his arms. Oh, but he was intoxicated! The spirit of Athalie, the old Athalie fond and faithful, was there like a fairy island set in that calm blue sea; his thoughts of her now were delighting birds, they rushed up into the sky that was all love, all her love, that embraced the island, hovered over the sea and called to the flashing birds.

Now he is climbing to the second floor of the villa. He knocks at the door and an old woman opens.

'Signora Beamish?' he inquires, and she points to one of the doors opening from a large hall. He taps upon it and enters.

Athalie, who sat by the window, knitting, was dressed as he had never seen her before; brightly, fantastically, so youthful and blooming was she! She just turned her eyes, archly smiling, towards him. Then her mouth opened and she whispered, 'Oh!' her cheeks filling with scarlet blushes.

'Hello!' he laughed, expectantly.

Athalie stood up, her colour deepening. The knitting dropped clicking to the tiled floor. She bent to

197

pick it up, keeping her eyes averted for a few moments longer.

'Didn't expect to see *me*!' he challenged heartily.

'No, no, I didn't expect to see you. No, I thought you were in England.' Laying down her knitting she went to him and was heartily embraced. 'Would you like some tea?'

Yes, he would like some tea. There and then the real purpose of his visit again rose up before him, but he thrust it away, down into some deep crevice of his mind like a guilty packet dropped slyly into a pit. He would leave all that for the present, for he could never face her irony if his suspicion were wrong, nor his own confusion if it were right. And so, over their tea, he gabbled of the long journey, of how much he liked Italy, and how pleasant her rooms were. 'Yes, but they are very small; my bedroom is smaller even than this,' remarked Athalie. She was pouring out tea, and her radiance was somehow dashed; she was like a child bothered by a problem in mental arithmetic. 'What are you going to do?'

'Do?'

'I mean, how long are you going to stay?'

'Stay? Why, that's what I've come to ask you!'

Athalie did not immediately reply, and she did not look at him. As she dropped lumps of sugar into his tea he saw on her ring finger a ring with a large ruby in it. He had never seen it before, and the guilty packet once more came rising up from its pit. Then she looked up. 'I mean, where are you going to sleep?'

'Sleep?' Absurdly he was like an echo.

'You see there's no room here.'

'Oh, but anything, anything . . .'

'No, there's no room at all.'

'Do you mean you don't want me, Athalie?' He fidgeted with his knees, with his collar, and he picked a match from the ash-tray and flung it out of the window. 'I can go to an hotel, I suppose? Ah!' he cried joyfully, jumping up, 'we'll both go, that's it, we'll both go to an hotel.'

Yet Athalie seemed unwilling, she murmured that she hadn't got her wedding ring with her.

'No? But that's stupid,' Martin said testily. They were in Italy, no one knew them! Athalie made no effort to bridge their difference.

'Look here,' the troubled man began once more. 'I'll go and buy another ring; come along.' He picked up his hat, but Athalie did not move. 'Won't you?' he asked. Apparently she would not. Her silence was unnerving; he put his hat down again. 'Or you could turn round that other ring you've got on. Where did you get it?' But Athalie was shocked at the suggestion. 'No, certainly not!' And it seemed as if in some secret way she was hugging the ring to her breast.

'Yes,' then he said sadly, 'just as I thought. Even if you had your ring, not then you wouldn't!' He jammed on his hat again. 'Would you?' Still she was evasive.

'I wish I hadn't come here. I'll go to the hotel.' As he lifted his bag Athalie got up and offered to show him the way. It was darkening, she switched on the light.

'No, it doesn't matter,' he uttered moodily; but with his hand upon the door-knob he turned and fired his last shot: 'Who's this man?'

'Man?'

'Don't keep repeating my words,' he dismally begged. 'You wrote about him. Not very much, but it was a bit startling, wasn't it? Have you anything to say to me about him?'

'To say?' Athalie stared at Martin.

'Yes, I suppose I ought to know.'

'But to say what?'

'Don't prevaricate, please. Is there anything in it — anything you ought to tell me?'

'There is nothing I ought to tell you,' said Athalie, with a suggestion of intense weariness, 'Nothing at all.'

'Well, I'm glad . . . or do you mean' — the examiner was ruthless — 'that you *won't* tell.'

'There is nothing I shall tell you — ever.'

'Humph. I see. Well, you needn't have said so much if you wanted to tell so little.'

'Ha, ha, ha!' Athalie rippled with laughter. He was astounded. 'Oh, it was only the funny way you said that,' she explained placatingly. 'You see,' she went on gravely, 'when you left me all alone in Wiltshire you bargained for "no restrictions".'

'I didn't bargain at all,' Martin asserted. 'Certainly not for this,' he added lugubriously.

'Didn't you insist on having absolute freedom? Wasn't that what you wanted?'

'Didn't I say you could trust me,' he replied steadily, 'as I trusted you?'

'What had I to trust to when I was forsaken? You got your way, you've had your fling, you've done what you wanted to do . . .'

'But I tell you,' he cried, exasperated, 'I've done nothing, nothing at all.'

'I don't ask you about that,' she sharply returned, 'what you've done, is done. I'm not inquisitive, I don't want any confessions.'

'But, Athalie! I swear . . . Good Lord, you don't dream . . .'

'I don't care!' shouted Athalie with finality.

And at that he could do no other than open the door and go, muttering as he did so, 'I'll come and see you in the morning — perhaps.' He slammed the inner door, and the outer door he slammed, and raging to himself, 'Perhaps, perhaps! Ho, ho! Humph!' he ran down the stairs and almost collided with a man guiding a mule cart passing close up to the door. Damn the fellow, it was dark, and the fool hadn't got a lantern; instead he was carrying a lit candle in one hand with a shade of paper wrapped round to keep off the draught. Even that was not necessary in such softly-breathing air; indeed it was a silken romantic night, the stars scrawling the heavens with their notation of immensity, the same stars still, although the shops were strange, the people queer, their language and their trees un-natural. It should have been a night. . . . Oh dear, oh dear! Only a couple of hours ago he was deeply in love; now he was in hatred, stung by the surprise of her coolness and baffled by the uncertainty of the thing he dreaded.

For half an hour he trudged about gazing at all the hotels, but unable to please his fancy until there were no more to choose from; then he went back and stopped at the first. His disenchantment suffered no abatement in the proximity — at the very next table — of a German family which had just strayed in for dinner, a little dumpy Herr whose patent-leather shoes were as wrinkled as his face, and whose white spats curled up at the edges like his hair and his nose; his large and solid Frau, draped entirely in lace — she was an antimacassar with a hat on — was trying to live down to her youth, but it was beyond her depth and she drowned before your very eyes. Whenever she made a remark to her husband he would first take off his glasses, hold them at half-arm's length, and meditate before answering very deliberately. Then he would dash *vino rosso* into his little mouth and gulp and gulp and gulp. To put down the glass was but an opportunity to grab a hunch of roll and cram it after the wine, and lo, it was gone, all gone, with the *hors d'œuvres*, the *risotto*, the *pollo alle cacciatore*, and the cream cheese that was to become part of the Herr for ever more. Their little boy, whose head was shaped like the end of a bolster, rustled about on his chair as if there were nettles in his breeches, and while his parents sipped their coffee he consumed a quantity of *éclairs*. First he would bite off the end and spy into the hollow fragment left as if it were a telescope; having allayed some itch of curiosity he would devour the body of the delicacy with an absent-minded air and suck, one by one, his long thick outspread fingers.

Beamish feared he was going to have a very unhappy night, but after dining he began to get drowsy, so off he went to bed and slept calmly, irresistibly, and unbrokenly. When he awoke he found himself still nurturing indignation against Athalie, and he determined not to run after her any more, he would just hang on for a few days and then go back to England without a word. For two days, then, he did not go to visit Athalie, and she, even had she wished to, could not visit him because she did not know where he was staying. Even on the third day, when he did go to her flat, she received him with reproaches.

'Why, why do you treat me like this?'

'But,' he stammered, 'I thought it was a mistake. So it was – you didn't want me.'

Passionately resentful she was. 'You make a fool of yourself, but is that any reason why you should make a fool of me? You come sneaking here, and then you hide away. It's mean and disgusting, it is. And I have had so much unkindness from you. Why do you behave in this absurd manner?'

'But I thought' – so bewildered was Martin – 'I thought I was in the way, that you didn't want me. And you didn't.'

Athalie's contempt was a revelation. 'No, then, I didn't want you, and I don't want you.'

'You married me. After all, I'm your husband,' he maintained sturdily.

'Heaven help you for a fool! Such a miserable thing you have made of our lives. Always you've had your own way, but it was never a man's way.'

'Listen, Athalie. I came all the way from England for you.'

'Yes, why?'

'I just wanted to see you.'

'Yes, but *why*?'

'I came for more than I can tell you,' he said. 'Oh!' she was bitterly impatient. 'You think I don't know why – but I know well enough!'

'I came, but you drove me away.'

Athalie eyed him, at this, as a schoolmistress eyes an idiotic infant.

'Let us go out!' she said petulantly. 'Let us go out! Shall we go out?'

The crumpled man put on his hat, and they walked together down into the streets. Silently all the way, under a long avenue of leafless sycamores, until they came to the market where the cheapjack's tiny boy was screaming: '*Una lira! Una lira!*' The honest burgesses were sauntering in the square, the seats of all their trousers mightily mended – not deceivingly, but with gusto, every patch coming boldly to the eye like a poster on a wall – and their women were bargaining at stalls for fruit that engendered a multitude of misgivings, for exhausted herbage and repellent fauna, for cheese and fish that would tempt neither cook nor cat – not in England, said Martin

to Athalie. On through the market to the sea they
went, idling up and down the piazza where elderly
people sat half-snoozing on seats, and infants harried
you with hard balls and soft balloons, while those
who did neither wandered laxly, enjoying their languor. It seemed that there was seldom any wind,
seldom any birds, and quite certainly never any
chimneypots in the little town. And it was all
exactly as Martin had imagined it would be,
coloured, queer, cosmopolitan, flamboyant, and
agreeable. A meek old man with a humpty back and
a meditative eye sat by a street corner roasting coffee
in a charcoal stove; there was a sweet smell. Horses
and rumbling carts went by musical with bells, the
barefoot carters cracking their whips; and there was
an Apollo with a huge blue-striped bundle bound
upon his back: he was crying in a loud voice that he
wanted — so Athalie said — to mend your mattress.

They sat down together upon the sea wall that was
warm as a hearth. Their antagonism had flown
away, though perhaps it had not flown very far, for in
Martin's mind there still hovered the thought of a
man, some man, who had impinged, or was about
to impinge — well, upon what? And who was he?
With gentle raillery he urged Athalie to tell him
something.

'What you are longing to hear,' replied she, 'is a
confession.'

'Well?' And he was prepared to hear it, his name,
appearance, age. But no, she would tell him nothing. Her downcast looks, as Martin pleaded for

205

something – he knew not what, but it was a desire for some certainty amid all things now so uncertain – her downcast smiling looks moved him to an emotion that was none the less charged with admiration of her bloom. She got up and sauntered away for a few yards, trailing her hand along the warm coping of the wall. How white her hands, how gracefully she moved, how newly alluring she was! No doubt she had written to the man telling him to keep away, or perhaps he was even now in view, watching them. It was ironic, this change in his wife, it was transfiguring her. Now he was the suppliant, and she was queening it in her escape from him. Soon she came back and stood beside him.

'When shall we go home?' she asked.

'When you like, dear Athalie, just as you please. Are you tired?'

'Oh, I mean when shall we go back to England?' Her gaze was turned to the sea, as if that blue immensity alone could contain her sad thoughts. 'I have packed my things.'

'Oh, Athalie!' Eager and breathless, he sprang up from the low wall. 'That's beautiful. Will you go? Let's go, yes, let's go. At once, can't we? There's a train to Genoa in an hour, and we can catch the Paris express to-night from there.'

No, she thought it would be better to catch the same express from their own station. 'Come for me in a cab in time to catch it to-night.'

'Yes, yes,' he said it joyously.

'Then good-bye until this evening,' said Athalie. With this smiling sally she went away, left him standing dumbfounded at the dismissal; but his relief at the happy turn of events vanquished that creeping grudge, and very good-humouredly he turned off in the opposite direction.

To while away the daylight hours he went nosing around for curios and souvenirs of the little *città*, lace things with Adam and Eve and the Serpent portrayed in cotton, and bangles and brooches of silver filigree, which he would give to Athalie as an offering for the deuce knew what! — but an offering certainly. Rejoicing emotions fluted in his bosom as he walked sharply from shop to shop. Athalie! Athalie! A handsome barefoot fishergirl mending nets sat sprawled on the pavement, her legs outstretched in the shape of a V, the torn net hitched over both great toes, the shuttle dancing marvellously from hand to hand. Tiny cherubim, in mundane attire, turned the wooden wheels in the ropewalk, wheels huge enough for Ixion and ancient as the Medicis, while the spinners handling hanks of tow sauntered backwards exuding threads as silently as spiders — until they stopped and shouted. Steep were the rocky lanes from the mountain-side, yet not too steep for the little swift Ligurian men who came and went like the angels on Jacob's ladder, shouldering their tubs of olive oil. But nothing in the streets or the people or the houses or on the seashore had power to interest Beamish now, not even the sign of *Factoria Acqua Gasose* over the ginger-

beer works, or the smell that pervaded all the land
like a mixture of coffee and cocoa. He went among
it unnoticingly, as if he had lived there for twenty
years instead of — as you might say — twenty minutes. Time and the blue air were enchantingly his.
Only a few dark and gaunt vessels in the port
dimmed the astonishing lustre of the hour, just as
the few bright yachts seemed to augment it. For
there was nothing in the mortal world one half so
real and fair as Athalie's devotion to him; he knew
now, he knew it all. It gave him the very accents of
joy, it gave him pride, the pride of a conqueror
whose conquest had been for ever, who had come
for his tribute of undying faithful love and had not
been denied. At least, not implacably! Even Athalie had her whims and fancies; but even these had
their ultimate felicities. Jove! it was a near thing.
though, however sweetly she had surrendered. Back
in England he could now go on with his studies once
more; they would ransack a whole county, he and she
together, although of course she would have to
learn a lot of important things: she wouldn't know,
for instance, — he couldn't expect her to know —
that the mouth of the Thames was once in Lincoln-
shire. As for this fellow, it would be better not to
mention him again, not to Athalie. No badgering,
it was only a passing fancy, nothing more. Let him
drop out of her mind entirely. Let him die — yes,
let him die a death like a damned cat in a canal.
(It was queer how seldom you saw a dead person;
he had only seen two in his life — and one of them

was his own father.) Yah! let him rot like a strangled cat.

It was a grand evening, fine moonlight it was, when he called for Athalie. And Athalie was waiting for him, dressed for travelling. He covered her face with kisses.

'Come, we must go,' she said.

'Yes, let us go,' Martin echoed. 'There's a fine moon and it's a grand evening.'

But all the way to the station she lolled back in the cab and never spoke a word. And of course there was nothing to *be* said, not much, really. Fine night though, grand!

The train that took them was packed so full of travellers that Beamish had to stand in the corridor for the first hour. A great nuisance, so many people going in the same direction. All the way to Genoa the train would now run close to the shore for a few minutes, now burrow under mountains for a few minutes, and then emerge slap into little towns hovering on the sea, and stop for a few minutes. Full and bright the moon, but it did not seem to light up the gulf; the water had no sparkle, there was only a gloomy movement of purple bulk. All the eastern heaven in the direction of Leghorn was menaced by a cloud as high and wide as ten thousand mountains, and every few minutes it was ripped by lightning that made no sound. But the white villas by the sea glimmered carelessly in the moonlight; the fine trees, the olives, the palms, were still, and you knew of the water only by the white foam squandering round the rocks. At one station perched on a ledge of a mountain Beamish could see down into a courtyard below him; there was a clothes line stretched across the yard, and on the line a pair of trousers inside out – how white the pockets were! – was hanging to dry. Immense and clear on the wall of a palazzo near by, the shadow of an ancient empty lantern hoisted above a gateway was thrown by a neighbouring street lamp. It was half-past nine, though the clock tower showed but a quarter to four, and the town seemed empty, lifeless, soundless, stone quiet, until the train moved again. Then the trousers on the line began to toss violently in a sudden thrust of wind, and the lantern shadow on the wall was waving to and fro. The train roared away into a mountain and on the other side slackened at a station covered with snow. One of the guards got down, picked up a handful, and scrutinized it closely and amazedly, as though he were peering at a watch with unbelievable figures; he stared for certitude again at the white glister under his feet, and gazed up into the clear heavens; then he brought his handful of snow back into the train and gave pieces of it to the wondering passengers – who tasted it. Beyond the next mountain, at the next station, there was not a vestige of snow; only moonlight, calm villas, trees by a dark sea, and a cloud full of lightning over Leghorn. The train emptied at Genoa, and soon Beamish was in the carriage alone with his wife, rolling inland from the sea.

5

It is known for truth by those who have commerce with fairies and the goblin sort that all their gifts and powers fall in the end to nothing, or even worse. Their bright gold turns to a shadow, to dead leaves their coin, the wine to air, the fine cloak to a wisp of hay, their joy to madness. Maybe in the heart of man there is some such demon president turning our hopes to vapour and our desires to dust. Possibly Beamish had bid too high, or his imagination was too low; whatever it was, long ere night came to an end some alchemy had effected a change: Athalie had shed her Italian charm with her Italian frock, and she was once more the old Athalie, placable, morose, subdued. Neither of them slept; they had both stretched themselves on the seats of the compartment and dozed and were rocked for hours. Dawn found them hurtling through magical Savoy, he disillusioned, she formal and polite – nothing more. How had all her extraordinary desirability withered? Was it only in combat with him that her beauty grew clear? For there was no change in him. Having borne her from probable disaster, had the glory been only in the achievement and not in what he had won? If he had retrieved only their old disharmony they had come together again to no end but calamity.

A still deeper flush of recognition awaited him after they had breakfasted together in the saloon. He had caught at the tail of an idea, seen as unexpectedly as a snake in one's path; he almost groaned aloud. The intolerable duplicity! Blind ass he had been! This tale of a man in Italy was a fabrication, a trick to win him back to her again! Oh, he had been beautifully fooled. Now she sat there looking ugly in her sly disagreeable silence, quite positively ugly, with a melancholy as if she had the bellyache. All a pose! She was secretly triumphant, because she had hitched her halter over him again. Her halter! Why, he had hooked it over himself, he had actually brayed for it, and she, the subtle wretch, was smiling in her dishonourable soul. She had told him this lie, she had seen him take it as a bird is taken in the trap of a devil, a meagre crawling devil, senseless and useless as the trap. She had even taken off that ring now, that idiotic ring that had so misled him; her fingers were bare. He had swallowed the whole damned foolishness.

For hours the concealed poison worked in his indignant mind, but in the afternoon he began to probe her. He had had enough of it; she should see!

'What are your plans when we get to England?'

'Plans?' She was smiling wanly.

'Yes, plans.'

'Oh, I have no plans,' replied she. 'What's the use of plans? They all come to nothing – now.'

'They do, they do. You don't seem very happy at coming back.'

'No?'

'Then why the deuce did you come?'

'I came because you wanted me, Martin.'

'But it was your suggestion.'

'Mine? Didn't you want me to come?'

'Don't prevaricate, please,' he adjured sternly, 'I hate it.'

'I'm not prevaricating.' She shook her head sadly. 'I came out to you at once, to get you out of a precious mess. I thought you were making a fool of yourself. This is the result.' He threw out his arms and was restless.

'I was happy where I was,' she said quietly. 'You thought I had lost my honour, or broken it, or something, didn't you? Let me ask you this: is my honour involved only to you?'

'What? Who else could it be to?'

'Everybody,' she cried, 'except . . . perhaps . . .'

He quivered at her hesitation, puzzled: 'Well? perhaps?'

'To you!' she burst out, 'you!'

Martin was silent for some moments; then he said. 'If you were so devilish happy why didn't you stop there? Why concoct such a lying tale to get me over there?'

'Tale?'

Beamish looked his unspeakable bitterness. 'This tale about a man. You hoaxed me; you know it well enough, and I know it — now.'

Athalie stared at him in silence.

'Such nonsense,' he continued, 'but I was weak enough to believe it. Oh, it deceived me, it's true. It took me in completely. I ought to have known you better.'

Athalie wrinkled her brow with dawning apprehension. 'I wonder,' she said, staring out of the window, 'whether you would be good enough to tell me what you are talking about.'

'Do you know . . .'

'No, I don't!' she snapped.

'I'm not asking a question, I am giving you an answer.'

'I don't want to hear it! You imagine now that I made up a story to lure you out to Italy, and then persuade you to take me back. That's it, is it?' He made no answer and she went on. 'I was a fool. I admit I was touched when you came. More fool I. I'd forgotten your self-conceit, I thought it was your love come back again. But it was only that you couldn't bear to be supplanted even in the feelings of a wife you hated. For you *do* hate me.'

'You seem to hate me,' he said moodily.

'I've only one regret in the world now, Martin. Do you know what it is?'

'That you married me?'

'No, that's *your* regret. For me that was good, for a long while — I give the devil his due. No, my regret is that I'm going back with you. I won't do it,' she wailed. 'I won't! I won't! All I want is to be rid of you, to see you no more. Oh, why did I let you persuade me? I have borne so much, and now I have thrown away. . . . Oh, I've thrown everything away!'

'Persuaded you! Good Lord, what about the trick you've played me?'

'Martin,' — even in her tears she commiserated him — 'you are a hopeless fool!'

But now they were nearing Dijon; thousands of railway lines seemed to be radiating eastwards. The train was slowing, soon the train stopped. 'Do we wait here long?' inquired Athalie, now quite composed.

'Don't know,' he answered, 'a little while, perhaps.'

She got up and strolled into the corridor, at which relief an emotion so easeful pervaded Beamish, soothing his ruffled plumes, that he smiled queerly and sighed with rapture. When she did return, in ten minutes or so, her coming was momentous.

'I'm not coming any farther, I shall stop here to-night.'

'Don't be absurd, there's no occasion to be so drastic; I quite understand. I'll get into another compartment if that will satisfy you.' Cheerfully, almost humorously, he said it.

'Don't bother,' returned Athalie. 'I'm not coming back with you.' She took her small case from the rack. 'I've just got them to shy my luggage on the platform. I'm not coming back at all. I can't stand you any longer, you revolt me.'

'But what, but what,' he began to stammer, 'but what in the world are you going to do now?'

She repeated with a sort of whispered passion, 'I can't stand you, you're insufferable. You close me in, in your own precious globe of emptiness, and I've got to smash it, too. The dullness was mutual;

I realized mine when you realized yours. I must thank you for that, I suppose.'

'Athalie,' he begged, 'don't say it.'

'I can't stop, the train will be going,' was her reply.

He grabbed her arm. 'Don't you stop me!' she cried fiercely, 'I'll fling myself from the window.'

'Hush, hush, be sensible, Athalie. What are you going to do?'

'I'm going back to Italy, where I had found happiness.'

She ran away down the corridor, and he was too awed to follow her. Desolated he sank into his seat where her valise had lodged. God bless! she had gone! Stupidly, vacantly, he read a notice over the door: *Nicht in den wagen spukken.* Over and over he said it, many times, until the train began to move. He sprang up, grabbed at his bag – but he did not lift it from the rack. He rammed his hat on his head – but then he dashed it to the floor. '*Spukken, spukken, nicht in den wagen spukken.*' Into the corridor he rushed, and pulled down a window, just as the coach glided by Athalie on the platform beside her trunks. He flung kisses to her as he passed, dozens. At that, she just smiled and waved a hand to him. He could have sworn he saw the flash of a ring on one of the fingers, a ruby ring. She was looking strangely lovely again as she passed away from him. *Spukken, Nicht in den wagen spukken.*

DUMBLEDON DONKEY

On a morning in early spring — the corn beginning to shine in the furrows, the sun bright, the air warm — a man is trenching a hedge ditch in the lonely fields near Dumbledon guidepost, a big angular countryman with a face almost as blue as it is brown and humorous blue eyes. His coat is folded on the bank and upon it lies his rush bag containing provender enough for an ox.

He peers through the bottom of the hedge into the field beyond him, and then unbending himself with a groan he stretches and breathes deeply. Taking up the loaded gun that lies hidden beneath his coat he creeps along to a gap in the hedge. Two or three hundred rooks are waddling like aldermen across the wheat, pecking soberly at the new spikes of green. The man with the gun shoots one of them — it seems to stumble and then it slips over. The black flock rises on leisurely, almost insolent, pinions until a second shot cracks upon their flight and another rook, tumbling down out of the sky, lies upon the green wheat with a vain movement of wing. The man returns to his trenching and with his spade he continues to smear blue mud from the ditch neatly upon the hedge bank, leaving a clean shallow channel behind him. The sun is bright, the air warm, and a lark in a frenzy begins to whistle.

By and by a dumpy little man in shirt-sleeves (and deep in middle age) came along by the hedge carrying a horse-whip in his hand. The digger looked up and called with great deliberation in a grizzled but gay voice: 'Hallo, Harry Munt!'

'Ah, Jim,' replied Munt, in a tone that sounded like a squeaky sigh.

'What are you arter in these parts?' asked the other, ''Tis a lonesome spot for timid chaps. A'n't you afeard o' being murdered?' He had a loud and cheerful tone.

''Tisn't so lonesome, Jim.'

'And ne'er a drop o' drink for a couple o' mile? You be keerful, Harry Munt. There be all sorts o' wild men going about the land — tinkers and gippoes and women as waunts to sell you a gridiron, and blind beggars a-walking to the races. You never can't tell what some on 'em be at, Harry Munt; and you might be done to your death in a fourpost bed.'

'No, Jim, no,' the little old man seemed to sigh, 'I've come down to catch Mrs. Bustin's donkey.'

'Ketch a donkey!'

'She wants me to drive her into Starn.'

'Well, that's a marciful fine thing to come ketching a donkey wi'!'

'What, Jim?' There was a look of botheration in Munt's eyes.

'Why, wi' a whip! He'll be rather fresh and frisky, I'm thinking; you won't catch a donkey wi' a whip in your hand.'

'Won't?'

'Not wi' a whip you won't.'

'We'll see, Jim Massey,' replied Munt, 'we'll see.'

He went away across the grass. It was a big field

and a rough field, with great tots of briers and thorn bushes growing all about it; around each clump the cattle had worn tracks as they ambulated, musing (it might be) upon the universe. Now the only tenant was the donkey meandering near the white palings of a farm-house that stood in the nearest corner by a vast ragged pile of yellow straw, a cloven hayrick, and a pile of black faggots with a blue cotton gown thrown upon it.

For some time Munt mildly ambled in the wake of the retreating donkey, cooing and gurgling: 'Come along, my pretty, come along, my bird.' The sun was bright, the air warm.

'He waunt have it,' bawled the big man from the ditch.

'He will have it, yes, he will have it,' returned the other.

The farmer's wife came and stood at the end of her white palings, clucking to some hens. She had a large face and many freckles, her sun-bleached hair was combed tightly to her head and then fastened in a wad like the top of a cottage loaf.

'Hee-haw! hee-haw!' roared Massey derisively when Munt at length began to adjure the donkey with some venom.

'Oh, if I catch you!' groaned the little man, tiring visibly, 'if I catch you! Ah, you devil!' he shouted to the defiant donkey, 'you blam rooster, I'll cut the legs off you!'

He cracked his whip furiously. 'Hey!' he cried, 'Ho!' he cried, and as the donkey cavorted with

pleasing extravagance Munt was gratified and slashed
the whip again and again. But he soon got tired of
that, it was useless, time was getting along, it was
hot, and he had a journey before him.

'Ho, you rooster you! Hey, you! I got to drive you
twice to Starn as 'tis, and now I'll drive you three
times, see if I don't, you blam rooster, you, and four
times I'll drive you, yes, I will, and I'll cut the legs off
you!'

'Why don't you come and help him,' called the
farmer's wife to Massey, ''stead of laughing there,
poor man, this hot day!'

'He must be crazy, ma'am,' said Massey indignantly,
'but I'll catch that donkey.'

He flung down his spade and very soon he delivered
the animal into the arms of the panting Munt.

'You blam rooster,' gasped that worthy man, 'you
give me a pretty coddle and now I'll give you a
pretty coddle.'

'Where's your halter?' growled Massey.

'I din' bring no halter.'

'Well, look arter him now you got him. I never seed
a donkey wi' such a wicked eye. You got him?'

'Yes, Jim, I got him,' and firmly grasping the
donkey by one of its ears Munt led it away.

'Look arter him now,' bellowed Massey finally.
Returning to the ditch he seized his gun, and although there were no more rooks to be seen he fired
a couple of charges into the hedge. Immediately the
donkey was seized by a paroxysm of extreme emotion; he brayed, he butted, his ears quivered, he

lashed his tail, his little hairy legs were thrust into the air at all sorts of angles; in short he pranced violently from the arms of Mr. Munt.

Of course he was caught again, for not even a jackass can evade the hand of destiny for ever, but afterwards (though it cannot be told for certain) old Munt must have treated him badly, perhaps gave him a good hiding, or drove him incessantly to and from Starn. Possibly some private anguish pressed upon the donkey's soul, or — you can't tell — old Munt may have poisoned him. Certain it is that what with one thing and another the donkey laid down at night and died, and the next morning he was found stiff and cold without a vice left in him, or a virtue either.

The good Mrs. Bustin, his mistress, sorrowed deeply; he was a spoilt donkey, but she was much attached to him. And that is not strange, for the world is full of respectable ladies who cherish a passion for some strange object or another, as likely as not an ass, though in the towns they can sometimes be seen riding on the tops of omnibuses with an armful of lilac, or bicycling out to the autumn woods for branches of dead leaves to put on a mantelpiece. Mrs. Bustin sent tearfully for Sexton Jethro. 'You can dig graves?' she began. 'I've dug many a score, ma'am, I warrant,' says he. 'Can you dig a grave for a donkey?' He said again he had dug many a score. So he and Munt were directed to inter the donkey in the field where he died, which was down near the Dumbledon guidepost. Somewhere adjacent to that spot Jim Massey, two days later, was topping some willow trees when Munt again approached him.

'Come and give us a hand with this dead donkey, Jim.'

'Where is it, Harry Munt?' the countryman asked.

'Only over in the long field,' Munt jerked his thumb in the direction. 'Just give us a hand, will you?'

'Surely you a'n't bin and started him off again, Harry, have you?' said the grinning giant as he picked up his coat and his bag and his axe (for he was a careful and wary man) and stalked off alongside little Munt.

'You'd think,' said Munt, 'that a man who's dug hundreds of graves would have more sense, but this grave ain't bin dug properly. It isn't big enough nor deep enough and there's not earth enough to cover him all up.'

In the long field Massey saw the new mound of earth from the four corners of which four little posts stood up. Jethro sat beside it earnestly scrutinizing the pictures in a newspaper, he took no notice of the two men. Massey stared at the small posts on the mound and saw that they were the four legs of the donkey. It had been thrown into its grave upside down, and though the earth had been heaped upon him his little stiff legs protruded from it, not very much, but they were still about a foot high above the ground.

'Well, that's a pretty piece of doxology!' commented Massey.

The sullen sexton made no reply, he continued to

regard his newspaper fixedly while Massey placed his basket on the ground beside him.

'Never knowed our Jethro was a larnèd man afore, but here he be a-reading big print and little print like a schoolmaster.'

The flattered sexton cleared his throat: ''Tis the *Weekly Journal*. I buys it sometimes for pictures, and sometimes I reads out of it, but mostly it's for pictures. 'Tis the only thing as ever I reads.'

'The *Weekly Journal*?'

'That and the Bible. I an't ashamed to tell 'ee.'

'When did you ever read your Bible?' inquired the inexorable Massey.

'Every morning I reads the Bible. Ah! Every morning! And I an't ashamed to tell 'ee that. But,' added Jethro with a sigh, 'if there an't any photy-graphs of old Sam's funeral in it I shan't buy no *Journal* this week.'

He raised himself up from the grass and they all surveyed the mound. It was neatly done, the donkey was buried, he was at rest, he was hidden – all but his four small legs; the hocks hung laxly, a little pitifully, as if appealing for something.

'What can we do with him, Jim Massey?' said Munt, enunciating a kind of husky hopelessness.

'Can't do nothing,' broke in the sexton, ''tis done and that's the end of it. We can't get him out again, we can't move him, he's wedged in as tight as a mossel o' cheese.'

'I'll show 'ee what to do,' said Massey grimly. 'One,' he said, 'Two,' he said. 'Three,' he said. 'Four,' he said. At each number he heaved his sharp axe at the little posts and the donkey's severed shanks rolled off the mound.

Munt picked them up one by one and held them in his arms.

'What shall I do with them?' he gurgled with a quaver of dismay.

'Pickle 'em!' roared Massey. And so Munt carried them away, but nobody ever discovered what he did with them. Jim Massey asked him often enough, often he asked, but Harry Munt never would tell him.

A THREE-HANDED REEL

IN THE THIRD DECADE OF THE NINETEENTH CENTURY a fusilier deserted from his regiment on the eve of its embarkation for wars in Portugal. Casting aside his forelock and martial gear Roland Bartlemas contrived to possess himself of civilian apparel, and made his way from Plymouth towards the interior, his intention being to trudge the lonely hill country that lies right across the southern counties. There he might travel in safety, as he thought, until he could reach his home in the Vale of Aylesbury.

He was not a coward, although the bare statement of his act may imply the contrary. The odds against complete escape were prodigious – he knew that well – and the punishment on capture was dire. Not war, it was not war he feared; it was the misuse of his life in ways unsought by him and despised. A plant strives towards the light it sees: what does a man strive to? Bartlemas hardly knew, but he knew that he had been jockeyed into the army by a trick while he was drunk in a market town of the Vale, and snatched from his young wife and the genial gear of home to toil in the harsh life of the camps. The early rankle of that injustice did not heal. Well built, freckled and fair, a vigorous countryman of twenty-five, he had kept a tiny farm and a hostelry which lay on the line of one of those old British trackways, the Icknield, whose uneager endless miles form an artery under the ridge of the downs, along which once streamed droves of cattle and sheep bound for metro-

politan markets from places even as remote as Wales.
Such hostels as *The Leather Bottel* were much used
in those days by the weary heavy-mannered drovers,
who penned the flocks for the night in the paddocks
of the inns.

A year or more had passed since he had left the
Vale, and now as he pressed on his eluding way
across the Berkshire uplands, from whence at last
he could view again the great Vale and the hills of
home, his heart leaped in his bosom, and a natural
satisfaction mingled with his triumph at having defeated, though still so precariously, the trick by
which his liberty had been won from him. Resentment never had abated; he was a gay countryman, he
was but a sullen soldier.

A day later he crossed the Thames at Wallingford
and soon regained the old trackway that turned
northwards under the Chiltern wolds and continued
green and long, a wide rough grassy track set between hedges or running open across solitary spaces
that knew no barrier. Towards nightfall he was
within sight of the inn. September coolness was in
the air, and the thick odour of sheep that had lately
passed. The stalwart gables and chimneys of his
house were sharp in the dimness; there was a light
in one of the windows. Hesitating and wary, he
crept to the back of the house. No voices. Then he
went in. His wife Rachel was there, and they kissed
long and fervently.

'Roy!' she cried through her tears. 'What's happened of you?'

And he sat down and told her. Trembling she was. A fine woman, stalwart as he, with fair hair too, and a rich tint of skin; a comely figure, with breasts so firm and fine — as Roland often said — that you could crack a flea on them.

'They were here only yesterday, some soldiers seeking of you,' Rachel whispered fearfully. 'They were after you. They swore you would be taken soon. Oh, what will they do to 'ee, my love?'

Bartlemas grinned confidently, and consoled her. He did not tell Rachel what would happen if he were taken up again, his mind turned away from so dread a prospect. Besides, he did not mean to be taken up. But he was alarmed. Who was staying at the inn now?'

'Nobody, only a drover man,' Rachel told him. 'Came along since noon with a flock of yoes. He's had a misfortune, though; a bough of a tree fell on him and broke his head open, poor man, so he's gone to bed.'

'Bough of a tree! There's not a wag of wind to-day,' Bartlemas said suspiciously.

'No? But there's yon crack in his head. Meg bandaged it up for him. The blood! He'll not set foot from here for days yet, I warrant. He groans and groans for the pain and the delay; he's behind time, it seems, and wants to get on. I think he said he was bound for Dunstable, but we can't get much out of him, he's so dazed.'

Bartlemas sat biting his fingers in silence. 'Where be the sheep?' then he suddenly inquired. 'Has he got a dog?'

'No, there was ne'er a dog, and there's only a few score yoes. They're out on the greens'ard.'

Roland got up. 'I'll go and have a look at 'em.'

'Oh, why?' whispered Rachel. 'Stay, you must be famished, Roy dear.'

'Only a minute or two,' returned her husband. 'This may turn out well for me. It will help tide me over for a day or two case the soldiers be watching around. I daren't stay here, and this is fortunate. Go find out who the sheep be for. Tell this chap I'm for Dunstable and I'll go off wi' un first thing in the morning.'

Bartlemas started towards the door. 'Don't tell him who I am. And just pop out now, Rachel, and see if coast be clear. I don't want to run into they soldiers.'

Throwing a cloak over her shoulders she kissed him ardently, and was gone outside for a few moments. When she came back nodding reassuringly, he stepped out across the old track to the field where the sheep lay. There was still light enough to perceive them. Bartlemas crept through a hedge gap and noted that they were yoes of the Hampshire breed, all marked with a letter H in blue ruddle on the haunch. Shearling ewes, about eighty of them, not in very good fettle; they were thin and lame, having no doubt been over-driven. A figure began to move slowly towards him from a shed in the corner of the field, and then stopped. He saw it was an ass. Bartlemas went to the shed to assure himself that no one hid there, then stretched his arms – part lassitude, part relief – and leaned against the shed. Above him the Great Bear had begun to twinkle, and evening airs were caressing the hedge of thorns. Beyond that sigh, and the cough of a ewe, there was no sound. How calm and peaceful, serene, secure, was all this; his own plight how perilous! They would never be able to resume life together here, they would have to sell their home and go far away, perhaps to America.

'They be for a Mister Oxlade of Dunstable, as far as I can make out,' said Rachel when he came again into the kitchen, 'but there's no understanding him, he's that queer.'

'Oxlade? Oxlade?' her husband repeated, 'I don't know such a man; but I'll take 'em, tell him. I'll bide in the loft to-night, 'twill be safer so, and in the morning I'll go, and I'll be back when the coast is clear. Give me some money, lass.'

She gave him money.

'Who's this Meg you've got here?'

'She's a daft girl I've got to help me, and for company.'

'Don't tell her who I be.' Then he said: 'I'll go to the loft now, and you can bring me a morsel to eat there secret, and put some in a bag for me to take in the morning.'

She did that and they slept in the loft together. Towards dawn he rose. 'Don't come wi' me, lass. I'll get 'em away quietly. Stay here. I'll send you word soon what we'll do together. Mayhap we'll have to go away from here. I won't be took alive. Goodbye.' And he kissed her softly and crept away. Later she heard the flock bleating, and the run of their many hooves as they passed out and away down the long green road.

After a while Rachel got up and descended from the loft into the yard. The sun was almost risen, 'twould be a fine day. She went quietly up to her own room, but although she was weary love and anxiety kept her from sleeping. A strange impulse made her get up again and go to the room where the sick drover lay. After listening at the door she tapped upon it. There was no reply; all seemed so very still within that she lifted the latch and peered into the gloom. Not a breath could she hear. The silence as she stood there all suddenly rushed over her, startling and suggestive. There was not light enough to investigate, and fear kept her from venturing farther. Leaving the door wide open she hurried downstairs, lit a rushlight and then returned to that dreadful silence. The drover lay on his back with his mouth wide open, a young slim ugly fellow with a black beard. He was fully clad, just as he had come into the inn. The bandage gave him a terrible aspect.

'I say,' whispered Rachel, but he did not reply or stir. She shook him slightly. 'Wake up.' But he did not awake. Rachel had never seen a dead man before, but there and then she knew that this one was dead. He did not breathe. Shaking him, calling him, had no effect, there was no life in him at all, and he was cold. Panic-stricken, she left him as he lay, fled through the open door back to her own room. There she locked herself in.

The danger of this catastrophe had immediately seized her, not its gruesomeness, but its danger to Roland. Oh, what was to be done now! For she would have to notify the death at once, and explain the drover's presence and the absence of his sheep! All would come out, and Roland would be tracked! The sun was risen up now, he was already a couple of miles away, she could never catch him up in time, and if she did he would not dare return with the sheep. They could not be abandoned, and if she drove them herself she could not get back before people were abroad, and any explanation of her possession of them would imperil her husband. She was distraught with apprehension. Whatever she did Roland would be caught and sent to the wars and killed. All because a rascal of a drover had died in his bed, a travelling rascal, whom nobody knew anything about or cared for. He was dead, and his sheep were gone. A curious possibility began to flutter in her mind. Could she . . . She might hide the body, she might hide it so that she need never give any warning of it at all. She might . . . His sheep were gone — well, he could be gone, too. With this wild project racing through her brain she snatched off her gown, dressed herself, and descended to the inn yard. Her mind was already made up, she would seize the chance of avoidance.

The sky was clear and earth was bright, the fresh blowing morn put a strange eagerness into the aspect of every hedge and hill. These hedges at hand seemed to be rushing along the rising of the track-

231

way – towards Roland – and the hills in a breathless
pause glowed with an intensity of lovely shape and
shade. Rachel went to the field where the sheep had
lain – the grass was cool to her bare feet – and caught
the donkey by the ears. After hitching him into the
shafts of a tiny cart that stood under the shed she
led him out of the field to the side of the inn. Into
the house she went again, treading like a cat, and by
and by came out staggering under an ugly burden
hung across her shoulders. She tipped the limp
drover into the tiny cart, covering him with sacks;
then drove off along the trackway, turning shortly
into a lane that led up into the hills. All the way she
kept muttering meaningless phrases to herself, mixed
even with snatches of song. The hill was reached,
the long slanting haul to the top was overcome.
There the lane became a mere grassy passage meandering amongst abundant furze and bracken that
stretched for many an acre; multitudes of rabbits
skipped there, and blackberries fruited like the vine.
Below and behind her the Vale lay in infinite holy
brightness, filled with hamlets and meadows and
shorn fields ticked with sheaves of corn. Every tree
and stook had a long shaft of shade. There was no
smoke rising yet from any chimney. But Rachel
scanned only the dark furze that sprawled like a con-
tinent across an ocean of hills, and no human shape
met her gaze. The cart was backed into one of the
innumerable alleys in the furze, where long blackberry briers came vipering across the path. Powerful
woman though she was she could not get the body

across her shoulder again, there was repulsion as well as physical difficulty, so she hauled him from the cart by the armpits, his legs dropping, one, two, and stumbled with him into the recesses of the furze, laying and leaving him in a nook where he might rot till the day of judgment. No one could ever find him. Then Rachel mounted the cart again and drove the donkey down the hill back to the lovely Vale, without a compunction in her soul, though she knew that justice is justice, truth is truth, and you cannot hack them about. But once you have closed the door on either you may as well shoot the bolt, there is no turning back. The cart was backed into the shed again, the ass turned adrift in the field again, and the young wife trod quietly back into the house, leaving the door ajar. Meg was still sleeping, it seemed, and Rachel, feeling more drowsy as the sense of relief deepened, went to her bed again and slept until she was roused by the daft maid.

'Missus, the sheep be gone! And the man wid 'um, the scampish man wi's head all blood.' Meg stood in the doorway, a young creature with foolish eyes and crooked body. 'He is gone, I tell you,' she repeated.

Rachel, drowsy and startled, sat up in bed. 'Gone?' Then her craft returned to her. 'Oh, yes, gone with his sheep, what a thief!'

Later on she primed Meg to say nothing at all to anybody about the defaulting drover, fearing that the foolish girl might blab the news of his destination to someone and thus put them on the track of Roy.

She was to deny all knowledge of the drover. 'I believe he be up to no good, and p'raps 'ull bring a judgment on us. He came with his sheep and went off with his sheep, but I don't want to be mixed up with it. If so be anyone inquires we must say . . . we must say that he did not come here, we have not seen him, you understand? He was a bad man, poor fellow, but the world's full of bad men and we have to make the best of 'em.'

Three days went by and Roy had not returned. Rachel was calm in appearance, but she was often to be seen throughout the day gazing along the green road, or towards the hills that lay so close, whence he might descend at nightfall. And her ears were for ever acock for news of soldiers.

On the fourth day after his departure Rachel drove off in her donkey chaise to the market at Thame, some miles off. She transacted her business and returned home in the afternoon. Meg met her in the doorway of the inn.

'I said he was bad, I told you, missus,' began Meg excitedly. 'That scampish man, that drover, bad and all and murder, too.'

'What! What do you say?'

'Murder!' repeated Meg with gleams of horrific joy. 'But he is taken, he's to hang, sure as doom.'

'Tell me at once, do,' urged the trembling Rachel, and Meg followed her into the parlour. It appeared that three men on horseback had ridden up soon after her mistress's departure to market. They were sheriff's officers from Dunstable and Wallingford.

They asked Meg if a man driving a flock of sheep had slept there on a certain night. No – she had said. Was she sure of it, could she swear to it? – they had asked. Yes – she had said. And then they looked at each other, and the Dunstable man had said – No, I thought not! and the Wallingford man said – No, *he* thought not. And they had written out and left a warrant, exhorting her mistress to attend the justices at twelve o'clock on the following day. A murder had been done, a body found with the head broken.

'But when did they find him?' exclaimed Rachel in terror. It was incredible that the body had been discovered already in such a wilderness of furze. The maid did not know; her vagueness maddened the mistress. All she knew was that murder had been done and the scampish man must be the man who did it. But Rachel knew that was not so – he could not be the murderer and the murdered too. Meg was insistent. 'Yes, and his name, it is Reuben Lynch.'

'Whose name?' asked the bewildered Rachel.

'That scampish man, they've agot him.'

'But he is dead, is he not?' cried her mistress.

'No, not him. He run away from here, but they ha' caught him at Dunstable.'

'But how could they? Who did he murder?'

'He murdered the man he stole the sheep from. He was driving the sheep at Dunstable, just the same number and marks, so they knew him.'

Rachel realized that it was inevitable for Meg to assume that the man arrested and the drover were one and the same, but she herself saw that Reuben

235

Lynch must be some other man: But who? And how did he get the sheep from Roland? And where was Roland? It was all mystifying and terrifying to Rachel; she was too much oppressed by the pitiful end of the drover, but after all the man was dead, dead men tell no tales, and no one could ever know of her part in the disposal of the body — not even Meg. She could deny all knowledge of him; having gone so far nothing should induce her to recant and betray her husband. He was still in danger, he could not be in a safe place yet, but perhaps he would come back to-night.

The topic of the murder raged in the tap-room all the evening; such rumours as came to hand were still more puzzling to Rachel. One asserted that the body had been found at the foot of Swyncombe Down, way back along the road, ten miles towards Wallingford. Another declared that the murdered man was a red-haired man with a hare-lip, whose name was Isaac Thorn. Rachel knew these things to be false, and it irked her not to give the lie to them, but she held her peace, though she held it scornfully.

Early next morn the carrier's van conveyed her to Wallingford, where they arrived an hour before noon. While standing amid the groups of people awaiting admission to the court Rachel gathered some additional news of the affair. It appeared that a drover had been journeying across country with a flock of sheep. His name was Isaac Thorn. Where he came from or whither he was bound had not so far been discovered, but he had been coming from the west

and going in the direction of London. Miles away
on the downs he had been joined by a stranger, some
rough man who was going the same road, and they
had travelled the pleasant miles very friendly together
until they suddenly fell a-quarrelling about the catching of a hare. From words they came to blows, the
blood was up, and they fought each other so ragingly
with their cudgels that Isaac Thorn was at last
knocked senseless into a ditch and left for dead. A
farmer passing in his gig had come upon him and
thought him dead, but he recovered under some
cognac, and was carried to the nearest house. Thorn
could only mumble thus much of the matter; beyond
this no more had been gleaned from him, and he had
died a few hours later. But Rachel learned that
Isaac Thorn *was* found near Swyncombe; he *was* a
red-haired man with a hare lip.

She breathed with infinite relief. This dead man
was clearly not the dead man she knew of, whose
body had not been found, and was still in the furze.
She could deny all knowledge of Isaac Thorn with a
clear conscience; at least, although her conscience
might not be clear it was not in any way venal. This
relief, however, only ushered in a new bewilderment;
it had lain almost unheeded under the stress of her
own peril, but grew into graver prominence at the
realization that her own dead man was still undis-
covered. How had the arrested man, this Reuben
Lynch, got possession of the sheep? The coincidence
of Thorn's murder aroused her deepest fears: had
Roland himself suffered a similar fate?

The court of justice stood by itself in the town
square, a pleasant place surrounded by shops that
gleamed with affability. The shops gazed cheerfully,
confidently, at the court-hall, but that noble building
appeared gloomy and aloof, as if its immune dignity
precluded all consort with so ephemeral a thing as life.
It was an oblong top-heavy building set upon a two-
step base of stone, its upper stories underpinned by
plain pillars that made a colonnade around it. The
church, all tower and gable, loomed close by, its white
clock marked with black figures. At a quarter before
twelve the loiterers began to go into the hall and
Rachel went in with them, into a dim chamber that
was full of private doors and benches and pews and
tables with many inkstands full of goosequills, chairs
covered with crimson plush, and ushers who talked
loudly to people who humbly whispered. Soon some
of those private doors opened, and lawyers came in
and sat at the tables and turned over bundles of docu-
ments as if their own lives depended upon it – as
indeed they did. At last the ushers shouted for
'Silence,' and in came the justices. There were five
of them, all dressed like other men; they sat themselves down at the long table on five crimson chairs,
and before Rachel knew what was happening a
wretched man was standing in the dock. It was her
own husband, charged under the disguised name of
Reuben Lynch, with the murder of Isaac Thorn. At
that revelation Rachel screamed aloud, and dropped
in a swoon. 'Poor thing!' said the people who carried
her outside and revived her, 'Poor thing! She says he

is her husband!' Oh, there was a hubbub about that, a great to-do about that, and the long and short of it was that Rachel returned to the chamber and her evidence was secured. The man in the dock — she told the justices — could not be guilty of this crime because he was not Reuben Lynch at all, because he was her own husband, Roland Bartlemas.

'Oh, wife,' the prisoner groaned, 'you've condemned me!'

So they asked Rachel what she could tell them about this business. She had instantly realized the danger Roland was in: she knew now that he had given a false name only because of his desertion, that he was not aware of the terrible complications newly arisen. Only herself was fully aware of them, and she had rather him be taken back to the wars than hang for a murder. There was no other way out, so she opened up and made a clean breast of her misdeed; told them all about the sick drover who had died at *The Leather Bottel*, and the way she had hidden his body in the furze. And they asked the prisoner if he was indeed Roland Bartlemas, and he confessed he was; but when they asked him why he had but now answered to the name of Reuben Lynch he hung his head and would not answer any more. And when they asked Rachel why she disposed of the dead man in that wicked manner instead of giving notice to the justices as by law required, she was confused and said she was afraid. When they inquired what it was she feared she was more confused than ever and burst into tears. At that Roland blurted out the truth about himself, for he saw it would otherwise go hard with them about the crime, and he did not want to suffer for a deed he had not done. He confessed that he was a soldier, that he had deserted and gone secretly home to *The Leather Bottel*, that the pursuers had been there only the day before him.

'I didn't know what were best for me to do, I was badgered. So there was the sick drover with the flock of yoes wanting to get on to Dunstable, and if he could not take them of himself I thought it a good ways to escape, for I'd be able to say I was a drover from far over in the west and no soldier at all. I went off with the yoes early next morning, but my great mischance was this crime against Isaac Thorn, which I did not know of, for the number of his sheep was known, eighty-one of 'em, all marked with a blue H. Soon as I drove 'em into Dunstable and asked for John Oxlade I was taken up by the sheriff's man. He asked me my name and I said it was Reuben Lynch, thinking it was the soldiers after me. I hadn't heard of this murder at all. I hadn't heard any gossip, I hadn't heard of Isaac Thorn, but of course there was no such person as John Oxlade and that put me in the fault at once. And that's the truth, for I was never a liar — anyone as knows me will tell you that. Good God! Why should I murder a living man? When I was told of this charge of murder against me I owned up about receiving the sheep from the sick drover at *The Leather Bottel*, though I did not give my right name, nor say I was a soldier. And this drover that I left sick in bed, I didn't know ne was dead until this moment, indeed I did not.'

Well, well! So they asked Rachel where she had hidden the body of the second man, and she told them: In the furze.

'Your husband did not know that he had died?'

'No,' Rachel replied,' my husband knew nothing about it, he had gone off with the yoes.'

'And you believe that this unknown drover caused the death of Isaac Thorn?'

'Oh, yes, he did,' she said, 'my husband knew nothing about that neither; nor I. This man had a wound in his head, which he said a tree fell on him, but he must have got it in the fighting.'

So the case was adjourned for the body of the unknown drover to be fetched from the furze. The five justices left their crimson seats and went back to their families, and Roland Bartlemas went back to his prison, while the sheriff's men accompanied Rachel to the furze on the hill. Ah! that was a plight for a poor pitiful wife, to go raking after the corpse of a rascal who had done murder, and he himself five or six days rotting. All the way in the sheriff's gig the sheriff kept asking Rachel about him: what sort of a man he was, and so on; and she gave a clear description of him – an ugly slim dark man with his head in a bandage. She described how she drove up the hill with the body in the donkey cart.

'By yourself alone?' the sheriff asked.

'Yes, all alone; 'twas soon after dawn, and I was home again before anyone was abroad, it's not far.

No one saw me or him, no one knew he was dead except me.'

The sheriff was accompanied by two of his men who rode behind the gig on stout black cobs. An hour before sundown they came to the top of the hill and the lane that became a grassy way and the alley into the furze with the long briers clawing across the path. Here they dismounted and Rachel led them into the secret alley as far as she could go, then stopped with a cry: 'Oh, he's not here, he's gone!' And true enough the body was gone. Rachel, turning round, saw that one of the sheriff's men had a queer grin on his face. 'Well, what did you expect to find?' he asked his mate. And then both of the sheriff's men had queer grins. They searched and they searched, but not a rag or a bone or a hair of any drover could they discover in that place. Rachel declared the body must have been stolen away, or he must have been alive after all, stunned only, and be alive somewhere now. 'Oh, what a cunning villain! How he has deceived us!' The sheriff's two men grinned queerly again, and shortly they all gave over the search and journeyed back to Wallingford, where Rachel found a lodging for the night.

Roland Bartlemas, as he was now called, was brought up before the justices again next day, and when the sheriff reported his failure to find the alleged body all five of the justices turned on their crimson cushions and whispered among themselves. 'Is there any corroboration of your testimony about this dead body?' was what they finally asked Rachel.

'My servant Meg saw him sick, and bandaged his head,' replied she; but the sheriff pointed out that they had already interrogated Meg, who was a natural, and she had declared that no drover at all had called or slept at *The Leather Bottel* on that day. In short it was agreed that Rachel's statement was a cock-and-bull story designed by the unhappy wife to shield her husband. She was a confessed liar, and so was he, and so evidently was her servant.

'But the sheep!' cried Rachel, scarlet with shame and indignation. 'My husband had the man's sheep, and that you can't deny!'

'No,' said the justices, 'but it is clear that he stole them from the unfortunate Isaac Thorn.'

And so her husband was committed for trial at the assizes to be held a fortnight later at Oxford. Meanwhile the owner of the sheep, Isaac Thorn's master, had not yet been found, neither had anyone come forward to claim the flock; the sheriff's inquiries were being diligently pursued, and by the time the trial came on it was expected that the owner would have been found.

Rachel returned to *The Leather Bottel*, a free but despairing woman. No action was taken against her concerning the body in the furze, because there *was* no body, it was a myth.

'The injustice, the wickedness of it all!' she moaned. 'There's not enough truth in the world for people to know it when they see it.' Back of her mind she knew that her own unwise action was the cause of all the trouble. She could blind herself no longer

243

to the terrible danger it had placed her husband in, and she was frantic because God had given her a holy burden -- conscience. She was a big pretty woman, but the bloom went off her; she could scarcely eat or sleep, she just pined and wept, or went up to the furze on the hill for long desperate hours seeking among its bushes. The crushing irony of events overwhelmed her. Truth was there, as plain as plain, but she alone knew it all. It was clear as the sun in the sky, but no one believed her. Again and again she told the story to the people she knew, or to anybody who would listen, whether she knew them or not, and brought the hapless grinning Meg to her support; but those people sat mute. No one would believe her, they could not; she was like a woman with a strange language wandering forlorn in a world where nobody understood her. If anything happened to Roland she would die of remorse and grief. Her dear sweet husband had come home to her and she had betrayed him. Pining and weeping and searching, the bloom went off her. Then there was the lawyer she engaged, spending long confabulating hours with him in a musty office that smelled of ink and cheese. Perhaps he believed her story, perhaps not, but he was not sanguine of the outcome, she divined that. The sheriff, too, although she besought him to search the country again and again, would not undertake it. Time rattled by until only a few days remained before the assize began, and her agony grew deeper and darker as the dreadful day grew nearer.

One morning she was attending to her duties in the
tap-room of *The Leather Bottel* when the door was
quietly opened and a slim dark ugly man with a
beard confronted her. He was smiling.

'God's mercy!' cried Rachel, her heart rocking in
her breast.

'You remember me?' asked the drover, for it was he,
the man whose body she had huddled into the
furze. 'I come arter my sheep. Where be they?'

'Sheep! Sheep!' stammered the young hostess,
recoiling from the apparition and rubbing her hand
against her heart to allay that tumult there. The
drover walked right into the room and Rachel
uttered a loud shriek.

'What! What's up, missus?' he cried, and then daft
Meg came running in. She stared at her wild-eyed
mistress and at the drover who sat himself down on
a settle.

''Tis the scampish man!' cried Meg. 'Where you
bin, hopping away like a flea on a sheet?'

'I bin middling bad; give us a drink,' said he in a
weak way.

Rachel went to her shelves and tilted down a flagon
of brandy. Two little glasses she filled, giving one
to the drover, and sipping herself at the other. He
sat silent.

'You're thought dead!' giggled the crooked girl.

'I bin middling bad.' He drew his hand wearily
across his brow. Although ugly, he was slim and
weak and did not look a murderer.

Rachel led Meg into the kitchen and whispered

fiercely: 'Run to the constable as fast as you can go and bid him come quickly!'

Away flew Meg, helter-skelter, but Rachel stood perfectly still in her kitchen, listening. There was fear in her bosom, she knew this was no ghost, this was a desperate villain, yet she wanted to bolt and bar every door to prevent him making off before the constable could catch him. That would rouse him, though, and she dared not let slip this certainty of Roland's deliverance. Never, never should he escape now; and so, taking a large pig-killing knife and hiding it in a pocket of her dress, she returned to the tap-room.

'Where be they sheep, missus?' he amicably inquired. Rachel stood behind her counter, with her hand in the pocket.

'There's been trouble about those sheep,' she returned steadily. 'You've been thought dead, you couldn't be found. A great pack of trouble it brought upon me.'

'Why!' said the little man, lifting his mild gaze on her. 'What all about?'

Rachel glared menacingly at him. 'You told me the yoes was for John Oxlade at Dunstable.'

'I told you!' he cried in incredulous tones. 'John Oxlade? That's my own name! There's no Oxlades at Dunstable as I know of.'

'Well, that's what you told me.'

'I disremember that, missus. Why should I tell you that? I come in here middling bad, I knows that, and I went to bed, and that gal put a bandage on my head, I knows that, but I can't recollect no more, not a scrap.'

'Oh, yes,' pursued Rachel. ' Oh, yes. You'd better freshen up your memory. I came upstairs to you and asked you that night where the sheep was to go. You kept on talking and rambling about them. They must be there, you said, they must be there; and I asked you where, and you said Dunstable. And I asked you what name, and you said John Oxlade. A friend of mine was going that way and he said he would take them for you, and I told you so, seeing you were sick and likely to be sick for days. And there's no keep in our paddock for a flock of yoes.'

'Oh,' he drawled thoughtfully, 'I don't remember a word of that, missus.'

'You'd better freshen up your memory, then,' repeated Rachel casually.

'I was all silly like, I'd had a big knock on my head . . .'

'A tree fell on it, you said,' interrupted Rachel.

'Ah, well,' the drover smiled, 'that was just a manner of speaking, a jokey way of saying it. It *was* a bit of a tree: I'd been fighting with some man and he struck me on my head with a stick! I expect I couldn't understand what you was asking of me. I expect I thought you was asking for my own name, for Oxlade's *my* name, *I'm* John Oxlade. As for Dunstable, well, I was to go *through* Dunstable, but the sheep are for Mr. Hallowbrass over by Hertford, that's where they're going.'

Again he drew his hand across his brow. 'I gave

247

that fellow a tidy crack myself, I left him stretched out for dead!'

'Oh,' observed Rachel coolly, but she dreaded to ask him about that conflict, and still more to tell him its shocking outcome. Her anxiety was maddening, but she had got him now and she would kill him if he made to get away.

'Whose sheep are they, where are they from?' she began again.

'My master is Mr. Stribblewell, down in Hampshire, Liphook, if you know it. A good master, too; he'll be wondering what's come of I. Ought to ha' bin back there a week ago. But perhaps he's not back himself yet – he went off into Wales same day as I started for here. Oh dear,' he said forlornly, pushing the drink away from him, 'I mun have no more of that, my head is bad. I was crossing Ilsley downs with they sheep, and I was jined there abouts by some travelling feller, a nasty ugly chap with red hair and a hare lip – I never did like that sort, but he was set on coming along of I, and so we drove the sheep along together for a day or a day and a half. His name was Isaac something or other, Thorn, I think. We was coming along by Swyncombe and a hare jumped off beside us, and I threw my stick at it and cut it head over heels, clean as a smelt. This joker threw his stick at same time and pretended that it was his stick that did it. Course it warn't so, but he was a very owdacious sort, and he snatched that hare out of my hand. Well, afore you could say Sweat! we was leathering one another for good and all; he was for killing me, surely, I could see that, oh, yes, a great strapping man, and he give me this blow,' – pointing to his head – 'but at the same time I give him the bitterest crack a man ever bore – well, he couldn't bear it, nor could you, no one could, and down he went. I didn't stop for no more, for the sheep had run off a long ways and I tore after them. Somehow I drove 'em as far as here, I just don't know how, and after I got into your bed I don't remember a thing till I woke up in some furze atop of yon hill. How did I get *there*?' he asked, looking stupidly at Rachel. Without waiting for her reply he continued, 'Well, I dunno; I only know I went to bed in your bed and I woke up in the furzes. I'd forgotten everything, sheep and all, and when I crawled out of the furzes I didn't know what all, nor where I was. So I tiggled on along the hills some ways, but I couldn't find nobody, and then through a wood, but I never met a creature till I come out of the wood into a bottom with a cottage in it, a very solitary spot. I fell down in a dead faint outside the cottage. An old shepherd lives there and his wife took me in, and they kept me in a bed as I was raving for a week. Arter that I got better, but everything was gone out of my mind, and I couldn't remember anything till this very morning. I was out for a stroll, and I happened to see the wood I'd come through, and I went through it again. Then I came to the furze, and gradually I found the top of yon hill, and I could see the green road and I could remember the country, and everything began to come back to me. So I run down a lane, and the very first

249

place I see is this house, and all I wants now is my sheep. But they were a good old couple, very kind to me they was.'

Only friendly feelings were surging in Rachel's bosom now, and she said to the drover: 'Mister, I fear there's trouble in store for you along of that man — he's dead.'

'What man?' he asked simply.

'Isaac Thorn.' And just as Rachel said this in came daft Meg and the constable, accompanied by a couple of powerful rustics provided with sticks. Oxlade had to tell over his story again, and then the constable took him away. Rachel flew off to her lawyer.

Well, of course, all was very well now and as good as over. Rachel went to the assizes in a confident spirit, and much astonishment ensued at the trial. Oxlade's master, Mr. Stribblewell, came forward and confirmed his man's statement. He himself had been gone into Wales, and knew nothing of the hue and cry. Isaac Thorn, it was discovered, was a ne'er-do-well, and as the blow had been struck in self-defence Oxlade was exonerated. Thorn's statement before he died had been confused, and it was now seen that much of it had been misunderstood.

Roland Bartlemas stepped out of the dock, free again. Rachel kissed him passionately, and murmured, 'All right, my love?' 'Yes,' he said. And there stood Oxlade beside them, in much concern at the account of what had happened to him while at

The Leather Bottel. To be carted off for dead and thrown into a furze like a dog!

'Course you thought I was dead,' he complained to Rachel, 'and it didn't matter, but it was a bad thing to do, any road.'

Rachel was covered with shame before him.

'Yes, I understands all that,' he replied to her defence, 'but it was a bad thing to do, any road. I'd a bin in a poor way if I hadn't met that old shepherd and his wife. They were good to I. Still,' he took her hand and shook it, and he did not look so ugly, after all, 'all's well that ends well. You didn't know,' he added, 'that's right.'

Rachel linked her arm in Roland's. 'Come, my love.' And they walked away. They reached the doorway, but there Roland stopped stone still. 'Ah,' he groaned. A posse of soldiers waited there. They came forward and took him. Rachel clung to his breast and screamed, but they took him from her, locked his hands together, put him into a military wagon and drove away.

Soon afterwards he was sent out to his regiment in Portugal, and there he was tried by a court-martial for desertion and condemned to be shot. And he was shot. Rachel did not hear of this until long afterwards, though.

THE SNARE

NAB BIRD, RETURNING FROM A VISIT TO THE GIRL of his heart, had walked a dozen Berkshire miles since breakfast, and what with the heat of the summer day and his happy thoughts he felt the need of rest and reflection and so lay down in a shady nook of furze on the edge of a common to sleep and dream of the girl to whom he was just betrothed — ah, fine dreams indeed, for she was all Nab's hope and fancy.

When he awoke he found a little girl staring at him. She had a pale dull face, short hair, no hat. Her frock was ragged; her face and arms were dirty, and heavy hobbed boots were on her feet; she was perhaps ten years old.

'Hallo!' exclaimed Nab, sitting up and pointing to a dead rabbit she was carrying, 'where d'ye get that?'

She made no reply, she only stared at the third buttonhole of his waistcoat which had been deprived of its button.

'Ay? What's time, little 'un?'

''S'three a'clock,' she said in a slow timid voice.

'Ju know where I can get some dinner?' he inquired.

She lifted her skinny arm and pointed to some buildings lying a little way back from the road. She then moved off in that direction, followed by our traveller, and soon they entered a small inn whose one public room seemed to be mixed with its private

252

domestic intentions. An enormous saucepan, without a lid, but crammed full of potatoes, was boiling
desolately on the dull but oppressive fire. The stone-
flagged room was stifling. The landlord was leaning
across the serving counter addressing a label. He
was a fat uncouth man, wearing an old felt hat but
no collar, a pair of spectacles but no coat, a waistcoat
without buttons, and a belt large enough for a horse.
Glancing over his spectacles, which hung so near the
point of his nose that they seemed windows for his
cheeks rather than his eyes, he noted first of all the
dead rabbit.

'Is it a buck?'

'Yes,' replied the little girl.

'Go on, draw it then,' he growled, and resumed his
writing while the little girl passed through the bar
into the kitchen of the inn. Nab Bird walked across
the room to the open window and remarked that it
was a fine day. If the observation called for a reply
it received none; the landlord's pen went on scratch-
ing horridly beneath his pulpy hand. A pipe that he
did not puff was stiffly fastened in the corner of his
mouth – it might have been a twig growing from
his face. Having brought his pen to its final scratch
he stood up, blotted his writing, and adjusted his
spectacles. Taking up the label he peered at it
and then struck upon the counter a blow of vexation:

'Garm it all, I bin and 'dressed it to *meself*!'

He crumpled the label viciously in his fist, flung it
across to the fire and commenced a new label.

253

'You ain't in no hurry, are you?' he remarked. 'I just waunts to git this 'ere label right.'

'Well, I ain't going up in my balloon for a minute or two yet,' Nab Bird remarked, winking at an almanac depicting a flock of gloomy sheep upon a snow-clad wold, 'but soon's you're disengaged, should like a drink, soon's you're quite at leisure.'

'Oh, ah,' said the man, 'shan't be arf a tick, my son.'

'And a bit of bread and cheese, or something,' added Nab.

He sat down and the room was quiet save for a bee that buzzed like an organ. He surveyed a high musty mantelshelf with a black empty wine bottle upon it and a clock with only one hand that hadn't the heart to move in such celibate isolation. There were three tables, magnificently scrubbed, three benches, and a lot of spittoons. An old field spaniel surveyed him with trance-like meditation, fixed him with a maudlin eye like that of a drowsy judge summoning him up. Her puppy became his devoted friend. It was a tiny fat monstrous-limbed creature that, as it reclined upon its haunches, looked as if it were sitting in an arm-chair. Its beautiful eyes kept him in a dream until the innkeeper thundered an expletive which I will only refer to and not actually mention, although the sweet satisfaction derived from its appropriate use renders it extremely popular. He thundered it and struck the inanimate counter a second blow of anger. Nab

stared coolly at him; the man took off his spectacles
and laid them by.

''Dressed the damn thing to meself *again*. Now
what do you waunt?'

'Half pint ale, please.'

'Half a pint?'

'Ah.'

'D'ye waunt bitter or mild?'

'Mild,' said Nab.

'Half a pint?'

'Yes,' said Nab.

'You'll be making yourself blooming drunk, if you
ain't keerful. Anythink else you waunts while I be
going there?'

'Yes,' said Nab reflectively, mopping his brow,
'there is.'

'What?'

'A pound of peaches and a bottle of jugged hare.
Not too many flies in 'em, neither.'

The fat man bellowed, 'Ho! ho!' remarking, too,
that he hadn't got any something peaches, nor no
something jugged hare, but if his customer waunted
summat to something well eat, why couldn't he
something well say so.

'Leave it to you, mister, leave it to you entirely,'
said the diplomatic traveller, 'and while you're gone
I'll write that label for you.'

'You will! Yas, go on then — theer's the address I
waunts it to go to, not to meself — I'll get yer summat.'

He departed. Nab noticed that though his feet
were cased in slippers he wore no socks, and the

255

seat of his trousers was brightened with frank, unabashed patches.

'I waunts two of them 'ere labels,' bellowed the voice from somewhere.

'Right-o,' called Nab, 'do ya a couple of dozen while I'm at it — last you a lifetime.'

When the man returned he brought a plate of fat ham, cold potatoes, bread, and the required jorum of stimulant. He placed them before the hungry fellow and proceeded to examine the labels.

'That's a nice crafty bit of work,' he granted, 'but I don't like them capital dees a'yourn. I can do a better one 'an that meself. I 'as a lot a practice wid dees.'

'Oh!' said Nab.

'Didn't yer see my name over door as yer come in?'

'No, I didn't notice.'

'You 'ave a look at it.'

'You tell me,' suggested Nab.

'No, you 'ave a look at 'im.'

There was a reflective twinkle in his awful eyes; they were afflicted with some disease and the lower lids hung down like two wounds, open and bloody. Nab stuffed a quantity of potato into his mouth and, fork in hand, departed to the doorway where he read that a licence to sell beer, spirits and tobacco had been granted to

DIDDIMUS DUDDRIDGE,

and having exclaimed thereat as appreciatively as the occasion warranted, he re-entered the room swallowing potato.

'What d'yer think a that?' grunted the Duddridge, adding that it was a something fine name to give anyone, waun't it?

'Well, if it comes to that,' declared Nab, 'mine is a something fine name, too. What d'ye think of Naboth — Naboth Bird?'

'Nebawth! I 'eard that name afore, I thinks — Shakespeare, ain't it? Ow ju spell it?'

Nab explained that it was a Biblical name, and he outlined the story of Naboth the Jezreelite, a piece of biography with which he was well acquainted. Mr. Duddridge meanwhile was sitting in front of the fire in an attitude of reflection; that is to say, his hands were firmly clenched in the pockets of his trousers, his knees were bent to suffer his naked heels to repose against the rung of his chair, his head was cocked judicially, while occasionally, without moving either his pipe or his head, he spat cleanly and cleverly into the grate just underneath the saucepan. At the conclusion the landlord, with an extravagance of epithet that was positively regal, entered a condemnation of the lady Jezebel that it would be difficult to transcribe, and unpardonable to publish.

'You bain't married, be you?' he asked.

'Not yet.'

'Well, never you be. I knows what women are.' He paused and his hearer added, 'I know, I know!'

'And *you* know what women are?'

'Ah,' said Nab.

'Women . . .' Diddimus began to harangue, but

paused for the commensurate utterance; to gain time
he removed the pipe from his mouth and spat with
perfect ferocity. Before he could resume the little
girl crept in, silently carrying the denuded form of
the rabbit. She had disembowelled it, skinned it,
and cleansed it, cut off its feet, inserted a peg of
white wood between the flanks of the stomach so
that its organs of economy could be scrutinized,
and now displayed her handiwork to the two men
with something like pride in her eyes.

'Thass a nize robbut, Nallie,' said Diddimus, taking
it from the child and gazing upon those edible
entrails with speculative pleasure. 'A nize robbut,
that is. Here you are, my gal.'

He gave her sixpence and she departed without a
word.

'Now take that gal,' he resumed, 'she's on-
natural . . .'

'Humph!' said Nab Bird.

'She is. Lives over there at that farm — they got her
from the workhouse — does everything a gal should-
n't ought, she do. Always knocking about with the
cattle and horses and the animals. She ain't fond uv
'em — she likes it 'cause she can order 'em about.
If you waunts to give 'er a treat you just set 'er to
kill a couple a pullets, or let 'er go ratting. She sets
all these robbut snares, and when she catches one
alive she strangles it slowly as she can 'cause she
likes to watch the funny look in the robbut's eyes.
'S'what she says! And that's just what women be
like if they gets 'old of ye. Don't you 'ave nothing

to do with no women or you'll be served like her robbuts be.'

The traveller smiled sceptically; had he not yesterday pledged his heart to a girl who was all his hope and fancy.

'You will, ah, my oath, you will; too something true, you will,' declared the fat misogynist, waddling away with the little corpse, adding as he went: 'thass a nize robbut.'

'So long!' cried Naboth Bird.

FISHMONGER'S FIDDLE

MAXIE MORRISARDE WAS NOT OF THE GENERATION of Morrisardes; what they were doesn't matter, save that one of them was a vendor of cheroots. Her paternal ancestry was Vole, her father and her father's father were Voles, but neither does that matter, for her mother had been a Crump. Here and now, for better or for worse, she was a Morrisarde set in a dominion of Voles. Aunt Vole and Uncle Vole. They had Christian names, of course, – Ethelbert and Ida – but they were the sort of people who never sported their Christian plumes, you always thought of them patronymically, and Maxie addressed them simply – Uncle, Aunt. And those respectable elderly retired Voles dwelt in a villa called *Crag Dhu*, half a mile from the sea front. It had blood-red bricks and a white gate. There was also a laburnum tree that never flowered, so it might just as well have been a pincushion; but still, it was a tree and it stood in the gate-corner of a plot of grass that framed an escarpment of mould whereon a dozen geraniums took seasonal holiday. And *Crag Dhu* seemed to hover over its garden, its gravel, and its coal plate, with benignity and pride. The next villa was in the occupation of a horse doctor, and was called *Phædra*. Except for this it was just like *Crag Dhu*, where the Voles lived; where Maxie Morrisarde was now living, and feeling much like one of those geraniums. That was absurd, for Maxie was married – in a kind of a way. She had been married truly and honourably to a one-time amiable tobacconist, who, however, after six months, had untruly and shamefully forsaken her by bolting to America, leaving Maxie without any tangible means of subsistence until she was rescued by her uncle and aunt. A ruffian, a serpent, he was; he had married her for her little fortune; a swindler he was, pimp, bloodsucker, criminal, and sponge; and he was doomed to the gallows; these things Aunt Vole so constantly avowed, vociferated and vouched for that in time even Maxie came to believe them. In her heart, too, Mrs. Vole believed him to be a bigamist, but of this she never breathed a hint to the deserted girl.

Mrs. Morrisarde had been a school teacher, a slight fair pretty creature, helpless, charming, delicate, and an orphan, when she married, quite suddenly, the first man who had made love to her — this scoundrelly tobacco fellow. Having no other friends in the world her gratitude to the Voles when they, as it were, adopted her was profound. Uncle Vole was a retired cattle dealer, hearty, connubial, and a Nonconformist. Aunt Vole was neither hearty (saving as to appetite) nor connubial (except by implication), but she was rather deaf and she was very nonconformist. Life to her was the world, the flesh, and repentance; packed with tribulation from birth to burial, with snares by the scheming of Satan in every hour of the twenty-four. All by the scheming of Satan. Mercy enough if you were alive, and miracle beyond belief if you were sinless. Aunt Vole sewed and sewed and glowered.

Now the Voles had a great rough hufty of a dog, with the name of Toots and the manners of a buffalo. 'What breed is she?' Maxie once asked, and Aunt Vole quivered all over as if Maxie had sworn at her.

'Breed!' she repeated, with hushing deprecation. And, really, when her aunt said it thus it did sound like something not quite nice.

'Oh, I only mean what sort,' floundered the flushed Maxie.

'Toots is a very good dog and bold as a lion. You must take her with you whenever you go out; you're safer with a dog, always.'

But Maxie did not go out alone, not at first; for a while her aunt always accompanied her with Toots, and inadoors the colloquy of Aunt Vole was as constant as the clock-ticks. Sometimes she felt a vague unease, would have liked to go out by herself to some quiet place by the shore and think her own timid thoughts for a while, but she was shy and unresisting. She did not know that freedom is never to be given, but only to be taken; she was like a child for ever beckoning to the things that did not come — tobacconists, perhaps. The tobacconist was never heard of more, and in time Maxie's freedom was enlarged, but there was generally a catechism.

'Well?' her aunt said at tea-time.

'Been a beautiful day,' bayed Mr. Vole, 'turned out capital well.'

'What do you think,' laughed Maxie, 'I saw a man with a 'cello going into a fishmonger's shop.'

Mr. Vole genially grinned.

'With a what?' Aunt Vole gazed curiously at the girl.

'Cello!' cried her husband.

'A great big fiddle.' Maxie made a gesture in the air with her two hands to indicate its gigantic size.

'Fiddle! Oh, I thought . . . humph.' And a silence followed in which the powerful crunching of lettuce became audible as an earthquake. Then Aunt Vole took up her cup and you could hear her gulping her tea – gallons of it. So Maxie took up her cup, and Uncle Vole his, and they all gulped together.

'What shop did you say?' inquired Aunt Vole.

'Fish shop!' shouted her husband.

'A fish shop,' said Maxie too. 'It looked funny, you know.'

'Fish shop,' echoed the elder lady, with a puzzled frown. 'What were you in a fish shop for?'

'I wasn't, aunt; I only saw him go in.'

'Where?'

'In Stamboul Street, I think it was. I was just passing by the fish shop and this man went in with a great big fiddle.' Again Maxie made a curve in the air with her hands.

'Did he say anything to you?'

'No, no, aunt, of course not.' A faint blush grew in Maxie's cheek. 'He didn't see me,' she added.

'What did they want with a fiddle in there?'

'Oh, I don't suppose he was anything to *do* with the shop,' explained the girl.

'They don't go into a fish shop for nothing,' Aunt Vole pursued, 'fiddle or no fiddle.'

'No, he must have gone in to buy some fish,' ventured her flurried niece.

'Oh,' rejoined aunt, 'Roman Catholic, I dare say. I shouldn't go that way again.'

Maxie felt as if she had been admonished for some questionable behaviour.

'The best fiddler ever I heard was old Fishel Ayres. Up at Cadmer End, t'other side of Kent, mother,' mused Uncle Vole. 'The master hand! He hadn't got no sense, and he wouldn't be told no sense. But he was the masterpiece with a fiddle; ah, good ocean! Never had an overcoat on or an umbrella, not if it rained bullock's blood. The last words he ever said to me was, "I shan't last many more years." "No," I said, "you won't if you don't take care of yourself." He'd only got an old policeman's jacket coat on, and believe you me he was dead in a week. Played the fiddle capital well, but you know: break out – and you break down. Those were his last words to me. Now that's a funny thing, ain't it?'

Aunt Vole had no pity for those roving customers. 'They are all for self, and no responsibility; they're no good, and you can't trust them. A man should settle down, he should settle down and bear his burdens, bear his burdens properly. That's what a burden's for.'

One morning Maxie took the dog with her and went to the pier. It stretched out into the sea quite a long way and was dotted with little cabins where you had your horoscope told or your photograph taken. Delicious it was on sunny mornings to hear

the thumps of your own feet and those of people
with parasols and fine-scented cigars all assembling
to hear the musicians, or to fish, or to dive, or to
go little journeys in rollicking little steamers.
Maxie had no wish to indulge in these accessory
joys; she was content to stroll up and down the long
planked pier, or to sit and divide the passing people
into those she liked – how few they were! – and
those she did not.

A small group stood silently staring at a man
sitting on a bench. He was covered with wild
pigeons, the birds hopping upon his head, his
shoulders, his knees, or picking peas from his hands
outstretched on either side of him. Only a few were
enjoying this vision of man and trusting birds; a
tiny boy with a hoop and a black velvet tam-o'-
shanter hat; a dame with a hare-lip and the austerity
of a judge; a stout gentleman in grey with a malacca
cane and a white hat; some sweethearts. Pigeons
pattered at the man's feet; he had a gentle face. As
Maxie came by the dog Toots bounded into the
group and snapped one of the birds in her jaws. The
other pigeons swooped away on thick flapping wings,
everybody shouted 'Brrr!' and the stout gentleman
fetched the wretched Toots such a blow with his
malacca stick that she yelped and dropped the bird
at Maxie's feet. It was dead.

'Oh, oh! What can I do?' cried Maxie to the man
who sprang up and confronted her. 'Is it dead, was
it yours?'

He picked up the dead bird and felt its breast, then

turned and dropped it into the sea. The boy in the velvet hat leaned over the railing to watch the feathered body floating and lifting with the waves. The man – he was not very old, he might have been thirty or thereabouts, with a pale face and thick brown hair – turned and stared at Maxie.

'I am so very sorry,' she stammered, trembling with apprehension, or disgust, or pity. Toots had vanished. 'You had better apologize to God,' the young man sourly said, walking away. Maxie was then still more abashed, for the people glowered at her; the little boy looked as if he was about to weep, and the stout gentleman swore that the dog ought to be shot or poisoned or cut in half; then he went stumping off after the young man, thumping his malacca stick dreadfully. Maxie fled off the pier, deeply angry with the young man. It was wicked of him to say such a thing to her, and she thought him quite nasty; but Aunt Vole, when the quivering girl related the misadventure to her, said it was only what you might expect from such people, that it was a dog's nature, and people ought to look after their birds better. So emphatic was she, that a flame of forgiveness at once began to flicker in Maxie's heart for the young man whom the birds seemed to love.

In a few days she ventured on the pier again. It was afternoon, and she did not take Toots with her, but still she had a faint fear that some passer-by would remember her as the girl whose dog had killed the pigeon. In that episode it seemed to her as if she had shared in a crime, dreadful and pitiful, and

266

that it would be long before the stout gentleman with
a cane and the velvet-hatted boy with a hoop would
cease to arraign her. Of the young man himself she
had come to think that he might even protect her
from them. None of these appeared, and no one else
affronted her. Then she audaciously paid twopence
to sit in a chair close to the band. At that moment a
solo was being played, a piece called *Wiegenlied* by
a composer named Schubert; so dreamy and beautiful it was that Maxie at the close even clapped her
hands with delight. Everybody else applauded too,
and so the player had to stand up in the midst of the
band and bow and smile. Bowing and smiling, with
his arm cuddling the neck of a violoncello, stood the
young man of the pigeons.

Maxie knew at once. In the act of clapping she
stayed as if she had been turned into that pillar of
salt, her two hands still raised, her lips parted, and
her eyes very wide open, for he was looking at her
now. She remembered his sad serious gaze when he
had reproached her about the dead bird; she remembered his going into that fishmonger's shop;
remembered too her aunt's warning words when
she had spoken to her of that. How strange! and
how clever of Aunt Vole! It was exhilarating, and
yet almost terrifying, to know he was that same man.

But nothing could have been less terrifying than
their conjunction as she was leaving the pier. The
music was over, people were sauntering off to tea,
and suddenly he walked at her side, lifted his hat
and chaffed her about her savage dog – where was

it? Had it been shot yet, or poisoned yet, or had she chopped it in half! No, yes; yes, no; confused delight allowed her no more indulgent replies; but when they parted at the pier gates she knew that she would meet him again as surely as if he had asked her to — which he did not — that he was splendid and clever, and that she must be careful not to let Aunt Vole know anything at all about it.

At their second meeting, as they took tea together on the pier, she told him of her marriage and her misfortune. Blackburne smiled: sympathetically, but he appeared to think it was funny. He was rather queer, but irresistibly friendly, and Aunt Vole had been quite wrong about him: nothing to do with any fishmonger at all, he only bought fish to eat. It was a pity, but all musicians had to, and he vowed that he ate like a horse. Each day he played on the pier three times, day in and day out; he was like a cart-horse, never free, and he would rather be a fishmonger, and he envied Maxie.

'Oh, but that is quite a mistake,' said the girl. 'I haven't any freedom.'

'Stuff!' cried Blackburne, so loudly that the waitresses turned and stared at him. In lower tones he went on: 'You married and so achieved a status. That's an important truth about marriage — for the woman. She links herself with a man and *ipso facto* becomes an individual. Until then she has only been a nuisance, bullied by her mother, badgered by her sisters, and spanked by her brothers — possibly even by her pa. You were freed of all those affectionate

ties, and then your man obligingly left you, so now
you are more free than ever.'

'He has left me alone, but not free,' murmured Mrs.
Morrisarde.

'Are you still fond of him?'

She shook her head. 'No, he is wicked.'

'Forget him then.'

'I have forgotten.'

And he did not go to church at all, how could he?
And he wasn't a Roman Catholic or anything like that.

'But Roman Catholics,' he declared, 'do at least
confess their sins to some real person; it's more than
the other sort ever do.'

'That's because they've got,' ventured Maxie, 'such
a lot to confess.'

'All the more to their credit then,' grinned Blackburne (whose other name was Arnold).

'No,' Maxie was positive, 'they confess, and then
they go and sin the more.'

'Well, if their consciences are clear! Of course,' he
jested.

'The only one who can forgive is God.'

'Who's He?' the implacable musician returned.

'You told me to apologize to Him.'

'And did you?'

'It was so rude of you, I thought.'

'There you are, you didn't!' laughed Blackburne,
but noting her solemnity, he quickly added: 'No, no,
forgive me; you were not to blame. And you would
never have anything to confess, nothing worth
hearing.'

269

'It isn't so,' cried she, 'no.'

'What! Shameful, shameful, Mrs. Morrisarde!' And he swore he would kiss her sins away — let her begin telling him at once!

He did not, he could not, give her those kisses then and there, but Maxie imagined them, and was secretly thrilled to be treated as a woman. Aunt Vole never would forget that her husband had run away, and her air imputed a blame to Maxie for that loss, as if she had been silly and overlooked something, something about his socks or his taste in cheese; without the anchorage of a husband of some sort she was a ship drifting, menaced by hazards all too dreadful to name but not too ambiguous to signify.

Maxie Morrisarde continued to meet her friend, to meet him daily, and to keep her aunt in ignorance of him. Concealment was like a 'worm i' the bud,' but still there *was* a bud, and it was opening, for although Arnold was absurd and tempestuous and spoke foolishly of God, he was handsome and careless and tender, and all her thoughts were of him.

Days of the week were days of timid bliss, but Sunday was a wretch for dullness. In the Voles' creed a visit to the pier on the Sabbath Day was an act verging on blasphemy, and their niece was no blasphemer, and no rebel. She had had a black serge father and a mother full of hymns; they died young, but they had not died soon enough — Maxie was no rebel.

Aunt Vole had put on her Sunday afternoon bodice; though her proportions were inelegant she knew she

270

was a woman with refined ideas. Uncle Vole snoozed in his easy chair; Maxie hymned at the piano, with the soft pedal down; Toots wandered disconsolately about the room, until Uncle Vole opened his eyes and commanded her to lie down.

'Lie down, Toots,' whispered Maxie, and Aunt, glaring up from a book, said 'Toots!' so sharply that it sounded like a sneeze. The dog complied, and silence settled on them all like a mist in a vacant garden. Ping . . . ping . . . ping chimed the time-piece bell.

'Ah,' Uncle Vole mistily murmured, 'it's three o'clock.'

'Humph,' sighed his wife, and Maxie sighed too, and went out into the garden to look at the geraniums. The thought of her marriage, so disturbing, so disillusioning, so inescapable, had lately begun to sadden her. She was filled with longings, restless as a bee in a window, for the afternoon was fair and languorous, the pier would be full of gaiety and the music would be sweet. How tiny, harsh and ridiculous the garden looked, how vast and blue the sky! Some clouds, in a small remote line, inched along the horizon; dark and flat underneath, but white and convoluted above, they were like travelling snails.

'Aunt,' said she on returning to the parlour, 'is it hard to get a divorce?'

As if the word were foul, fouler even than the word 'breed,' Aunt Vole flung it away from her. And from Maxie too.

'I just wondered,' temporized the niece.

'How could you! No modest Christian girl could wonder or talk or think of such a wicked thing. At least I hope not. Whatever did you get married for?'

'It costs a bushel of money,' Uncle Vole sat up. 'Good ocean! It costs a fortune, my girl!'

'We may thank God for that,' his wife added.

'I could go to work.'

'What? I can't hear!' shouted Mrs. Vole. 'What could you work at?'

'I could work at something, I could save. I don't like him, and he doesn't want me.'

'That makes no odds, you've been joined,' declared Uncle Vole, 'it's in the Book.'

'Besides, you're separated *now*.' Her aunt was quite impatient with her.

'He doesn't want me, he has been so bad to me.'

'Suppose,' cried Aunt Vole, 'suppose he came back again?'

'I couldn't bear it, he has been bad to me.'

'Or suppose he sent for you, as of course he might as soon as he settles down and pays his debts? Then you would be together again, and just as happy as ever you were.' Aunt Vole could travel upside down as easily as a wasp on a ceiling, and you dared not remind her of this for she could just as easily sting you.

'Aunt, I believe I hate him.'

'No, you don't. You can't, not your own husband! I never heard of such nonsense. I don't know why

272

the Almighty allowed a Christian girl to marry such a wretch — but He did; and you've got to carry your burden. That's what a burden's for! Oh, Maxie, no, no, no!'

'Listen to me for a minute, my dear,' began her uncle. 'One of our leading butchers died last Tuesday, Roland Dean. I spent many a happy half-hour with him. And he used to keep a dog called Brisket chained up in his yard, very savage it was. There lived close by a soft-hearted man who wanted to make friends with the dog, and kept on trying to persuade Roland Dean to let it off the chain, just for an hour now and again. Well, every dog has his day, and so after a lot of jaw tackle Roland Dean did let it off, and the first thing Brisket did — what do you think? Flew at him! Flew at the soft-hearted man — Budge his name was — and nearly limbed him. That's a fact. And always afterwards that Brisket was so savage whenever she saw Budge that he had to give up going past there altogether. So you see! Things should be left alone. Stay as you are, my girl, you're safer. Break out, and you break down.'

Maxie, timid and unfortunate, felt like an insect caught in a web that the spider has forsaken. But her delicate beauty throve, for in those hours snatched almost daily with Arnold was all the life and wonder she desired. Morning or afternoon — she could not meet him at night — in the intervals of his playing they would sit together and murmur and smile, and he would say the most absurd, the most

delightful things. And coming or going, the lively
streets crowded with people crudely gay or graci-
ously dignified, the very dust on the worn pave-
ments printed with a thousand footfalls, the sweet
air, the wide sea rolling a collar of milky surf along
the shore, were full of an enchanting savour; her
soul seemed to caress all these things, and her dark
fancies were lulled.

'Look!' he cried one day as he greeted her, 'to-
morrow I'm to have a holiday. You must spend it
with me. We'll go along the shore, miles and
miles . . .'

But already she was shaking her head, denying
him. It would have been difficult in any circum-
stances, but to-morrow would be Sunday.

'But you must!' he cried. 'What! I've a hundred
things to tell you and ask you. Are you afraid?'

'Yes,' she answered meekly.

'Afraid of those wretched Voles! Pouf! I'll teach
you!' And he was so contemptuous and jocular and
headstrong that she had to consent. She dared not
tell her aunt, and it was impossible to think of an
excuse for such an absence — on a Sunday, too!
How it was to be done she did not know, but she
did not care now; she had promised. In the morning
she slipped guiltily out of *Crag Dhu* before her aunt
could interrogate her, and ran to meet Blackburne
waiting by the sea.

They made off in a westerly direction far along the
sands. The air was windily bright, the tide was low,
but the waters were dull dark green, except for the

tufts of foam the wind tossed upon the strand. All over the soft wet shore were worm-like knots of sand, and tiny recesses beside them like sunken cups with a hole in the middle.

When Arnold asked her what excuse she had made to the Voles she answered that she had not told them at all, and did not know what the outcome would be.

'Tell them the truth,' he said, 'I will come with you.' And he kept on singing, or beating stones into the sea with his stick. 'Tell them the truth.'

By and by they came to a village, all cabins and nets and husky canvas-clad fishermen. Beyond the village was a river, with an old wooden bridge crossing it. The river was wide and they sat down upon its grassy margin before going over. Some way off was a chalk pit scooped out of a green down, so white that it dazzled the eyes, and beside it were tall black chimneys. Nearer there were fields, vacant save for a few writhen trees. And in the middle of the river, where it widened to take the sea, lay a pear-shaped island of sand uncovered by the ebb; nearly an acre of flat smooth sand, like bleached gold, washed by blue crinkled waves. On that silent isle hundreds of snowy gulls were scattered, standing motionless, snoozing in the sun, intensely white, like a drift of divine flowers, and among them a few rooks intensely black.

'Enchanting,' murmured Blackburne, 'how lovely!'

'They are like crocuses growing,' Maxie said.

'Yes, indeed,' the man replied. 'That is how our

sense of beauty sometimes drugs us – by analogies; by things that in their beautiful deceit remind us of things different but in their likeness. The voice of the forest is like the voice of the sea, the rhythm of a hill is the green wave, the torrent of storm is the anger of God, and so on. Here are birds that make you think of flowers. Pure nonsense! It is all unnatural; it is only man's strange faculty for making an ass of himself.'

One of the gulls came soaring above them, and as it slid by on motionless wings it lifted one of its pink feet and scratched gravely at its tilted neck. Arnold lounged beside Maxie and meditated solemnly. She did not understand him, but the sunny solitude was sweet, and she was happy.

'You cannot catch beauty,' he went on. 'She never affirms herself or asserts herself. Beauty is that which is denied – isn't it so?'

'I don't know,' said the girl, 'I know so little.'

'Ignorance is bliss, my dear, truly. What makes for happiness? Not knowledge. Knowledge only realizes that it doesn't know very much, and that what little it does know it doesn't know very well. You just take up life and opportunity, learn the way to do things and keep life in order – that's all.'

'It seems to me God does all that *for* you.'

A deeper pink flush spread in her cheeks as she said it. 'He is wise. To pray for them that hate you and to forgive your enemies is noble, and that is wise too. You pretend not to believe in Him, but in spite of it your spirit *knows*.'

'Perhaps, my dear priestess, perhaps. For a man's emotions are exposed not merely in his relations with his fellows; they are most nobly expressed in his denial of the world in which he lives, and in his sense of his soul's relation with – its perceptions, its concurrences with – that ideal kingdom of which he only dreams and wonders. Yes,' he mused, but as if not speaking to her and communing only with himself as he gazed at the vision of the birds, 'beauty is that which is denied. Man so loves the world that he craves this unbegotten beauty, not as a sign of his mystical relationship to God, but as a sequel and a solace to his own mute misgivings. Without this we are but stocks and stones.' He turned to her, smiling. 'You may not understand this. I hope you don't.'

'I do! And it means that you are a Christian.'

'Oh, chuck, chuck! You've no more brains than a frying-pan. But oh, Mrs. Morrisarde,' he leaned on his elbow closer to her, 'I'm deeply fond of you.'

Her blush deepened as she slipped off her wedding ring and tossed it into the river. 'Don't call me that,' and she put her arms around him. He swore that she had a soul as sweet as any of the white birds, and the body of a queen – which was going rather far, perhaps, but not really absurd, maybe.

The wind had fallen and the heat was increasing when they journeyed over the bridge. A mile or two along the road they found an inn and a haughty bar-maid with bedevilled eyes and lustrous hair, who said she could not provide them with lunch but that

they might have sandwiches. They sat down in the
bar and ate them. Arnold drank beer and Maxie
drank wine. Presently they heard steps approaching
the open door and a voice lustily singing a song about
the Queen of Poland. An elegantly dressed man and
a lad came in together, flushed from swift walking,
their boots covered with dust.

'Foo!' said the gentleman to the barmaid, 'Foo, hot!
The barometer is – ah – quite a lot, I think. In the
shade, you know. Foo, dash it, yes!'

He had a large freckled face and triangular eyebrows, with a tough chestnut moustache; his voice
was large and angular, too.

'What can we have to drink? How's that blister,
Jamie?'

The sylph of the barrels replied: 'Anything you
care for.'

'Well, yes; it must be something we care for. You
haven't any egg flip? No, you haven't any egg flip.
Then a bottle of melodious beer, if you please, with
a few chromatic splinters in it.'

Leaning upon his walking-stick, he crossed a leg
and sung again:

> Oh, the Queen of Poland is my queen
> And I'm her Salamander.'

'Jamie, have a bun? Isn't it hot, foo! What have
you done with your orange? Jamie, spotless treas-
ure, they haven't any buns, so what now, eh? Cocoa!
Oh, but Jamie, you can't; it's Sunday, it's rude. No,

what you want for your complaint, my darling, is is . . .'

'I said some ginger-beer,' the boy interrupted loudly.

'Ginger-beer! Oh, God bless me, yes. If you please, madam.'

'Oh, the Queen of Poland is my queen,'

sang the gentleman, winking – or appearing to wink – at Mrs. Morrisarde.

Arnold and she walked in the fields again, inland, far from the sea, towards a town where they could catch an evening train for home. Fragrant and alluring their track was, fragrant and tender those untiring hours, with the glimpse of a kingfisher as it dashed from a rock into the bosom of a stream; rabbits, watervoles, ducks; the forlorn beggars who all cajoled pence from Blackburne: 'I'm powerless, abject,' he cried to her, 'they conduct their peaceful raids upon my charitable emotions'; the cottage where they got tea from a widow whose man had been massacred by Zulus; the churchyard stone to a sailor who had been 'done to death by Neptune; Maxie felt she could go on roving thus for ever in so bright and free a world, to hear and see all the absurd things and all the beautiful things with the man she loved.

But in the cool of the evening: 'Tell me,' Blackburne suddenly urged, 'what can we do about this husband of yours? Can't you divorce him?'

She stopped quite still, facing him; not looking at him but staring back along their travelled road. So far they had come already, so very far! They were in a long thin white rambling road, its herby borders fringed with ragwort and succory. A willow brook dribbled along one side, and endless fields ranked with stooks of corn stretched on and on. The sun was going down, the daylight moon which had ghosted in the sky for hours was triumphantly hovering. So alone they were, so quiet it was, that their very footsteps had seemed to crunch the peaceful air. Her hand was laid upon his sleeve in a slow caress.

'No,' she said, 'it's impossible, Arnold.' She had come to accept her aunt's horror of divorce; not for its hideous publicity, but because it defamed God's will. Like all timid people she took a reason that had not been hers, and made it her own, multiplying its intensity. Never, never, never! And with that dark question hopelessly argued there and then between them she felt she was a miserable woman, deeply sinning. Blackburne pleaded and scoffed and stormed, but she cried on his breast and declared she must never see him again.

'I believe, you know,' said he, 'that in seven years you are free to marry again provided you hear nothing of him in that time; you are free.'

'Is that true?'

'I have heard so, in seven years, yes.'

'How strange!' She was smiling, almost placidly. ' That's not long.'

'Oh, no – the week after next!' But his sarcasm crumbled at her gaze. 'Dear love, I want you.'

'Yes, yes,' she murmured.

'Do you know? Do you want it, too?'

She was bewildered by his caresses. 'Oh, what do you want, Arnold?'

'A lover, a wife, a mistress,' he whispered, 'whatever you can be to me.'

'If I gave you everything it would not be enough.'

'Come and live with me, Maxie. I'll care for you dearer than any husband.'

Her refusal was the softest ever uttered, but it was the ultimate answer.

With her arm linked in his they walked on rapidly until they got to the railway station, where they sat and waited for their train.

'Don't hate me, Arnold.'

'No, of course not,' he returned moodily. 'Isn't this an ugly, rackety, exasperating hole? And that cursed engine boasting and heaving and crashing with its millions of empty trucks!'

Half an hour later they parted at the gate of *Crag Dhu*. Should he wait to see if she were flung from the door? No. In the gathered gloom she pressed him to her as if bidding an eternal farewell.

'Don't go, Maxie. Come away now!'

'It has been a sweet little holiday,' she whispered, and then ran off along the garden path.

As she entered the house Aunt Vole appeared in the passage, bonneted and cloaked and wild-eyed. With a stupid shriek she heaved herself upon the errant girl and burst into tears. 'Oh, Maxie, darling child!' Little Mary Fitchew, the servant, stared from the end of the passage like an owl.

'We thought you were dead!' sobbed the extraordinary, the surprising, Aunt Vole. 'Dead drowned!'

'Oh, Aunt! I'm all right, I've only been out with a friend.'

'Or that you had run away!'

'No, no, aunt, I'm all right.' At this unexpected reception she almost wept herself; but she patted her hysterical aunt and hushed her. 'I ought not to have gone, I know; I ought to have told you, didn't I?'

'Tell me, come into the parlour and tell me everything,' adjured Aunt Vole. And there Maxie told her everything.

'Dear, dear!' was her aunt's comment. 'And your uncle is scouring the town after you.'

'Let me go to bed,' said the distracted girl.

'Oh, but wait for your uncle, won't you?'

'No, you tell him, aunt.'

'If you wish it, child. But promise me, promise me this, promise you will never see that man again.'

Maxie sat silent for a few moments. 'I'll go away, aunt, a long way away, and get work.'

'Oh, you uncle wouldn't hear of that. Do you want to leave us? We are fond of you. And what work could you do now? And your husband — don't forget him — what would your husband think of this?'

The pretty sinner bowed her head in tears, while Aunt Vole, who envisaged a soul tottering on the brink of destruction, went to a shelf and reached down a large heavy book.

'You will promise?' she urged, with strange unfamiliar gentleness.

'Yes,' said Maxie.

'Lay your hand on the book.'

Maxie laid her hand on the open book. She was the creature of her environment, always. With her lover she had no fears, for he was fearless. With the Voles she laid down her pride; and she swore on the book as Aunt Vole directed her. There at the end of one of her fingers a verse met her glance:

'My heart panteth, my strength faileth me: as for the light of mine eyes, it also is gone from me.'

Her aunt kissed her, and then startlingly knelt down as if in silent prayer. But Maxie did not join her. She sat staring at invisible things, a wonderful sunset shining with eternity, and far-off ineffable joys. Seven years! Seven years! And there was a stupid man with triangular eyebrows who kept winking at her and singing:

Oh, the Queen of Poland is my queen,
And I'm her Salamander.

'THE BOY OUGHT TO HAVE A CRICKET BAT, TOM,' said Eva Grieve to her husband one summer evening. He was a farm labourer, very industrious, very poor, and both were so proud of their only child that they sometimes quarrelled about him. They all lived together in a tiny field that was shaped like a harp and full of sweet grass. There was an ash tree in it, a water splash, a garden with green things and currant bushes in corners; and of course their little cottage.

'He can't play cricket,' Tom Grieve replied.

'Not without a bat, he can't; he ought to have a bat, like other boys.'

'Well, I can't buy him no cricket bats and so he can't have it,' said Tom.

'Why, you mean wretch . . .' began Eva with maternal belligerence.

'For one thing,' continued her mate, 'he ain't old enough — only five; and for another thing, I can't afford no cricket bat.'

'If you had the true spirit of a father' — very scornful Eva was — 'you'd make him one, yourself.'

So Tom chopped a cricket bat out of a slice of willow bough and presented it to his son. The child hardly looked at it.

'Course not,' snapped Eva to her sarcastic husband, 'he wants a ball, too, don't he?'

'You'll be wanting some flannel duds for him next.'

'I'll make him a ball,' cried Eva.

Eva went into the fields and collected wisps of sheep's wool off the briers for her firstborn, and bound them firmly into a ball with pieces of twine. But the child hardly looked at that either. His mother tossed the ball to him, but he let it fall. She pelted him playfully with it and it made his nose bleed.

'He's got no one to play with,' explained Eva, so she cut three sticks for a wicket, and in the evenings she and Tom would take the child out into the harp-shaped field. But the tiny Grieve did not care for cricket; it was not timid, it simply did not care. So Eva and Tom would play while David stood watching them with grave eyes; and at last Tom became very proficient indeed, and so enamoured of the game of cricket that he went and joined the village club and no longer played with Eva; and the child wouldn't, so she was unhappy.

'He likes looking at things, but he doesn't want to *do* anything himself. What he ought to have is a telescope,' said Eva. But how to get a telescope? She did not know. The village store had stocks of hobnailed boots and shovels and peppermint drops, but optical instruments were not in demand, and Eva might for ever have indulged in dreams – as she constantly did – of telescopes that brought the interior of heaven itself close up to you as clear as Crystal Palace. But one day she went to a farm auction, and there had the luck to meet a great strapper of a gipsy man, with a husky voice, a long ragged coat and a depressed bowler hat, who had bought a bucketful of crockery and coathooks and odds and ends, including a little telescope.

'Here,' Eva approached the gaunt man,' is that telescope a good one?'

'Good!' he growled. 'Course it's a good 'un, and when I say it's a good 'un I mean the gentleman's gone to Canada, ain't he? And he don't want it. Ho, ho!' he yelled, extending the instrument and tilting it against his solemn eye. 'Ho, ho! I give you my oath it's good. I can see right clean into the insides of that cow over there!' Forty people turned to observe that animal, even the auctioneer and his clerk and his myrmidons. 'I can see his liver, I can. Ho, what a liver he has got – I never see such a liver in my life! Here, . . .' he dropped the glass into Eva's hand, 'two shillings.'

Eva turned it over and over. It looked perfect.

'Have a squint in it,' roared the gipsy man. 'Go on, have a squint at me!'

Eva was too dashed in public to do any such thing. 'How much do you want?'

'Look here, ma'am, no talk for talk's sake. Two bob.'

Eva quickly gave him back the telescope.

'Eighteenpence, then,' wailed he.

She turned away.

'Come here, a shilling.'

Eva took the telescope and gave the gipsy a shilling.

Home she went, and David received the telescope on his birthday. It occupied him for an hour, but he did not seem able to focus it properly, and so he only cared to look through it from the wrong end. He would sit on one side of the table and stare through the cylinder at his mother on the other side. She seemed miles away, and that appeared to amuse him. But Eva was always taking peeps with it, and carried it with her wherever she went. She would look at the trees or the neighbouring hill and discover that those grey bushes were really whitebeam; or tell you what old woman had been tiggling after firewood in the hanging copse and was bringing a burden home; or who that man was riding on the slow horse through the shocks of barley. Once when she surveyed the moon she saw a big hole in the planet that no one had ever mentioned to her before; and there wasn't a man in the moon at all. But David could not contrive to see any of these wonders, and after a while the telescope was laid by.

A singularly disinterested child was David; not exactly morose, and certainly never peevish, but how quiet he was! Quiet as an old cat. 'He'll twine away!' sighed his mother. Gay patient Eva would take him into the spring woods to gather flowers, but he never picked a bloom, and only waited silently for her.

'Look at this, I declare!' cried she, kneeling down in a timber lane before a strange plant. When its green shoots had first peered into light they pushed themselves up through a hole in a dead leaf that had lain upon them. They had grown up now to four or five inches, but they still carried the dead constricting leaf as if it were a collar that bound them together;

it made them bulge underneath it, like a lettuce tied with bast only it was much smaller. Eva pulled at the dead leaf; it split, and behold! the five released spears shot apart and stretched themselves flat on the ground.

'They're so pleased now,' cried she. 'It's a bluebell plant.'

And Eva, singular woman, delighted in slugs! At a threat of rain the grass path in the harp-like field would be strewn with them, great fat creatures, pearly or black, with such delicate horns. Eva liked the black ones most.

'See!' she would say to her son. 'It's got a hole in its neck, that little white hole, you can see right into it. There!' And she would take a stalk of grass and tickle the slug. At once the hole would disappear and the horns collapse. 'That's where it breathes.' She would trot about tickling slugs to make them shut those curious valves. David was neither disgusted nor bored; he just did not care for such things, neither flowers, nor herbs, nor fine weather, nor the bloom of trees.

One day they met a sharp little man with grey eyebrows that reminded you of a goat's horns. There was a white tie to his collar, shiny brown gaiters to his legs, and an umbrella slanted through his arm as if it were a gun.

'How is your cherry tree doing this year, Mr. Barnaby?'

Mr. Barnaby wagged his head, and gazed critically down at Eva's son.

'There was a mazing lot of bloom, Eva; it hung on the tree like — like fury, till it come a cold wind and a sniggling frost. That coopered it. A nightingale used to sing there; my word it could sing, it didn't half used to chop it off!' Then he addressed the lad. 'Ever you see a nightingale part its hair?'

David gazed stolidly at Mr. Barnaby.

'Say — No,' commanded Eva, shaking him.

The boy only shook his head.

'No, you wouldn't,' concluded the man.

'There's no life in him. I'm feared he'll twine away,' said Eva.

For David's ninth birthday she procured him a box of paints, and a book with outlines of pigs and wheelbarrows and such things, to be coloured. David fiddled about with them for a while and then put them aside. It was Eva who filled up the book with magnificent wheelbarrows and cherubic pigs. She coloured a black-and-white engraving of The Miraculous Draught of Fishes, every fish of a different hue, in a monstrous gamboge ocean; a coloured portrait of David himself was accomplished which made her husband weep with laughter; and a text, extravagantly illuminated, *I am the Way, the Truth, and the Life*, which was hung above David's bed. To what ambitious lengths this art might have carried her it is impossible to say, the intervention of another birthday effecting a complete diversion. This time the lad was given a small melodeon by his fond parents, but its harmonic complications embarrassed him, baffled him; even the interpretations of

'All hail the power' or 'My Highland Laddie' which Eva wrung from its desperate bosom were enough to unhinge the mind of a dog, let alone poor David.

David seemed to be a good scholar, he was obedient and clean, and by the time he was due to leave school at the age of fourteen he had won the right to a free apprenticeship with an engineer who specialized in steam-rollers. How proud Eva was! Tom too, how proud!

Yet he had not been at work three months when he was stricken with a spinal infirmity that obliged him to take to his bed. There he remained a long time. The doctor prescribed rest, and David rested and rested and rested, but he did not get better. At the end of a year he was still as helpless. There was no painful manifestation of disease, but it seemed as if his will were paralysed, as if he had surrendered a claim on life which he did not care to press. Two years, three years rolled on, and four years went by. The long thin youth, prematurely nipped, and helpless, was a burden like the young cuckoo that usurps a dunnock's nest. But even the cuckoo flits, and David Grieve did not. For seven years thus he lay. There were ill-speaking folk who hinted that he was less ill than lazy, that his parents were too easy with him, that he wanted not rest but a stick. At times Tom, who had begun to feel the heavy burden of years, seemed to agree, for there was nothing the brooding invalid was interested in save brandy. For years he was indulged with spoonfuls of brandy in lieu of medicine, and a long row of bottles in

Eva's kitchen testified that the treatment had been generous. It had, to the point of sacrifice. Decent steady-going people the Grieves had been, with the most innocent vices — for vice comes to all — but at last Tom had to sink the remnant of his savings in a specialist doctor from London. To the joy of the devoted parents the doctor declared that a certain operation might effect a cure.

So David was bundled off to the county hospital and operated upon. For a while Eva breathed with gaiety, an incubus was gone; it was almost as if she herself had been successfully operated upon. But soon, like a plant that flourishes best in shade, she began to miss not only David but the fixed order his poor life had imposed on her. His twenty-second birthday occurred as he was beginning to recover, and so they sent him a brand-new suit of clothes, the first he had had since boyhood.

DEAR SON, (Eva wrote to him)

We are pleased to hear of you getting so well thank God we are very pleased and miss you a lot but cant expect no other you being our only little pipit. Your father has bought you a suit for you to ware when you get up and you can walk   a drak serge like himself   what a tof. And will send them by the parcel post off next week. Look careful in the pockets.

And God bless love from

TOM and EVA.

He looked careful in the pockets — and found a half-crown.

It was on an April day that he returned to his parents, very much enfeebled, neither man nor child. Seven years of youth he had foregone, his large bones seemed too cumbersome for him and adult thoughts still hung beyond his undeveloped flight. But even to him the absence had taught something: his mother had lost her sprightly bloom, his father was setting towards the sere. Both of them kissed him with joy, and Eva hung upon his neck in an ecstasy of tears that made him gasp and stagger to a chair.

Restoration to vigour was still far off. Sometimes a villager would come in of an evening and chat with him, or invite him to a party or a 'do' of some sort, but David did not go; he was frail, and as it were immobile. He was on his feet again, but hardly more than enough to convey him about the harp-like field. Restless and irritable he grew; his life was empty, quite empty, totally irremediably empty. The weather, too, also unmanned him; summer though it was, the storms of rain were unending and he would sit and sigh.

'What is that you're saying?' asks Eva.

'Rain again!'

'O Lord,' says his mother, 'so it is. Well!'

The grass was lush in the field, the corn grew green and high, but the bloom of the flowering trees was scattered and squandered. Whole locks of laburnum would lie in the lane, the blossomy cream of the quicken tree was consumed, and the chestnut flowers were no more than rusty cages.

But on one brighter eve he suddenly took a stick and hobbled off for to take a walk. The wrath of the morning had gone like the anger of a good woman. The sky was not wholly clear, but what was seen was radiant, and the shadows were august. Trees hummed in the bright glow, bees scoured the blooms without sound, and a tiny bird uttered its one appealing note — Please! For half an hour he strolled along a road amid woods and hills; then the sky overdarkened quickly again, and he waited under a thick tree to watch a storm pass over. Clouds seemed to embrace the hills, and the woods reeled in a desperate envy. Rain fell across the meads in drooping curtains, and died to nothing. Then, in a vast surprise, heaven's blue waves rocked upon reef all gold, and with a rainbow's coming the hills shone, so silent, while the trees shone and sung.

There was no song in the heart of the desolate man; his life was empty, and even its emptiness had a weight, a huge pressure; it was a fearful burden — the burden of nothingness. Grieve turned back, and when he came to an inn he entered and drank some brandy. Others there who knew him offered him ale, and he sat with them until his sorrow fell away. But when he got up to go the world too seemed to fall away, his legs could not support him, nor his mind guide him. Two companions took him and with his arms around their necks conveyed him home.

'He's drunk, then?' uttered Tom harshly.

'No, it's the weakness,' cried Eva.

'That's it,' corrected one of the men. 'That beer at *The Drover* ain't worth gut room. If you has five or six pints you be giddy as a goose.'

For a week David could not rise from his bed, but as soon as he was up he went out again, and as often as he went out, he was carried home, tipsy. Tom took his money away from him, but that did not cure him.

'He's mad,' said the father, and at last Tom took the suit of clothes, too, rolled them into a bundle, and went and sold them to a neighbour.

So David Grieve lies on his bed, and his mother cherishes him. Sometimes he talks to her of his childhood and of school-treats he remembers on days that smelt — so he says — like coco-nut. Eva has ransacked her cupboards and found a melodeon and a box of paints and a telescope. The sick man watches for her to come and feed him, and then he sleeps; or, propped against a pillow he hugs the melodeon to his breast and puffs mad airs. Or he takes the telescope, and through the reverse end stares at a world that is not so far away as it looks. Eva has taught him to paint inscriptions, but he repeats himself and never does any other than *Lead, kindly Light*, because it is easy to do, and the letters are mostly straight ones.

A DIVERSION WITH THOMAS

'THE TOWN ITSELF IS ENCHANTING, VERY SMALL and shy and delightful; it just smirks and snoozes — you know! And it has history and all the suitable monuments, priory, ramparts, manor, alleys and gateways, a tower where a marchioness was smothered, and a guild of something or other. I beg you to realize that you can't rush into a spot like that by train, you dare not; it's a shrine; you must draw nigh reverently and behold it. . . .'

'I understand you.'

'You understand, yes; I assure you it cannot be properly enjoyed apart from a congenial approach, it is, well, I put it for simplicity, like a supremely heavenly kidney in the heart of a superb steakpie. We will go,' declared my friend Pondicherry, hooking a compass to his watchchain and pocketing a map, 'on foot. The day will be fine and hearty.'

Pondicherry was a man of great parts but small person, guardedly rotund, with a face that seemed unused to amusement. He was always as spick and span as a new envelope and at least once a day he polished the gold or gilded parts of his spectacles with a piece of soft leather which he concealed in his purse.

'Yes, on foot let us go,' agreed I, reflecting that a visit to an Ancient Place is always a job for a pilgrimage, which is never anything but a job for the feet. I took my stick, he brought out his umbrella. The same obscure movement of genius led him to bring his son, a modest lad, Thomas by name.

'Exceptionally intelligent, that child, really,' explained Pondicherry to me. 'I find it so moving to watch his mind unfold. What is a father if he is no more than a parent? Absurd. He must be guide, philosopher, friend, a refuge, an encyclopædia, in fact the whole bag of tricks in one. It is delightful; far be that day when he no longer needs me. I say the whole focus of society must be upon the *genus* boy; it responds. Dear me, how that child responds! Would you believe it . . . ?' And so on, and so on.

Away we went until we came to a hedged lane, a wide grassy track, so exceeding full of ruts and stones and hillocks and mud as to make our travelling a matter of some discomfort.

'I never set foot upon a Roman road,' began my friend —

'Is this a Roman road?' I exclaimed.

'Oh, yes, the genuine article,' declared Pondicherry, 'straight from the Cæsars. I never set foot upon a Roman road but that some essence of history creeps from boot to brain and I march with Agricola and his cohorts.'

'True, I understand such thoughts, a sort of amnesia of time; but this Roman way has so little of my notion of a road that I feel all the swords of all those cohorts must have been whacked into ploughshares which have never ceased ploughing here.'

'Father,' interposed Thomas, 'what is a cohort?'

'A body of soldiers.'

'I thought it was a fowl.'

'A fowl, my boy! But you know what a fowl is?'

296

At that moment a loud and vehement country-woman hailed us. 'Be they your boys?' She appeared from a small house set between an orchard and a couple of yards, one of which was full of pigs and the other of dung. 'Be they your boys?' she raged. We declared that we knew nothing of any boys; what boys?

'Thousands an 'em, just gone by, not five minutes. They like a flock of locusts; two bushels o' codlins stole from my archard and a duck trod on, it's murder. Be they your boys!'

Mr. Pondicherry again said 'No.'

'Then whose be they?' roared the violent woman.

'I haven't the least idea,' replied he, 'this little lad is my only offspring.'

'I don't care whose they be or what they be,' cried the fury, shaking her fist at my friend, 'they ought to be poisoned, that's it and all, the dirty devils, ought to be chucked into purgatory, straightaways, so there!'

I led my friend and Thomas away to safety, explaining to them that we were apparently in the track of some rascally boys and were being blamed for their misdeeds.

'Father, what is a purgatory?'

'A kind of half-way house to the deuce knows where. As a matter of fact there is no such place.'

'I thought it was a swimming-bath.'

'A swimming-bath, my boy! But you know what a swimming-bath is.'

We heard, not far ahead it seemed, noise of shouting and the sound of bugles, a gamut unmatched for profane indelicacy. Advancing towards us was a fat sheep, incredibly nimble, pursued by a man of whose nimbleness the sheep made mockery and scoff.

'All my ship be going the Lord know wheres,' cried the panting distracted drover, 'all through a gang o' boys – be they yourn? May they be fog-lasted. You putt 'em at a job o' work, master, or I'll have their blood. I had to come back for this 'ere 'un, I had to come back.'

'Ah,' chimed Pondicherry affably, 'so this is the one more than the ninety and nine.'

'Ninety! There's three hundred ship in that flock, or there was, fog-last 'em; there should be when I gets 'un back, however. Be they your boys, master?'

'No,' said Pondicherry hurriedly, and we began to help the man with his animal. But getting it back was not so easy as getting the camel through the eye of its peculiar needle. I am persuaded that it was not man's first disobedience nor the fruit of that forbidden tree, not Eve, not Helen, that first brought woe into the world, but a sheep; when sheep first stepped into Eden peace popped out of it. In short this one exhibited an aversion to walk anywhere at all, and as for progression in the destined path its disapproval was as a mighty bastion. The man slipped a belt from his waist, and buckling it round the neck of the beast he began to hale it forwards and we to push it from behind. After immense exertions the sweating drover begged us to go and collect his flock, somewhere up the lane, and drive them back to him. Only by such means could this monster be persuaded. 'She'll go with 'em, but not without 'em. And keep all your boys from me or their blood I'll have, I will.'

So we went on and soon espied sheep. Sheep were in the lane, in the fields to the left, and in the fields to the right more sheep revelled and wandered, terribly dispersed.

'Good heavens!' protested Pondicherry, 'let us get on with our journey, it is a hopeless job, we shall never get those sheep, we shall never get anywhere. Leave the old wretch to do the best he can with his ewe.'

So we did this and hurried on, shamefully silent, thinking of the drover.

'Father,' piped little Tom, 'what is a ewe?'

'A ewe is a female sheep.'

'I . . . I thought it was a tree.'

'A tree, my boy! But surely you know what a tree is?'

We left the Roman road but we did not leave our difficulties. Other occasions, several, heaped all their opprobrium on us. There was a man with onions from Brittany, an interview with an unconvinced and unconvincible policeman, and then that astounding altercation with a suffering charabanc party. We renounced and denounced those boys; we solemnly, indeed excessively, paraded our entire dissociation from them, but the applewoman had overtaken the drover, the drover had connived with the policeman, and the policeman bore down upon the charabanc party. We escaped molestation, but our hazard had been fearful for we could not invoke a single impartial witness.

'Why, oh, why,' groaned Pondicherry, 'should we be confounded with this horde of envenomed ruffians? We haven't even seen 'em! Is it because Thomas is with us! I suppose so. It's a devilish bad joke, you know. Let us slip into the fields and go along by the river. Our whole adventure is in peril.'

Into the fields went we, but how futile. It was by the river that we ran into an outlier of these mythical miscreants, fifty skull-caps, each with a coloured knob atop, blue, yellow, green, red, white, and beneath each cap walked a larrikin of the *genus* boy. He had a bugle or he had a bat, had a ball, a stick, a yell, in truth the quintessential demon pranced and cavorted. Conspire as we would we could not escape them and anguish dropped from Mr. Pondicherry's eyes as we approached the Ancient Place in the tail of a particularly exasperating troup of the fiends.

Pondicherry almost sobbed: 'It is one entire horror to me. This horde, this rabble, has been let loose upon us. It is tragic, the whole spirit of the place, the sense of the past, the eloquence and dignity of history is being smitten, as it were, in the nose, smack! It is tragic, the very soul of poetry is wounded.'

Pondicherry was right, these imps were everywhere, whooping in alley and garden, swarming in the priory, massing upon the tower where the marchioness was smothered, and hobbledehoying on the bridge. The ramparts were racketed by assault, decorum outraged, glamour mocked, and pandemonium established. The places of mere refreshment were denuded of every bottle and bun. By heavens, it was impossible to obtain the small relish of a ginger-pop for the exhausted Thomas, and so in pain and discomfiture we turned our back upon the Ancient Place and retreated to the station. Behold! Boys were already on the platform before us; behind many others were joyously marshalling for the train.

'No, I know nothing of these monsters, sir,' declared my friend Pondicherry to the stationmaster very abruptly and passionately. 'They are,' he continued to me, 'the curse of society, a blight, a catastrophe. May I be switched!'

Then a tall man came upon the platform. It was an old acquaintance whom I had not seen for a couple of years. I went up to him.

'My dear fellow,' he cried, 'is that you? Well, well!' After a few exchanges I learnt that he was now a master at the famous school in the neighbourhood. He had come over in charge of two or three hundred boys.

'I have seen them,' I murmured, 'a band of vipers, indeed.'

He grinned: 'Yes, rather a handful. I arranged for them to walk over, just to tone them down, six miles, you know. I came over by train this morning

301

early so as to get the town to myself. Adorable place, isn't it? So calm, so mature, so full of languor, just exquisite, don't you think?'

'My friend,' I exclaimed with emotion, 'come and tell it to Pondicherry, come.'

We moved through crowds of boys who seemed suddenly transformed into well-looking modest youths of behaviour and breeding. They touched their skull-caps to my friend murmuring 'Good afternoon, sir,' with almost an excess of politeness. As we approached the Pondicherries I heard the one unto the other say.

'It's a decoction for killing bugs, Thomas.'

'Why, father, I thought it was a bottle.'

'A bottle, my boy! But surely you know what a bottle is?'

I HAD NOT TAKEN MORE THAN SIX PACES ACROSS THE bridge at Waterford, that is to say I had not lived longer than two minutes in Ireland, when I was accosted by a big poor man in old boots — so very old indeed that he moved like some soft-walking spirit — who offered me his assistance in a voice at once colossal and husky. I was grateful, for to be strange and weary in a city at seven o'clock of the morning, with the sunlight lying on the flats of the houses heavily yellow, and the air not kind to coughing people, is no sort of a way to be beguiling the hours of your ease. So I was very grateful to my friend who wanted to guide me to an hotel, he saying *this* to me, and I looking already like the third part of a tramp:

'To the Imperial Hotel, sir, you should go, patronized by Royalty and all the officers of Europe.'

We approached that hostelry, but the number of its windows and the gravity both of its appearance and my own abashed me, and it was in another quarter I decided to choose my lodging. So I handed my friend threepence. He surveyed pathetically the contents of his palm, and scrutinized me with those mild blue eyes.

'Ah, begod, I can't get a drink with that . . . it's sixpence a pint in Waterford!'

'But you could,' I said, 'you could buy a banana with it.'

He gazed at me uncomprehendingly, and I hast-

ened to give him another twopence, which left him
with still a margin for anxiety.

In the afternoon I walked to the top of Yellow
Road, where there was to be a hurling match, and
there I met a young man standing outside of his
house. Discovering that I was a stranger he took me
to walk with him. He was a curious youth with a
voice that fluttered from high falsetto and plunged
to gruff profundity.

'You are a bit of a walker,' said he as we paced
along, the sun shining very clear and straight upon
us. 'You are a boy for the walking,' and he wiped
his neck and eyes.

'I am used to it,' said I. 'It isn't at all uncommon for
me to do my thirty miles a day.'

He looked ahead reflectively. 'Thirty miles is a
great way to walk. Would you believe it, I took a
drove of heifers from Clonmel to Waterford a fortnight ago in one little bit of a day.'

'How far is that?' I asked him.

'Thirty-one miles,' he said, 'and forty-three cattle,
or maybe forty-two . . . thirty-one miles!'

'I did a good journey myself a week or two ago,' I
said. 'I walked a matter of forty miles in a little
over ten hours.'

'And the next day,' he continued, 'I drove two
hundred and eighty-three sheep from Ballyporeen
o Carrick.'

'Is that very far?'

'About forty-one miles,' said he. 'It was in the
afternoon we did it . . . they were . . . they were

very good sheep and we sold them well. It is dry walking.'

We approached a shop and entered. I bought a half-pint of Guinness, which was given me in a stone bottle commonly used for ginger-beer, while he took a pint of porter.

'Whisky,' he said, 'is no drink for chaps the like of us. Now we can stop when we are half drunk agin we fall, but whisky is a dangerous drink, it defeats ye. If you're fond of the walking I could take you a little walk on Thursday next.'

'Yes, I should be very pleased,' I said, 'on Thursday.'

'Ah,' he cried, 'we'll have a right ramble, a cushy day! We'll get two sticks and I'll take you to Thulgare, and bring you round by *The Sweep* and so on to Mornington. Come along now.'

We marched upon the road again. 'Grand country about here, and I'll be showing it you. There's a fine bit of corn now,' said he, starting at lah and running down the me ray doh of his voice.

Now I had it in my mind that I could grow better oats on the roof of a hencote than the crop I saw in the field he indicated, but I did not want to wound him, so I said, 'Ah!' as if the prospect delighted me.

'What would ye think it 'ud thresh out to?'

I could not say.

'Ah, but give a guess.'

I'd no knowledge of such things.

'No? I suppose ye haven't. Well, on Thursday then we'll have a right ramble, a cushy day.'

Soon we approached a young bull straying in the road.

'There's a nice bull,' he said.

'Ah!' said I.

'Now, what would you think is the worth of that bull?'

'I don't know.'

'But put a price on him now, go on!'

'Twenty pounds.'

'Ah, you might as well offer a ha'penny! Forty guineas is the worth of that bull. Oh, he's the boyo, he is,' he screamed, and shouting harsh words at the animal he leaped towards him with horrific gestures that put the fear of seven-and-twenty devils into the heart of the bull, who leaped over the low hedges and was never seen again. We went on in silence until he began murmuring half to himself, 'On Thursday then. . . . I'm a man of me principles, mind ye . . . we'll have a right ramble . . . begod it is hot! . . . a cushy day. We'll get two sticks . . . two little twigs . . . and I'll take ye to Thulgare.'

He stopped, and took me by the arm. 'Now, what do ye think of that mare?' he said, remarking a female horse that stood in a field with a foal beside her.

'A beautiful animal,' said I.

'Put a price on her.'

'Fifty pounds.'

He spat before me with fine facility, looking sternly in my eyes.

'A hundred guineas is the worth of that mare,' said he.

Again we walked on, 'and I'll bring you round by *The Sweep* and so on to Mornington.'

Ah me, the many things I promised to do for him! To deny him led to such unending argument that I promised a thousand promises which I couldn't fulfil if I had had a thousand good intentions, which I had not. As, for instance:

Would I take him to Duncannon on the steamer?

And to the boxing-match on Friday evening?

Would we go to Tramore together?

Would I give him a pair of old boots?

And find him a job in England?

Am I an angel now to be dangling largesse, or the Lord Himself come to be dropping sweetness and fatness upon him like a stray bird in a nest?

We came back to the town and he prepared to leave me:

'On Thursday, then, we'll have a right ramble, a cushy day. Give me sixpence,' said he. Search my pockets as I would I could but find fourpence ha'penny, and with this I endowed him.

2

It *is* a long way to Tipperary, and I suppose it *was* the song that sent me there. Wondrous, is it not, the insignificant motives that inspire some complicated efforts?

'Let you be giving me a penny, sir,' said the old

woman to me. I had but just started upon that sunny journey, and she hailed me.

'Let you be giving me a penny, sir.' I gave it. 'May the Great God take ye to heaven, sir,' said she, and then I wished I'd given her a shilling, for, thought I, if I get to heaven for a penny, the Lord Himself might forgive me a great deal for the odd elevenpence.

And, indeed, then I am specially blessed, for as the old woman goes wending away I stand looking back at her, and there by the highway I see a little group of farm buildings and trees just sitting across the top of a low bank, so very green, soft as silk it was, with no blemish upon it. Across that green some white ducks go a-travelling; the wind blows their voices to me. There is, too, a line of poplar sprigs, very slender and fan-like, their stems no bigger than altar candles, and they sigh like women in their grieving.

I got out a post card, one of those rarely tinted and admirably chased with a golden edge which I carry for the purpose, and, licking my pencil stub like a greengrocer's boy, I made a poem, one of those things with no rhyme in it, and with rhythms like a mangled corkscrew, with some lines as short as a full stop, and some unending ones on which you peg out very sweet notions as indiscriminately as a washerwoman hangs out her underwear, and then magnify with an exclamation mark.

'Go on, now,' said I to myself then, and go on I did, like a sheep. It is not uncommon to feel yourself convincingly bullied by yourself into doing the thing you would not want to do. I'd love to be standing in that place, with a coin of gold in my hand, this very minute, until I'd become a pillar of salt with looking at it, but I went on until I came to the borheen.

Now, a borheen is a lean lane, full of deceitful notions, with hedges as high as a workhouse wall and brambles like the midriff of a great fish. Within a borheen the travelling stranger is beset as completely as the slice of meat in a sandwich, no more view of the surrounding world, no more will of his direction. Does a serpent twist? Then a borheen is a serpent bereft of its reason. What is the longest thing in the world? A borheen, for it's longer than a sad Sunday. In ten miles or in twenty miles you may happen upon a cabin. You approach it, you drop a glance over the half-door, and you perceive an old, old woman sitting on some steps leading to a loft. There may be a pig sitting before her, apparently worshipping her, and there will certainly be hens, very furtive hens, and a cauldron. The old woman regards you with apprehension, with awe. You ask to be directed and she tells you to go on and inquire at the next house. You indulge this vain pursuit for as long as your sanity survives, or until you meet a pig coming towards you. There will be no more than just room for him to pass you, and so you will stand like one Christian meeting another, or like any man with a gush of charity in his breast. But this pig will fear you, he will turn tail, and behold you have a pig upon your hands, for, wherever you go now, you have upon you the appearance of driving that poor pig before you. You will endeavour to conciliate him, or persuade him of your passionate friendship, but there is no mortal man can appease a pig and it not wanting. He will behave like a Kaffir, and finally you will dislike him — and tell him so.

'A great nuisance was that pig to me,' I said when I regained freedom upon the high road once more, 'and a great pity that I only bought a pennyworth of blessing of that good old woman. I'll go no more into those borheens, so go upon your journey now.' And I was just going when I heard the stir of a vast noise behind me. A great grey ass was standing in the road and braying as if he were the king of all asses, as indeed he was, for, look you, along the road a car came flying with military persons in it. The horn went Honk! Honk! but the ass went He! Haw! and lay down in the road before them, lashing his heels as if he'd tear the skin off the sky, and screaming triumphantly as the car came to a stop upon his very neck.

'Get out of it, or we'll break your heart,' yelled the soldiers, and the car pumped noises at him like a big gun, but the ass trailed his carcass in the road with no fear at all, until someone leaped out of the car, kicked him where there was no dignity, and then pushed him into the borheen, where, I thought, if he meets that little pig of mine, it will not be Greek meeting Greek, for its just Ajax to a sunflower that he will destroy my little pig and devour him. 'But go on now,' said I to myself, and I walked on into Tip, where I got some interesting food – but it was queer feeding. Better a fly in the ointment, believe me, than one in the blancmange. You will always have a cosy for the teapot in Ireland, and a slop basin, but there will be something odd and incinerated about the teapot; there will always be insects in the milk, cracks in the cup, and things in the sugar basin besides sugar!

'Waiter,' I said, 'this tea is very weak!'

'Is it, begod, sir, then I'll just put another half-pound in it,' and, taking from his waistcoat pocket a thimbleful of tea wrapped in a screw of paper that had once contained tobacco, he emptied it into my teapot, saying soothingly, 'It 'ull be all right now.'

In the evening I went into a bar. She had eyes as soft as darkness and a voice like a singing swallow. 'A drop!' I cried to her, for she was reading on a book and did not heed me. When she had given me the whisky, she resumed her book.

'May I be stricken to my doom this minute,' said I, quite to myself, 'if it is not poetry and new poetry that girl is reading.' At that a handsome young man came in and stood before her.

'Good evening, Mary.'

'What is it you're wanting, Peter?'

'Stout,' said he; 'and what is it you're reading, Mary?'

'Poetry,' said she; 'listen to this, Peter,' and she read out, in the soft voice that was like the singing of swallows, some verses. Mary went on reading the poems, and there was no laughter upon the handsome young man; we were both filled with delight.

Pleasant thoughts I had that night as I pulled the quilt up to my neck, for pleasant it is to sleep in a country where the very donkeys are valiant, and even the barmaids woo you to the muses.

3

Currency notes, like time and tide, wait for no man, and when a small packet of them has the itch for exchange there is none can say it nay. At least so it happened to me when I had been walking for all a week in Wexford and Wicklow. Mine *would* go — oh, how they would go! I would turn a black one into two red ones, and they'd fly off like little pigeons, swift birds with the large appetite of turkeys, until I became savage with impecuniosity. So I cast about in my mind for some notion of replenishing the lean pocket, or of dealing with the situation. Meditating fitly I approach a board that bears a bill upon it, a bill with strange blue words beneath a handsome woodcut of a bull prancing and breathing out smoke, a sweet figure indeed. These were the words:

Hould that one!
Tear the skin off him!
    and take it to
James O'Loughlin,
Who gives best prices for skins and hides.

Well, I had little stomach for such jobs. I looked into the fields where there were grazing heifers and fat steers, but there was not one mild old cow, or even a calf, that I was prepared to dispossess of its only garment just for the profit of myself and this Mr. O'Loughlin.

I walked on a mile until I saw another bill tacked upon a tree, about a man at Carrick who was clamouring for:

> *Five thousand tons of Blackberries!*
> *Get 'em! Get 'em! Get 'em!*

I studied his invitation, but I concluded there were not five thousand tons of blackberries in the rolling world, leave alone any part of Ireland that I could step across before they were all gone. And what was the use of a couple of pounds in a handkerchief to a great blackberry captain like that! Besides, there were no blackberries to be got yet, they were only just podgy little green buds squeezing on the twigs.

So I proposed to myself a resolution: I would not spend a penny before the fall of night, and I'd wait till my stomach was barking before I would give in to it. (*Carried.*) Isn't eating a wretched means of keeping the life jogging in your bones? And it is not healthy. I considered the fields in their beauty upon either hand of me. 'Observe,' said I, invoking the unconscious sky, 'all these things are living — yes, they are thriving — upon air and mud, and not toiling nor spinning nor starving; air and mud!'

I became curious about that, and thoughts began to unfold within me.

'Who has heard,' I said in my large manner, 'who has ever heard of pangs or of hunger among the green leafy things that live on air and mud? Nutriment! Why the rich carrot is buried in it. Who ever heard of an elm tree suffering from neurasthenia, or of a cucumber with a debilitated lung? What vegetable product ever went mad or contracted chilblains? Are there pills for potatoes, or plasters for parsnips? Before the hardy but excellent onion the paregoric drop pales its utterly ineffectual fires. Take the gorgeous dandelion: that incomparable beast may have its bad moment when bitten by a cow, but it has, I am persuaded, a pleasant pastoral immunity from pains in the back. Isn't eating the wretchedness! I will not spend a penny before the fall of night.' This was in the early morn. Alas, a good resolution that lasts longer than one o'clock becomes a penance and no virtue at all. Vows are made, not with the intention, but with the expectation of being broken. Crossing a mountain range, I saw not a soul nor the sign of it in the miles behind me, nor in the miles before, and I tell you the bird of hunger was roosting on my breast. I bore it until I could stand no longer, and I sat down to contrive in my mind the kind of meal I would have if I ever came to a place where I could lavish my rich money. There would be a beautiful girl to wait upon me, the table to be set like snow for the linen, and like a Jew's pantry for the silver. And she

would speak to me like this, with all the notes of a
dove in her wooing voice:

'Chops?' she would say.

'Two of them,' say I, 'and a bottle of stout,' I say.

'One?' says she.

'Two of them,' say I.

There would be loaves in dozens, bastions of
cheese, and little round ounces of butter. All of it
would be consumed by me. In time I awake from
this dream and shuffle upon my courses, going on
from hour to hour until at last I have put the mountains behind me and come upon a road. Upon this
I go on and on, and from mile to mile, meeting not
a soul or the sign of it, until suddenly, hard upon
five o'clock, I see a little round thing lying in the
road. You remember that footprint in Crusoe's
island? This was an onion. Here at last was
humanity, and if this irascible herb was a sign more
pungent than propitiating it at least denoted the
possibility of a meal with some grace, however pro-
vincial. When I got to the place there was no tea
in it, and no beer in it; whisky there was and welcome, and I with no food in me since the clock was
nine! 'I have,' said the old lady — Anne Kennedy
was her name and beguiling were her ways — 'I have
some lemonade and some bread and butter.'

'Lay on, then,' said I. She was a very sweet old lady,
and she produced a loaf so huge that she lifted it
with difficulty; a yard long it was, and nigh upon
two feet wide. It would have been the fair snack
even for Magog and his twin brother with the ugly

name. Here it was, then, and hot from the oven. 'This fine drink,' I said, 'and this fine food, may be the destruction of me, but here goes – if I die in five minutes.'

However, I did not die, and I was in Dublin itself by eight o'clock, where a queer adventure befell me.

4

In Dublin I was driven by necessity to lodge in a mean crooked little hotel, that had bullet holes in its windows, where I ate sausages and eggs until I nearly burst, not with pure joy of such food, but because I was almost hungry enough to eat a billy-cock hat. On a tramping journey the egg dogs you like a punctual ritual of flagellation; it is flung into all your meals like the apple of discord – that regrettable pippin; fried out of truth into toughness it becomes not meat but mendacity. Were there any adoration left in me, I would adore as the jewelled prop of the world any maid who produced for me a tin of sardines, or even the mere shavings of a nut.

But listen now to the two men who are talking behind me as they shuffle the cards for a game.

'The pigs I bought this morning, James?'

'I seen 'em.'

'Four pounds each, James!'

'Ah!'

'They'll do well, James.'

'They'll do well in twelve months.'

'They will, James?'

'No doubt at all unless something comes on 'em.'
'And it won't, James?'
'It should not.'
'Well, James, pigs are pigs.'
Somehow that conversation decided me.
'Madam,' said I to the house lady, 'could you put me up this night?'
'Well, I could and I couldn't.'
I waited.
'There is but the one room left, which you may share with Neal Callaghan, a very pleasant boy.'
'Neal Callaghan,' I thought, 'I would do a great deal for a man with a name like that – but . . .'
'Yes,' said she, 'there *are* separate beds.'
'Thank you, ma'am, I'll be pleased to share with Neal Callaghan.'
So she took a candle and me up two flights of stairs, a few steps down, a little bridge to be crossed, round a corner or two, and again up a flight, for all the world as if we were a couple of domestic hares deceiving some kind of a hound, till we came to a room which was numbered 14. Two beautiful white beds were in it.
'That will be yours,' said herself, pointing to the one by the window. I left my satchel there and went to walk abroad in the city of Dublin, where the gutters were lined with ragged children and women offering things for sale. There were a thousand arms outstretched and voices crying:
'See the three rich apples!'
'The four fine plums a penny!'

'A penny for that onion!'

The distracting thing about Dublin, as about all Irish towns, is its domestic architecture. It doesn't merely decay, it is smitten by a disease from which there seems to be no recovery. The walls fall in — let them fall. Is there a conflagration — well, then we go, and the ashes are triumphant. If a window is broken, it is like the vow of a bad woman — broken for ever. Calamity here is progressive. I said as much to a Dubliner.

'Begod, then, ye should see the slums of Belfast!' said he, implying that even if Dublin were Sodom there was a very complete Gomorrah elsewhere.

I bought some Sein Fein papers, and went home. Creeping in unobserved I seized a candle and sought my room. His lordship was already in bed. He lay with his back to me, but I could see from the corner of my eye that he was slumbering. A slight fellow he seemed, and, thought I, if he does misbehave I'll have no difficulty in subduing him. So I did off my clothes and was just taking a last peep in the glass to see what sort of a face the sun had left me when the voice behind me said:

'Are ye sure ye're in the right room?'

Just those simple words, nothing extravagant about them, but, by the Lord, I was badgered to the heart — for the voice was the voice of a woman! What could any man do there in the shame of his undress?

'I stood stone still, let time run over me.'

318

Then I sat upon the bed and put some decency upon me.

'Yes, oh, yes, it is my room truly,' and, taking the candle, I pulled back the door.

'There you are,' I said, lighting up the number triumphantly, 'No. 14, my very own room, and I think you'd better be going.'

She turned round to me at that, smiling with excellent eyes — a fine white-handed girl with a mouth of sweet shape.

'That's nothing,' she said, 'next door is 102, and my sweetheart is in No. 79.'

Very friendly she was, and yet I sat down upon her bed and urged her to leave. But of course she was disinclined.

'I will not,' said she, and there was no moving her from it.

'Shut the door,' she says, 'and don't be making a noise, for me sweetheart's in a room somewhere on this landing.'

'Your sweetheart! God help me!'

'Oh, there's no harm at all in the world.'

'Is your sweetheart Neal Callaghan?'

'I never heard that name on him,' she said, 'but it's a good thing I heard *you*, or what would I do in the morning when I woke in my innocence and see you lying across there!'

Indeed, that was a serious thought, but I could see her shaking with her laughter under the quilt.

'I'd not be rising against you were gone — how could I, under the Lord!'

'No more would I,' I said to her.

When I had finished my dressing, I went to the landlady and told her of my misfortune. Confessing her folly, and screaming with glee at my recital, she made a good explanation to me. She led me to another room where I was abed and sleeping till the clock was one, when my Neal Callaghan came in with the madness of drink raging, skinned to the very eyes. He flung his hat out of the window, and his collar into the ewer; the candle slipped from his fist and his foot crushed it. He lay on his bed smoking a shag of a pipe, and letting a blather of whisky and jockeys out of him. He cursed me for some minutes and groaned for hours – did not I, too!

Late it was when I went to my breakfast, and there in the big room sat the girl with a tall fierce-looking man. She glanced a smile at me, but I looked beyond her, for I thought in my subtle simplicity it would be awkward for her to explain our acquaintance.

Eggs and eggs again I ate until at last the couple rose and went towards the door. I durst not raise a glance to her, but as he passes the young man bows genially and cunningly to me.

'Good morning, sir!' says he.